Turning the Tides

by

Nell Castle

Turning the Tides

Cover Art by *Kim Mendoza*

The Wild Rose Press, Inc.
PO Box 708
Adams Basin, NY 14410-0708
Visit us at www.thewildrosepress.com

Publishing History
First Mainstream General Edition, 2017
Print ISBN 978-1-5092-1452-5
Digital ISBN 978-1-5092-1453-2

Published in the United States of America

"What are you doing here?"

Lounging against the shelf of toys was the bartender from Whistler's Grille.

Lee stared at the man on the floor. Even in khakis and a button-down shirt, he radiated a sex appeal at odds with the tiny trucks and blocks surrounding him. If she'd found Cleopatra playing with Kaleb on the carpet, she couldn't have been more surprised. "Are you a friend of the family?"

"I'm the guardian ad litem." He extended his hand. "James Kilbourn. But friends use my middle name. Bricker." His smile didn't reach his eyes. "You're Lee Anya Cooper, the parent educator?"

She leaned down to shake his hand, uncomfortably aware of her blouse gaping as his rough, warm palm closed over hers. "Lee to my friends." She straightened, her pulse beating in her throat. "So you're a trained guardian?"

His eyebrow rose. "So you're a trained educator?"

Her cheeks flushed. *Of all the rotten luck.* The one person she needed to win to her client's side was the man she'd rejected the day before.

Praise for Nell Castle

"Nell Castle's *A LEAP OF FAITH* is a beautiful novel…a believable and satisfying romance, and so much more. Highly recommend."

~*Kimberly Keyes, author of The Trouble with Tigers*
~*~

"Refreshing in its portrayal of the characters involved in Sophia's life. These were people I could meet at any time. Real people, with real hearts and real mistakes. By the end of the first chapter, I was hooked."

~*Melissa R.*

~*~

"You can't help but love Sophia as she struggles with issues that all of us know so well! You will never expect the situations Sophia finds herself in."

~*Peggy L.*

~*~

"A beautifully written book…Tender, light hearted and a twist that I didn't see coming."

~*LAS Reviewer at Long and Short Reviews*
~*~

"Nell Castle spins sweet stories that touch the heart. If her new books are as warm and engaging as *A LEAP OF FAITH*, I will happily follow her characters anywhere."

~*Colleen L Donnelly, Amazon #1 Bestselling Author*

Dedication

To CHK, and late-night walks to Mister Donut;
to the blue chair and wavy hair;
to Neil Young, Harold and Maude,
gin gimlets, and The Guess Who.
Your laugh rings through
so many of my best memories.

Chapter One

The painful screech of a garbage truck's brakes pierced his brain fog.

Bricker peeled open one sleepy eye. Early morning light magnified every detail of the foot resting inches from his face at the bottom of the bed. Baby blue toenail polish. The delicate curve of an instep. Bristles of stiff, black hair sprouting above the ankle.

This was closer than he needed to get.

A headache clamped his skull with a vise grip. Taking a deep breath, he rolled himself off the bed and managed to land upright, his toes sinking into the softness of a shag throw rug. Tangled sheets wrapped the slumbering figure of a woman he barely remembered from last night's bonfire. His blue-striped boxers peeked out from beneath her pillow. Holding his breath, he plucked them from under her cheek.

She tossed red curls from her face, her eyes still closed. A soft snore rattled the back of her throat.

Swiping his T-shirt and jeans from the floor, he escaped into the hallway. Careful not to click the door shut behind him, he donned his boxers. With his shirt clenched between his teeth, he slid into his jeans without so much as losing his balance. Now for the zipper. Nothing roused a sleeping woman faster than a zipper. To mute the sound, he tugged the slider tooth by tooth.

A sudden squeak of hinges jolted him. The door to his left swung open. He froze, hoping he wasn't about to meet Mr. Redhead in the worst possible circumstances.

But a tall, long-legged blonde emerged instead, wrapped in a fluffy yellow towel. Looking up with wide blue eyes, she spread her fingers across the top of her chest where the terrycloth exposed the swell of her breasts.

His gaze locked on her protecting hand as he yanked the zipper to the top stop. He relaxed his mouth into a slow smile, dropping the T-shirt into his waiting hands. "Didn't mean to scare you." Flexing his arms above his head to offer her a good, long look at his pecs, he pulled his arms through the sleeves. He winked before ducking his head through the neck hole, emerging with the hint of a leer. "Looking for someone to scrub your back?"

The blush spreading across her cheeks made her even more attractive. He crossed his arms and leaned a shoulder against the wall. The next move was hers, but he was pretty sure what it would be. When he heard the bedroom door open behind him, he whipped around his head.

Bundled in bedsheets, the redhead's lips curled into a sneer. "You know what? You can just lose my number."

Covering her smile with her hand, the blonde darted one last look at him before she fled into the bathroom.

The redhead slammed the door in his face.

"Already lost it, darlin'," Bricker murmured as he strolled down the hall and out the front door into the bright light of day. Wincing, he rubbed his forehead. He was getting too old to be partying like this. The redhead better have done the driving last night.

A breeze stirred the jasmine bush tumbling over the yard's retaining wall. The sidewalk was shadowed by a grouping of Queen palms near the front of the property. During the summer in south Florida, this was the best part of the day. He usually slept through it. Before he could open the door to his truck, he was pelted in the side by a flying object.

"Don't come back!" the redhead yelled from the porch.

He leaned over to retrieve his sandals and straightened to salute her, a shoe covering his hand. The door on the empty porch vibrated with the violence of her exit.

Climbing into the driver's seat, he checked himself in the rearview mirror. He pushed long, tangled hair back from his forehead and winced at his bloodshot eyes. Just another night on the beach at one of Austin's bonfires. A few hours in the sun, dozing and fishing off the end of his boat would take care of that. He slid his feet into his designer flip-flops and started the truck.

It was already a good day. He was going home with all his clothes and his shoes, too.

****

Pushing her long black hair off her face, Lee staggered to the front door and threw it open. Her eyes squeezed shut against the onslaught of the southern sun. "Go away!" she yelled in the direction of a crowing rooster. She slammed the door shut with a satisfying whack.

Why did morning have to arrive so *early* on

Pomegranate Key?

Shrugging on a terrycloth robe, she stomped into the kitchen to turn on the coffee. As she did most mornings, she banged her hip against the counter. She couldn't open her eyes until she had coffee, and after six months, she still hadn't memorized the layout of her rented bungalow.

When she'd taken the new job with Mangrove Family Services, she'd had to learn the ropes fast. And there were a lot of ropes. She squinted around the high-ceilinged living room, at the stacks of boxes, the canvases leaning against the bare ivory walls. A sigh escaped her lips. One day, she'd get around to unpacking.

The coffee was finally done. Balancing her mug in one hand and her laptop in the other, she elbowed open the front door and settled at the glass table on the porch. In just a few hours, the heat would be unbearable. But at six am, a cool breeze whispered through the fronds of the scraggly dwarf palms framing the pebbled path of the housing compound.

Regal and deliberate, a rooster pecked its way around the path connecting the four small wooden bungalows. His red comb jiggled on top of a dirty beige head.

Lee eyed him with distaste as he passed by. "I've painted better roosters than you." While she sipped coffee, she checked her social media notifications. Her eyes focused as she Liked the pages of an old college friend here, a work acquaintance there. She stopped at her sister Brett's entry. For Throwback Thursday, she'd posted an old picture of the family titled "Twenty-three years ago."

4

Lee recognized the photo, one of her first after she'd arrived from Korea at the age of two to live in northeast Pennsylvania with her new family. Her fine, straight black hair was girded into a whale's spout on top of her head. Her full lips were caught in a quaver as she gazed into the lens of the camera. Unshed tears threatened to spill over her broad cheeks.

The rest of her family leaned in, competing to see who could get closest. Her sweet-faced mother, Irene, rested a plump, protective arm over Lee's shoulders to ward off pre-teen Brett. Blonde and tanned, Brett stood a little too close with wet hair and a bathing suit. Her brother, Conrad, touched his new baby sister's arm.

Dad must have taken the picture, Lee thought. She Liked the photo and added a correction: "Twenty-five years ago." Just like Brett to shave a few years off Lee's age. Would she ever believe her little sister had grown up?

Fetching her second cup of coffee, she called voicemail to hear any overnight messages from the office. Becoming a parent educator hadn't exactly been a lifelong dream when she found the employment ad online. The location was what caught her eye: Bellamy, Florida, on the Gulf Coast. Her family demanded to know what she'd do with her undergraduate degree in psychology. According to the ad, this job required just a four-year degree in social work, education, or psychology. Bingo! Perfect solution to cold Northern winters *and* family interference.

So what if the position required her to link needy families to local resources when she'd never set foot in the community? Or provide parenting education to single teen mothers when she'd never so much as babysat? She was a fast learner. Her supervisor, Janna Wilson, was willing to take a risk because she thought the young mothers would find her easy to relate to.

She was making her way pretty well. So far, she'd read all the child development materials in the office. During the three-week training process, she studied the labyrinth of social services offered through county and nonprofit programs. She observed how the seasoned social workers in her office operated. Then she copied what they did. To a girl who'd known no English, who'd been adopted into a family of high achievers, impersonating others was old hat.

The log of client calls proved typical. Breanne was canceling today's visit. Kayla needed diapers before payday on Friday. A new client wondered if their meeting could be rescheduled. But Lee had to press the phone against her ear to understand Amber Maly between her sobs.

"Lee, you have to help me." Amber's quiet voice was ragged with tears. "DCF took Kaleb." Her voice rose, high-pitched and panicked. "They're charging me with abuse and neglect. Dan and I got a public defender, and he told me to think of someone who can testify on my behalf. Call me back."

As if the phone burned her fingers, Lee dropped it on the table. Amber Maly was *not* a poster child for mother of the year. She'd been referred to Mangrove County Family Service's parenting program after DCF, the Department of Children and Families, ended its investigation into concerns raised by her son's pediatrician. Amber had agreed to work with a parent educator only to get the agency off her back. Now she was back under the microscope again. And she wanted

Lee to go to bat for her.

Lee sighed. Of all the mothers she worked with, Amber was one of the least sympathetic. She rarely smiled, and her voice was a steady monotone. Trish Nichols, the Children's Services worker who'd referred Amber to Lee's agency, had called her "emotionless and cold," closing the case only after knowing a worker from Lee's agency could keep an eye on the home situation.

Emotion like she'd heard from Amber in the voicemail was new. Lee had to admit, the young mother *did* demand too much of her son. But Lee was protective of Amber. Unlike a lot of Lee's teenaged clients, Amber was eager to learn about child development. Over time, Lee hoped Amber would develop appropriate expectations for a toddler. But if Lee was forced to take the stand now, she couldn't claim Amber had shown a lot of progress. She tapped her fingers on the glass surface of the table. The first thing to do was talk with her supervisor. Maybe Janna could help her find a way to avoid testifying. Lee lifted her mug and sipped her coffee. Cold now.

From underneath the porch, the rooster gave another grating squawk.

Her hand jerked, and coffee slurped over her chin. She slapped a bare foot against the wooden porch plank, satisfied when the rooster fluttered back into the clearing. Wiping her face on the sleeve of her robe, she gathered her belongings and headed inside.

****

A few hours later, Lee led her boss into Whistler's Bar and Grille. Tucked at the end of a quiet street, the bar was known by locals as the island's best spot for fresh seafood and an ocean view.

"The view of the local fauna isn't bad, either." Janna snickered as she slid into a booth.

Lee followed Janna's gaze to the man straddling a tall chair at the bar.

Burly-chested in a snug T-shirt reading 'Bellamy Fire Department', his dark hair cut short and tight, he raked his gaze over them.

Lee frowned at her menu. "Don't encourage him." She put her phone on silent and slipped it into her purse, hoping for some uninterrupted counsel from her supervisor.

"Come on, live a little." Janna removed her lightweight black shrug and drew back her shoulders to invite attention to what lay beneath her tight gold camisole. Her skin, deeply tanned, bore the faint, erosive lines of middle age.

Lee widened her eyes, the corners of her mouth quirking. "I thought we were here to talk about work. Not pick up guys." Janna's husband of twenty-odd years had left her for a younger woman a year ago. From her co-workers, Lee caught a definite whiff of disapproval at Janna's attempts to reclaim her youth with tight clothing, online dating, and dance clubs.

Janna gave a little wave to the bar and brought her attention back to Lee with a triumphant smile. "Yeah— but I've still got a *pulse*." She scanned the appetizer menu. "Have you tried alligator yet? It actually does taste like chicken."

Lee wrinkled her nose. "No, but I've learned to like conch fritters. I'm not in the mood for anything fried today, though."

Her eyes brightening, Janna glanced up from the

menu. "Don't look now, but here comes the main attraction."

Swiveling her head, Lee found her gaze level with the zippered crotch of their server. She snapped her face back to center, eyes wide with embarrassment.

Janna smiled upward, her wavy, highlighted hair falling back from her face. "My friend here says she likes your fritters. What kind of fritters were those, Lee? Co—?"

"Conch!" Lee choked out, her face burning. She glared at Janna, struggling to control her voice. *"Conch* fritters. And no, I don't want any today."

Surveying the menu with a wicked smile, Janna gave a tiny shrug.

Lee looked up as she began her order. "I'd like a—" Her words sputtered, and she cleared her throat. "A garden salad with oil and vinegar on the side. And hummus with pita bread, please."

While she waited for Janna to finish ordering, Lee clamped her gaze on the napkin holder at the center of the table. She'd seen their server once before, at the public beach concession a few weeks ago. Balancing a flimsy container of fries, she'd caught sight of him coming toward her. Tall, slim, and bare-chested, he had sun-kissed hair that grazed his bronzed shoulders. The muscles of his torso rippled like a predatory cat's.

Riveted by his approach, she stumbled right into a small boy in her path. Lunging, the man grabbed her elbow, bending his knees to reach her with the grace of a shortstop fielding a grounder. He smiled, the gap between his top front teeth the one concession to human imperfection. And maybe his nose was just a little crooked; she couldn't say, because she'd been hypnotized by eyes as blue as the Gulf waters over his shoulder. Eyes so deep and warm she could fall into them. Clutching her half-empty box of fries, she stuttered a word of thanks and fled.

Returning to her friends on the beach, she kept a lookout for his return. He was gorgeous, yes; but his smile had melted her. She traced his arrival at a blanket several yards away. She spied him handing a water bottle to a beautiful girl in a bikini, and her heart sank. Enjoying the rest of the afternoon with her friends had been hard. She glanced behind her to see the man lathering his hands with lotion and running them over the silky curves of his companion's backside. Lee shivered to imagine his long fingers soothing and cooling her own sun-warmed skin.

Her envy evaporated at the approach of a second woman in a see-through cover-up. The woman's angry words were flung into the wind. "Cheater. Two-timing bastard. Slimy." Lee couldn't make out the whole argument, but from the outraged expression of the bikini girl, Lee had gotten the gist.

The man stalked off the beach without a word to either woman.

Chancing another look now, Lee wrinkled her nose. Janna was doing her level best to attract his attention, and he wasn't missing one detail of her show.

His gaze dipped from her lips to her cleavage.

Lee cleared her throat until he glanced in her direction. She raised her brows so high, she felt air behind her eyeballs. "If you're not too busy, could you get me some cranberry juice?" His answering smile was practiced, oozing with charm.

"I'm sorry, ladies." His voice was playful, with just

a hint of a Southern drawl. "This isn't my day job. We're shorthanded, so I'm running some tables to help the other server. I'm off my game, I'm afraid to say." Placing his hand over his heart, he shook his head, his thick hair a curtain of silk.

Janna's back arched like a cat's at his attention.

Lee breathed a short, irritated blast through her nose and handed him the menus. She pointed her attention to Janna. "Let's talk about my client, okay?" She pulled a tablet from her bag, averting her face from their server until she heard his footsteps retreat.

Janna sat back, composing her face into a more professional expression. Flirting or not, the director of parenting education for Mangrove County was serious about her job and her staff. "Amber Maly. She lives out past the railroad tracks off of Route Ninety, right?"

A registered nurse, Janna visited the home of every family who entered the program. Lee nodded.

"Dark hair? Pale? I remember her." Janna frowned. "She had a flat affect. No expression."

Lee grimaced. In elementary school, her nickname had been "Stone Face." A high school biology teacher had once pointed to her as an example of the "lack of genetic variation" in some ethnicities. "Because she's Asian, Lee's eyes aren't as expressive as most of ours," he'd told the class. Her raised middle finger when he turned his back made her classmates laugh. But she'd resented his casual stereotyping. She shook her head, coming back to the present. "But you can't tell what Amber's like just by looking at her face."

"True," Janna conceded. "You get a more accurate idea once she opens her mouth. Like yelling at her toddler during potty training."

This was just why Lee dreaded the prospect of testifying for Amber. "She used to put Kaleb in the corner every time he wet himself," she admitted. "But she's stopped punishing him for accidents. We've talked about appropriate expectations."

"So what are the new charges?" Janna's mouth, set in a grim line, brightened into a welcome as the server approached with their drinks.

"One sweet tea, and one cranberry juice." He slid a glass in front of Janna and placed the other at the side of Lee's tablet.

Condemning him with a shake of her head, she thrust away the glass from her device.

"Sorry." But he seemed amused, folding his arms and sitting on the table behind him. "Don't you ladies get a break from work to eat?"

"This is a *working* lunch." His patronizing use of the word "ladies" irritated Lee. Who did he think he was, interrupting their lunch to flirt? God's gift to women, no doubt.

"So you can write it off on your taxes, am I right?"

The dimple in his chin twinkled right along with his blue eyes. To think she'd found this guy attractive. God, he was nothing more than a walking stereotype. She glared at his cocky smile.

He backed away holding up his hands with the palms out.

"Lee!" Janna giggled as she took a sip of her iced tea. "Give the poor guy a break! He's just being nice!"

"Come on, did you see his name tag? 'Bricker?' He should go back to starring in adult films." Now she was just being malicious. Lee blew out a breath, forcing herself to refocus on her client's problems. "Trish

Nichols, Amber's caseworker from Children's Services, said the incident occurred at Gloria Marshall's house. Gloria's a special needs foster mother for the county. Do you know her?"

Janna nodded, pressing her glass of iced tea against her forehead. "They place crack babies with her. Kids with profound delays. How does she know Amber?"

Lee glanced at the background information she'd collected when she first met her client. "Amber's husband, Daniel, was the best friend of Gloria's son. Daniel had a bad home life, so Gloria unofficially 'adopted' him into her family. Amber says Kaleb calls Gloria 'Grandma,' and she's like a second mother to Daniel."

Rolling the sweating glass across her flushed cheeks, Janna shrugged. "At least Amber's got one good role model. So what happened at the house?"

Janna already had a negative opinion of Amber. Lee's newest update wouldn't help. She cleared her throat. "Mrs. Marshall called Children's Services when she saw Amber shaking Kaleb for wetting the bed. Kaleb was taken to the hospital for a CAT scan, but no evidence of brain damage was found."

Janna set down her glass. Iced tea sloshed over the side. "Let me guess. Amber denies shaking him."

Patting her napkin over the puddle, Lee nodded.

"And the County is taking the word of one of its most valuable foster mothers over a mother who's already been investigated. Can't say I blame them." Janna shrugged.

Her body tense, Lee swallowed hard. "Amber's been charged with something else. The ER nurses found welts over Kaleb's diaper area." She winced.

"Like he'd been whipped."

Just then, the kitchen doors flung outward and their server appeared, holding a tray over his head with one hand. "Ladies, I'm approaching," he called from across the dining room. "Warning, please secure your electronic devices. The establishment will not be held responsible for damages to personal belongings as I unload this tray."

Lee swept the tablet back into her bag and rested it against the leg of her chair. As she raised her head, her attention was drawn to an exposed strip of skin above his waistband. Racing upward like a lit fuse, her gaze found the bulge of his bicep as it balanced the tray. She lowered her eyelids, taking a deep breath. Her brain knew this guy was bad news, but her body was operating on a different vibe. She'd be damned if she let it show, though.

Janna giggled as he glided to their table with exaggerated care and placed each plate with a flourish.

"May I refill your drinks, ladies? Sweet tea for you." He flashed Janna a brilliant smile before turning to Lee. "Nothing sweet for you. You're more…sour." He snapped his fingers. "Cranberry juice, wasn't it? Could I get you some more?"

His face was a mask of politeness. Lee lifted her chin, feeling her face flush. "Just bring the check." Here she was, figuring out how to help a mother accused of child abuse. But this guy kept thrusting himself into the spotlight. Now he was angry that she'd put him in his place?

"Yes, ma'am." Dipping his head in mock obedience, he sauntered back to the kitchen.

Janna bit into her grouper sandwich, her brows

knocking together over the bridge of her nose. Her gaze bored into Lee as she chewed. She held a napkin to her lips and swallowed hard. "If I were your age, I'd be getting his phone number. But you act like he's something you found stuck to the bottom of your shoe."

Lee snorted. "He's a sexist. I told him this was a working lunch, but he doesn't care. He cares about satisfying his own vanity." She spread hummus over a triangle of pita bread and popped it in her mouth. She'd been so charmed by his smile. What an idiot.

Janna sucked on her straw. "You're only young once, Lee. Why not enjoy it?"

Before Lee could respond, she saw the server approach with their check. Despite his smile, anger glittered in his eyes.

"I suspect you'd like to get back to work without any more annoying interruptions, so if you'll just settle the bill now, ma'am, I'll leave you alone."

"Great." Lee extracted cash from her purse and tossed it on the table.

As she passed her credit card, Janna cast their server an apologetic look.

He gave her a polite nod and returned to the register.

Janna kicked Lee beneath the table. "Well, *that* was awkward," she whispered.

"Did you catch his 'ma'am' comment? How old do I look?" Lee flicked the bills to the center of the table. "I don't know why I'm even leaving him a tip."

They were silent when he returned their receipts, Janna scrawling her signature and handing it back with a hopeful grin.

A polite smile plastered on his face, he left without

another word.

A nagging sense of shame bothered Lee as she finished her juice. Was she angry at the guy for being a shameless flirt, or angry at herself for being taken in by his smile?

Janna glanced at her watch. "We have ten minutes. So Amber beat her little boy. With what? A belt?"

Lee shook her head to clear her thoughts. "I don't know. Hearing she's hit Kaleb with *anything* surprises me, though. Amber's always said she doesn't believe in spanking."

Janna hooted. "Welts and bruises don't lie."

"I know." Lee sagged back against her chair. "But she swore she'd never hit Kaleb because of her own abusive mother. Don't get me wrong—I know Amber is too harsh with him." For half a year Lee had been teaching Amber to use positive reinforcement, instead of punishment, to influence her son's behavior. "She's still learning how to be a better parent."

Janna raised a skeptical eyebrow. "I don't understand why you're so worried about Amber. Kaleb's the one I'm worried about."

"I'm worried about him, too." Lee leaned forward, shaking her head. "But the idea of the state taking a toddler away from his mother…" She trailed off, tracing the tines of her fork through the oily remains of feta cheese and olives. She had one memory from her time in the Korean orphanage. A long row of metal beds lined the sides of a plain wooden dormitory room. Huddled on a thin mattress, she'd clutched a blanket under her chin and squeezed her eyes shut to block out the unfamiliar, mud-caked walls, crying out a name… Even now, her lips moved, trying again to retrieve the name time had stolen.

Janna ate the last of her sandwich and scraped her chair back from the table. "If you're subpoenaed by the Court, you just tell the truth. They'll want to know if Amber met with you regularly, if you saw food in the house, and if she ever laid hands on her child. Those kinds of things."

Lee pushed aside her plate. She hadn't eaten half of her lunch. "I don't have to give an opinion on her mothering skills?"

Janna shrugged. "They might ask what you think about Amber. Or they might not. If you're not comfortable offering your opinion, just tell them what you're teaching her." Janna tapped the back of Lee's hand. "Don't worry too much. The guardian ad litem's report is what the judge relies on."

The term sounded vaguely familiar. Lee bit her lip. "What's a guardian ad litem?"

Leaning back in her chair, Janna slid her purse onto her lap. "They're appointed by the court to represent the child's interests in a custody dispute or in cases of neglect and abuse. You said Amber's got a public defender, right?"

Lee nodded.

"Then this is a serious charge. Otherwise, she'd have been assigned someone from Legal Aid. The court will definitely assign a guardian." Dropping her napkin on the plate, Janna stood, peeling the black shrug from the back of her chair.

"Do I need to talk to the guardian?" Lee took a final swallow of cranberry juice as she rose from her seat.

"If you're called, and if the guardian asks your

opinion, you'll get your chance to say something positive about Amber. If you want to." Janna waited, half-turned toward the door.

For a moment, Lee considered requesting a to-go container for her meal. On second thought, she'd rather go hungry than tangle with the server one more time. He was behind the bar, talking to the man in the fireman T-shirt.

As Janna passed in front of the customer, she slid her arms into her wrap, drawing attention once more to her cleavage.

"Good day, ladies." The customer glanced at Lee, a smile dimpling his cheeks.

The server dipped his head toward Janna. "Thanks for coming in today." With a noncommittal nod at Lee, he wiped an invisible spot on the counter with a polishing cloth.

Wearing a frozen smile, Lee followed Janna out the door into the blast of afternoon heat.

Chapter Two

"Fresh fish coming through. Look out," Bricker called, opening the front door to his mother's elegant home. He padded across the decorative inlaid tiles of the foyer to the larger squares of the living room and kitchen. A trail of damp footprints marked his path behind him. He swung his bucket of fish into the ceramic sink.

Hector Flores, his mother's home companion, emerged from the lanai. Sliding open the glass doors leading into the family room, Hector tsked. "Your mother won't like you putting fish in her sink."

His voice, soft and cultured, carried a faint shade of his Cuban heritage. Bricker clapped his hand against Hector's. "You're right. Is she up?"

Stepping around the kitchen bar to peer into the bucket, Hector nodded. "Red snapper?"

Filling a glass of water at the refrigerator, Bricker took a long drink, and then nodded, looking into the older man's face. "How's she doing?"

Hector hesitated, tilting his head from side-to-side. "She's taking a little longer to get through the morning routine. She needs to stop and rest more often. But she's doing well."

Bricker ran a hand over his face. His mother had been diagnosed with relapsing remitting multiple sclerosis years ago. Although the symptoms of her flare-ups—vision loss in her right eye, hand tremors, and dizziness—went away when the episodes passed, she struggled with muscle weakness. Numb feet made walking difficult. "Ma!" He called out to the eastern wing of the house. "Do you need help?"

A door opened in the hallway across from the dining room. "No, I don't." His mother's voice, low and strong, called back. "And I'd better not find fish in my sink." The thump of a walker accompanied her words as she approached the family room.

"I'll take care of it." Hector lifted the bucket from the sink and vanished through the doors of the lanai.

A moment later, Corinne Kilbourn appeared under the archway. Her long brown hair, streaked with silver, was drawn into a ponytail, revealing high cheekbones and intelligent eyes. Her nose wrinkled as she paused, her breath labored. "More fish," she finally said.

"What else?" Bricker reached around the walker to hug her, planting a kiss on her forehead.

"How will you ever get a girlfriend if you always smell like bait?" Her gray eyes sparkled with affection.

"No shortage of girls around here, Mother. I just met a new one last night." Sliding the walker to the side and placing his palms under her forearms to steady her, he steered her to a bar stool. He opened the refrigerator and poured her a glass of orange juice.

"I don't mean a tourist. I mean a serious girlfriend." She sipped her juice, her gaze steady on her son's face.

Bricker forced a smile. "Why would I want a serious girlfriend, when the frivolous ones are so much fun?" Despite himself, his memory returned to the encounter with yesterday's lunch customer.

Lee.

He'd seen her before, at the beach, although he doubted she remembered him. Watching her was more interesting than talking to the girl at his side. Lee held the attention of all her friends, a potent charisma he could sense from yards away. Her straight black hair swung between her shoulder blades, chasing after her head as she chatted to whoever was on her right and left. Every few minutes, the wind carried her laughter over the beach—peals of pure joy, high and clear as sleigh bells. Her body shook with giggles that wouldn't quit. Just when her air seemed about to give out, she'd stomp her feet in the sand and laugh even louder. Adorable was the only word to describe her.

When he saw her head toward the concession stand, he offered to buy his date some water so he could follow. He had the great luck of being close when she tripped over a kid darting in front of her. One muscled thigh sprang from behind the skirt of her white halter swim dress as she struggled to hold her plate of food. He grabbed her arm, feeling the muscles of her biceps tense against his fingers. The Cupid's bow of her lips parted, her irises dark and velvet. Her black hair slid over the delicate bones of her shoulders. A dusting of white sand sparkled an invitation from the hollow of her throat down to the satin collar of her sleeveless cover-up. During the long moment he touched her, he sensed the power in her small frame, like a bird ready to take flight.

She nodded her thanks and wheeled toward the beach, fries held aloft as she picked her way across the sand. Probably a tourist he wouldn't see again. Disappointed, he returned to his blanket only to get into a row with a woman he hadn't seen for a year. When he watched his date grow angry too, he left. He'd never promised either of them anything but a good time.

Too bad, though. He could have listened to Lee laugh all day.

Yesterday, his heart had flared when she sat at his table. He wanted to spark a little back-and-forth with her, a little snappy patter. But more than anything, he wanted to draw out her raucous laughter.

Instead, her lunch companion pulled out all the stops to get his attention. He'd had no chance to find an opening with the girl from the beach. She took an instant disliking to him. And every word he spoke made matters worse.

"Because you're past thirty, and I want grandchildren."

Corinne's words knocked him back to the present. "Don't look at me." He narrowed his gaze, shaking a finger at his mother. "You've got a daughter with good childbearing hips. Go nag her."

"Ha." Corinne gave a dismissive wave. "Tatum's not ready to be a mother. She's too wrapped up in her career."

Bricker opened the refrigerator and removed a carton of eggs, a block of cheese, and a small bunch of asparagus. Producing a medium saucepan from a lower cabinet, he placed it on the burner. Coating it with a skim of olive oil, he chuckled. "The world of high finance doesn't keep office hours. And my little sister isn't the type to sacrifice her free time for a baby."

Corinne sighed. "Can you imagine Tatum changing a diaper?"

Bricker rinsed the asparagus and snapped the stalks

in half, discarding the thick ends into a compost container on the side of the sink. "Imagine her chronically sleep-deprived." With an exaggerated shudder, he lifted the pan by the handle to roll the crisp asparagus tips back and forth.

"See, this is why *you* have to get married. Look what a good husband you'd make." His mother swept her hand toward the stove.

Bricker shook his head. "Most women around these parts are looking for more of a lifestyle than a bartender can provide." With one hand, he cracked and emptied four eggs one after another into a bowl. He whisked in a little water from the sink and poured the mixture over the asparagus, clamping on a lid while he shredded the cheese.

"So retake your bar exam. Get a job in a law firm. Make a good living." His mother leaned over the counter, her smile bright.

"Are we doing this again, Mother?" His bored tone was deliberate. He took the lid off of the pan to find the edges of the eggs had crisped. With an expert thrust of his wrist, he flipped the eggs to brown on the other side.

"I know better than to talk to you about working in your father's firm. Even though he built it to make you a partner one day. But I know"—she interjected, waving her hand—"you want to be your own man. Fine. You could work somewhere else. Heck, you could be a public defender or work for Legal Aid. Just make use of your law degree, instead of pouring drinks at a bar for a living."

Twisting his neck to face her, he forced his voice to stay calm. "I've told you, Mother, I don't want to be an attorney. I *like* working at the bar. I like sleeping in late.

I like meeting pretty new tourists. I like spending my days off tooling around the islands on my boat. For some reason, I like bringing home fresh fish to cook for my mother, even though she hassles me about my choices every time I come around."

Corinne raised a placating hand. "I don't mean to hassle you. I just want you to have a family and be happy, the way your dad and I were happy. I know Dad would want the same."

Bricker carried a plate with a large slice of the omelet to his mother, a fork balanced on top. "Maybe I'm not looking for my happiness to lead me straight to a fatal heart attack at the age of fifty-four." As soon as the words were out of his mouth, he cursed himself for saying them.

His mother's smile vanished, and a tell-tale blush of red rose up her throat. She drew her lips into a thin line.

Why did he have to open his big mouth? He closed his hand over hers as it rested on the counter. "Sorry, Mom." He squeezed her hand 'til she relaxed and leaned her head against his shoulder. He stood still a moment longer, breathing in the magnolia perfume Corinne had worn for as long as he could remember. "I just stopped by to drop off the fish. Hector's taking care of it at the outdoor sink. I've got stuff to do this afternoon." He planted a quick kiss on her cheek and eased away his hand, heading to the garage door through the kitchen. Pivoting, he gave a little wave.

"But aren't you having breakfast?" She leaned over the counter, forehead creased.

"It's for you and Hector. Bye!" He shut the door before she could argue. Standing still in the cool retreat of the garage, he pushed sticky hairs away from his forehead and exhaled. He knew better than to talk to his mother about Dad. Pounding his fist once against the rubber garbage can, he strode outside into the relentless heat of the morning.

****

Lee drove slowly along Hyacinth Street in Bellamy, the mainland town just over the long bridge from Pomegranate Key. Amber's apartment was buried among rows of nondescript wooden buildings in Highland Park. Tall palm trees and a few scraggly pines provided the only refuge from the sun, and the brown shingles of the residences had faded to gray. Instead of front lawns, Lee saw only sandy patches of ground with tumble-blown weeds.

Her stomach growled. Could she squeeze in lunch before her appointment? Checking her GPS for the closest lunch spots, she spotted Whistler's Grille. Only one-and-a-half miles away, just a quick jog over the bridge back to the island. Her cheeks flamed at the memory of yesterday's encounter with the bartender. Terrible idea. He'd sooner poison her than wrap up a to-go meal. She glanced at the clock. In this neighborhood, her fastest option for lunch would be whatever meat was pruning on a convenience store rotisserie. Scrabbling for her purse with one hand as she steered with the other, she found her tin of mints and popped two in her mouth. They would have to do for now.

Spying the number 232 above a broken porch light, she drove into a space beside her client's dented and scratched red car. She stepped with care over a bed of fire ants streaming into the sand from the crumbling cement stoop in front of the door. Her knock was short and quiet. She'd been taught to avoid the loud rapping of knuckles identified in poor neighborhoods as the "cop knock." As the door swung back, she glued on a polite smile.

Amber was small, no more than a hundred pounds. Her inky black hair was thick and wavy, and today it needed a good washing. Brown eyes squinted from her pale face. She held the door open, and blue veins pressed against her wrists. She shivered in her tank top, eyes filled with tears.

Her surrender to emotion caught Lee by surprise. "Hey." She patted Amber's shoulder. When she saw the girl flinch, Lee dropped her hand. "You'll be okay."

The girl nodded, drawing her lips together in a severe line and dropping her gaze. She pivoted from the entrance into the open room of the apartment.

When Lee closed the door behind her, the apartment shrank into darkness, its one window hidden behind a panel of brown fabric. Only a rectangular outline of light was visible.

Lee's eyes adjusted to the dimness, finding Amber climbing under a jumble of blankets on the sagging couch beneath the window. The building, thermostat-controlled by the landlord, was always cold during Lee's visits. A coffee table littered with crumbs and empty soda cans leaned against the couch. Lining the wall perpendicular to the couch were milk crates stuffed with action figures, plastic building blocks, and puzzle pieces. Lee seated herself on a plastic green lawn chair in front of the TV, angling it to face Amber. The distant hum of an electric razor was audible from down the hall.

"Dan leaves for work in a minute."

Lee waited for Amber to continue, but her face had regained its habitual blankness, staring toward the kitchen. She stifled a sigh. "Why don't you tell me what happened at Gloria Marshall's house."

Amber's eyes flashed, hard and brittle. "She's trying to make me look like a bad mother so she can keep my son. Nobody believes me because DCF thinks she's a saint."

Lee tried again, keeping her voice calm. "Were you visiting the Marshalls?"

"We had to stay over there for a few days while our hot water heater was replaced. She invited us. We never should have said yes." Amber scratched at her shoulder.

Even in the dim light, Lee could see an angry splotch rising against the girl's pale skin. She cleared her throat. How to mention the allegations without alienating her client? "I spoke with Trish Nichols from the Department of Child and Family services this morning. Mrs. Marshall claims you were shaking Kaleb when she passed the bedroom. Since she saw the bed was stripped, she assumed Kaleb had an accident."

"She's full of shit." Amber's voice was fierce. "I mean, he did wet the bed. But I would never shake Kaleb. I know about Shaken Baby Syndrome. You can kill a kid. She's lying."

Lee nodded. Appeasing a client was more productive than arguing, she'd learned. But the truth was, as a DCF foster mother, Gloria Marshall had a lot more credibility than Amber. "The CAT scan didn't find anything. But the medical examination found red welts on Kaleb's bottom, like he'd been whipped by a belt."

"Not a belt." Amber twisted her plain gold wedding band, her gaze fixed on her fingers. "It was a track from a race car set."

Without blinking, Lee stared at the younger woman. She'd been trained to look for solutions when her young clients made parenting mistakes. To avoid being judgmental. Now she struggled to keep her face from betraying her revulsion. "I was always impressed by your commitment not to hit Kaleb the way your mom hit you." Lee was relieved to hear how quiet her words sounded.

A spasm passed over Amber's face. "We spanked him the night before, because he threw a miniature car at one of Gloria's special needs kids. It hit her face and made her bleed." She glanced at Lee, her thin lips quavering. "We were protecting her from Kaleb. The only reason he got spanked with the race track was to make sure he didn't hurt any of those kids again. And then Gloria makes up this big freaking lie about shaking Kaleb, just to make sure DCF would come after me."

Lee closed her eyes, covering her mouth with her hand. So Amber admitted to beating Kaleb. Hard enough to leave welts. A fist of anger welled behind her ribcage. Had she wasted her time working with Amber all these months? Or, even worse, was she just terrible at her job? She swallowed hard. During training, she'd been told over and over not to expect miracles with the clientele. Her job was to be a guide, not a judge. Lee opened her eyes, clutching the couch cushions and painting on a reassuring smile. But before she could speak, a door creaked from the hallway.

The silhouette of a man, short and stocky, emerged from the darkness. He paused at the doorway. "Hi." He nodded to Lee but spoke to Amber before Lee could say hello. "I have to get to work. Did you make my lunch?"

Amber jerked her head toward the counter.

Dan picked up a thermal lunch bag and poured coffee into a travel mug. "See you tonight." He glanced at his wife before he left, but her gaze was fixed on the carpet. The apartment was blasted with heat and light for a brief moment before he shut the door behind him.

Amber faced Lee again in the dim light. "Mr. Wonderful."

Detecting a ghost of a smile on Amber's drawn lips, Lee smiled back, happy for any release of tension in this glum room. "What do you do all day here without a car?"

Amber shrugged. "I'm still doing school online for my GED. I can't concentrate right now, though. I wish *I* could escape, like Dan." She snorted. "You know what's really unfair? Dan told me to spank Kaleb with the piece of track. But the one DCF's coming down on is me, because Gloria's poisoned them against me. She'd never let anyone accuse her precious Daniel of anything."

Same old story. Someone else was always to blame. When would her clients learn to take responsibility for their choices? "You're in a tough spot, Amber." Lee chose her words with care. "DCF investigated you once before. You needed to keep your nose clean. Even if Gloria's accusation can't be proved, finding those welts on Kaleb's bottom makes you seem"—she widened her eyes to soften the word—"abusive."

Amber threw up her hands. "I wouldn't even have done it if Dan didn't tell me to. He was afraid Gloria

29

wouldn't let us stay there if one of her kids got hurt. Figures. I get the blame for this, too."

Her monotone was undercut with a thrum of insecurity and unhappiness. Lee's gaze softened. She wanted to believe the young mother. "Did Dan tell Mrs. Marshall the spanking was his idea?" Why would the investigation focus on just the mother if the incident occurred when the father was in the room, too?

"He said he did." Amber's gaze was bitter. "He says being spanked as a kid was how he learned respect. Gloria feels sorry for him, because she thinks his parents were monsters. Dan is always a victim in Gloria's eyes."

Lee pressed cold fingers to her temples. "If she cares about Dan so much, why would she make up a story to hurt his wife and jeopardize custody of his son?"

"She wants to get rid of me. Isn't it obvious?" The words exploded from Amber in an angry burst. "She wants Dan and Kaleb to move in with her. She wants to be the only woman in Dan's life."

Lee lowered her eyelids. If Amber hoped to get back her son, she'd have to learn to keep her paranoia in check. In the six months Lee had worked with the girl, her progress had been slow. No matter how often she was told her toddler needed affection and approval, Amber still reacted too strictly to Kaleb's behavior. What were the chances she'd learn to be appropriate now, with her back against the wall? Lee tapped a finger against her lips. "When do the support classes start?" Parenting classes were the first step for a parent whose child was taken into custody.

"Next Tuesday." Amber whipped the blanket off

her lap and threw it to the floor. "And guess what? *I'm* the only one who has to go."

Lee lifted her eyebrows. Dan had been a witness to the beating. Why would DCF excuse him from mandatory remediation? "That's really weird. Normally both parents have to take the classes."

"Gloria Marshall's influence again." Amber's lips twisted into a cruel smile. "She told the caseworker Daniel's a good dad, and *I'm* the one who needs help."

"Wow." Punishing one of two parents. Talk about a recipe for marital conflict. She leaned toward Amber. "Don't let this case come between you and your husband. You have to be a team if you want Kaleb back. Try not to take out your anger on Daniel." If she didn't know better, she'd wonder if Mrs. Marshall *was* driving a wedge between Amber and Daniel—although no one at the Department of Children and Family services would ever believe it. On the phone, Trish Nichols had as much as said Gloria Marshall's testimony was beyond doubt.

"He'd just better remember where *his* loyalties are." Amber poked the tip of her pinky into her mouth, the cuticle jammed against her top front teeth as she chewed. "He's allowed to go over to Gloria's and see Kaleb whenever he wants. I get one hour of supervised visitation a week."

Frowning, Lee shook her head again. This whole legal process seemed biased against Amber. "Any chance they'll increase visitation if you cooperate?"

"I'm hoping they will." In the moonscape of her complexion, Amber's eyes were two deep wells. "My attorney said he'd work on it."

Lee retrieved Amber's folder from her work bag.

Empty cans clinked against each other as Lee cleared a small space on top of the table for a stack of release forms. She handed Amber a pen. "If you want me to speak to your attorney or anyone else, you have to sign these papers. By the way, Kaleb's two-and-a-half year developmental screen is coming up."

Amber nodded. "You could visit Kaleb at daycare, even if I'm not there."

Just last month, Lee had helped Amber enroll her son at ABC Preschool. "Good thinking." She passed Amber another release form to sign. "Has the guardian ad litem called yet?"

"I don't think so." The part in Amber's hair was a vivid white line as she bent her head to write her signature.

"Well, make sure you answer your phone when she does. Her opinion will hold more weight with the judge than anyone else's, because her job is to represent Kaleb's best interests—not his parents', and not Mrs. Marshall's." Lee had researched guardians ad litem last night. In Florida's judicial system, they were trained volunteers who spoke with the most important people involved in the case—including the child.

"Everybody takes Gloria's side." Amber signed another release and handed it back, her eyes bleak.

"Well, not me." Lee hoped her face showed more confidence than she felt. "I work for you. I won't lie for you, but I'll let the court know you're always here for our appointments, and you're always interested in learning more about child development." She smiled with false good cheer as she gathered her papers to leave.

Amber wobbled to a stand, her expression

crumpling. She wrapped her arms across her chest, hugging her thin shoulders. "I hate being here without him." Her whisper was keen with pain. "I never wanted to hurt him the way my mother hurt me. I was doing better, wasn't I? With your help?"

Her expression was urgent and vulnerable, pleading for approval. Lee swallowed hard. "Definitely. But if you love your son, you have to cooperate with this investigation. No matter how unfair you think it is, you have to keep your temper and just be a loving mother to Kaleb when you see him. Okay?"

Amber nodded, tears spilling onto her gaunt cheekbones. "Okay. I just want him back." She wiped at her face with the back of her hand.

Lee squeezed Amber's cold arm. "We'll get back your boy."

For the first time today, Amber smiled, the crooked tips of her teeth just visible from behind her lips. "Thanks." She opened the front door to a flood of sunshine.

Her pupils contracting, Lee winced. She stopped on her way out the door, her hand shading her eyes from the sun. "Do yourself a favor, okay? Open your curtains and let in some sunshine."

Amber's smile widened. Covering her mouth, she shut the door.

Lee climbed into her car, for once relishing the stifling heat. She wrapped her hands around the warmth of the steering wheel. Amber's apartment was as cold as a tomb.

Chapter Three

Lee glanced at the time. Two o'clock. No wonder she was starving. She steered her car out of Amber's neighborhood, heading south toward the shopping area. She just had time to pick up a quick bite to eat before meeting her next client. The local supermarket had recently added a dine-in deli. Nothing fancy, but a place to cool off while she ate.

In line at the supermarket deli counter, she checked her voicemail. *Great.* Her next client had canceled—a perpetual nuisance of Lee's job. But at least she wouldn't drive twenty-five minutes south and be stood up.

She sat at a booth and bit into her meatball sandwich. A little dry. She dipped it in the marinara cup and took another bite. Maybe she'd get her paperwork done early today. Lee glanced out the window. She wasn't far from Kaleb's day care center. She *could* stop in, see how he was doing, and tell him his mom missed him. She sighed, swaddling the half-eaten sandwich in wax paper and tucking it in her purse. She'd eat it for dinner if it survived the heat.

The preschool playground was empty when she arrived fifteen minutes later. No wonder—on a blistering summer afternoon in south Florida, kids' sweaty bodies would stick to the slides.

Her release form in hand, Lee asked to speak to the

preschool director. She was shown into the office of Mrs. Lattery, an energetic woman with a salt-and-pepper beehive. "She's completely inappropriate." Mrs. Lattery's penciled eyebrows rose high for emphasis. "She offers her son nothing but negative attention. Last week he built a tower, and when it fell over, he started to cry. She told him to quit acting like a baby, or she'd take away the blocks. Of course he cried harder, so she took away the blocks and told him it was his own fault."

Classic Amber. Lee clenched her jaw. Mrs. Lattery was right to be critical, of course, but like all the other home visitors in her office, Lee was protective of her clients. "Amber loves her son, but she's young and has a lot to learn. Have you seen her with Kaleb very often?"

"Just twice. Before he was put in Mrs. Marshall's custody, his dad was the one who usually picked him up. Now Mr. or Mrs. Marshall picks him up, and he's happy as can be to see them. He gets a lot of visitors since DCF has been called in. Only his mother's visits upset him."

Lee stifled a sigh. Amber made enemies wherever she went.

Wiping an embroidered handkerchief over her nose, the director pinned her gaze on Lee. "At her visit earlier this week, I expected an emotional reunion. I knew she hadn't seen Kaleb since Child and Family Services removed him from her custody. Instead, she sat at the lunch table and told him to stop socializing with the other kids 'til he finished his broccoli. Can you imagine?" The director's voice hit a high note of indignation. She blew her nose like a trumpet, wadding the handkerchief and tucking it in the waist pocket of her blazer.

"Amber's not…comfortable with public displays of affection." Lee leaned across the desk. Maybe if she could establish a bond with the director, she could diminish the negative impression Amber had made. "But she's been very open to learning how to be a better parent." *As open as a closed book can be.*

Mrs. Lattery tsked. "All I can say is, the girl needs a *world* of parenting education if her little boy has a prayer of developing normally. *And* therapy," she added with a nod. "For both of them."

"Thank you, Mrs. Lattery," Lee answered with a polite smile. The director's mind was already made up. "Could I see Kaleb now?"

Mrs. Lattery led her past Hush-a-bye Corner, a cozy, carpeted nook framed by shelves laden with picture books, past the lunch area with its long table and miniature chairs, and over to a more active section of the preschool identified as Builder's Town by a red banner hanging from the ceiling.

A waist-high wall of shelves enclosed an area dedicated to wooden trucks and blocks of every size and shape. A little girl of three or four, her cheeks freckled and her hair flaming red, crawled around a colorful cardboard skyscraper with a small wooden wagon in her hand. Next to her, a wide grin on his elfin face, was a small, thin boy with brown hair and pale skin.

Lee nodded her thanks to Mrs. Lattery. Kaleb hadn't noticed her yet.

Tilting his head, he stared at the cardboard construction on the center of the rug. A shy smile lit his face, and he nodded to the left.

Lee's gaze followed Kaleb's, but she could see only a pair of men's brown loafers jutting into the children's circle. Someone was stretched on the floor near Kaleb. Was it Gloria Marshall's husband? Lee didn't relish the idea of a conversation with the Marshalls today. Steeling herself, she followed a path around the shelves of blocks to enter the play area.

Kaleb's smile fell away. Two lines formed a deep groove between his eyebrows.

Placing her hands on her knees, she leaned her face closer, her smile wide. "Hi, Kaleb! Your mom told me I could find you here."

Kaleb tucked his chin to his chest, ears protruding from his fine hair.

Awkward. She hadn't developed much of a rapport with Kaleb, relying on the toys in her bag to keep him close during her home visits. She straightened, her gaze sidling to the scuffed brown shoes and up the man's slacks. She stumbled backward, into the sharp corner of a cabinet. "What are *you* doing here?"

Lounging against the shelf of toys was the bartender from Whistler's Grille, his hand frozen in mid-air as he retrieved a block from the shelf.

Lee stared at the man on the floor, her mouth agape. Even in khaki pants and a casual button-down shirt, he radiated a sex appeal at odds with the blocks, trucks, and tiny construction signs surrounding him. If she'd found Cleopatra playing with Kaleb on the carpet, she couldn't have been more surprised.

His smile tight, he aimed his attention on Kaleb, pointing to the cardboard tower. "You need to guard the wall, little guy. Before your friend drives a truck into it."

Seizing the cardboard block, Kaleb raced to place it on top. His expression solemn, he shielded his hand in front of the wall.

With a sweet smile, the little girl rolled her truck around the perimeter of the building.

Lee floundered for an explanation. "Are you a friend of the family?"

"I'm the guardian ad litem." He extended his hand. "James Kilbourn. But friends call me by my middle name. Bricker." His eyes glinted.

She leaned down to shake his hand, uncomfortably aware of her blouse gaping as she brushed her fingers over his.

His palm, rough and warm, squeezed her hand and then released it. "Are you the parent educator? Lee Anya Cooper?"

"Lee to my friends." She straightened, her pulse beating in her throat. "So you're a trained guardian ad litem?"

His eyebrow rose. "So you're a trained parent educator?"

Her cheeks flushed. "Sorry. I just didn't realize you were more than a bartender. I mean"—she hurried to correct herself—"I'm surprised you're the guardian. How did you know my name?"

He shrugged. "I read the file. Figured I might want to check in with you at some point."

Of all the rotten luck. The person she most needed to win to her client's side was the man she'd alienated the day before. *Great. Time for a heaping helping of humble pie.* She swallowed hard. "So you've met Kaleb already." Her voice pitched high, she held her hand out to the little boy.

Kaleb shrank against the shelf, his pale brow furrowed.

"Come on, Kaleb! Don't you want to shake my hand? I won't bite!" Lee's lips stretched against her teeth as she smiled.

But Kaleb slithered farther along the shelf, his gaze locked on hers 'til he bumped into the opposite corner.

"You're not real natural with kids, are you?" Bricker whispered.

Lee whipped her hair over her shoulder and opened her mouth to retort. Then, thinking better of it, she swallowed her indignation. *Please, kid, could you work with me?*

Bricker rose, two blocks in hand, and sat near the fortress. Placing the bricks on the highest rampart, he dusted off his hands. "There. Nothin's gonna knock down my wall." He nodded, his gaze fixed on the bricks.

A smile breaking over his face, Kaleb sneaked to the tower and swept off the two top bricks with the palm of his hand.

Feigning indignation, Bricker knelt in front of the fort and guarded it with his body. He shook his finger at Kaleb. "If the fort comes down, all its bricks have to be put back."

Lee watched Kaleb's expression as he cocked his head. The satisfaction he'd gained from building the fortress battled with the temptation to destroy it.

"What do you think, Kaleb?" Bricker asked. "Do you want to keep going and make it bigger, or do you want to knock it down and build another one some other time?" His tone was neutral. Either option seemed okay.

"Knock it down." Kaleb's voice was soft and shy.

"Knock it down, and then we'll put away the bricks?" Bricker asked.

Kaleb nodded.

"All right, then." Bricker retreated to the shelf. "You'd better watch out," he told the red-headed girl. "The demo crew's moving in."

She backed up as Kaleb, a joyful smile on his face, ran into the center of the fortress. The cardboard blockade crashed to the floor. He collapsed, laughing, in the center of the destruction.

Pulling up Kaleb by his hand, Bricker high-fived him. "All right, little man, let's get these bricks put away so you can play outside. You hand me the bricks, and I'll hand them to Ms. Cooper. She can stack them on the shelf. Like a chain of helpers, you get it?"

Lee knelt as Bricker tossed her a block, careful not to meet his gaze. She'd written him off as an egotistical womanizer. But she'd never met a man more gifted with children. And children could smell *phony* a mile away.

Kaleb giggled and hummed as they worked.

When the last brick was handed down the chain, Bricker dropped to his knees. "Good work, Kaleb. I see you're a man who can build, *and* you're a man who cleans up after himself. It's been a real pleasure to meet you." His gaze warm, he extended his hand to the little boy.

Kaleb thrust his hand into Bricker's and chortled as Bricker's big hand pumped his small arm up and down.

"Now let's shake hands with the nice lady who helped us clean up." Bricker rotated his broad shoulders to include Lee in their circle.

Kaleb's smile faltered, and his hands dropped to his side.

"Go ahead, buddy. Shake her hand to say thanks for her help." Bricker nodded at Lee, raising an eyebrow to encourage her.

Lee held out her hand. Bricker had already witnessed Kaleb rejecting her once. She'd never recover her dignity if he snubbed her again. *When in doubt, kiss up.* "You built a great fortress, Kaleb. I liked watching you knock it down, too."

A tiny smile playing at the corner of his lips, Kaleb brushed his fingertips against Lee's. Then he dropped his hand, gluing his gaze back on the carpet.

Lee rose, tugging at her skirt. At least he hadn't run away.

Bricker stood and tousled Kaleb's hair, bringing back the smile to his upturned face. "Why don't you go outside to the playground, and I'll go talk to this nice lady. I'll come back and play with you again real soon." He raised his hand for one more high-five, following with a low-five that made Kaleb giggle.

The boy ran to the door of the playground and disappeared.

In his first visit, Bricker had gotten right past Kaleb's defenses. In six months of weekly visits, Lee hadn't gotten as close to the anxious little boy. *Looks like there's no one this guy can't charm.* Her lips twisted. She'd have to find a way to deal with Bricker Kilbourn.

He glanced from Kaleb's retreating figure to Lee, his expression cool. "I suggest we go outside to talk."

Blanching at his formal tone, she nodded. As she

led Bricker through the child care center, she fought the urge to pat her hair, forcing her hands to relax as she made her way to the school's entrance.

Bricker stepped to Lee's side and opened the door. The full heat of the day engulfed them the moment they were outside. The blacktop shimmered with waves of heat, distorting the surface of the parking lot like a funhouse mirror.

Lee swept a lank strand of hair behind her ear as she eyed the lot. "I don't think talking out here is such a good idea. I'm already melting."

"Northerners," Bricker said under his breath. "Well, how about we talk in my truck with the air conditioning on?"

Lee's palm shot up. Alone in the front seat with this guy? Close enough for him to hear her heart beating? No, thanks. "Why don't we stand under a tree in the shade?"

Bricker nodded his chin toward the tall, thin palm trees scattered on the outskirts of the lot. "Those? They don't throw enough shade for a pencil."

Sweat trickled down Lee's cleavage as Bricker waited for her decision. Clenching her fingers into a fist, she blew air toward her forehead. "Okay, fine. Where are you parked?"

Crossing the blacktop was like wading through lava. Lee's gaze clung to Bricker's back like an invisible lifeline as he strolled ahead, tossing his keys in one hand as if he'd never been more comfortable.

As they approached a black SUV, he tapped the hood and opened the driver's door, hopping inside.

The truck rumbled to life, and Lee recoiled. As she rounded the vehicle to enter the passenger side, she saw

Bricker bound from the truck to help her.

"Isn't black the worst color for a car in this heat?" She was too hot to stop herself from grumbling.

His answer was a pointed stare at the door as he waited for her to get in.

She lunged upward, her heel slipping on the running board.

He shot a hand to her waist, steadying her.

The shock of his unexpected touch raced through her system. Off balance, she tumbled sideways onto the seat, jerking her feet inside. Righting herself with all the dignity she could muster, she glanced to where he stood outside the door.

An amused smile played on his lips.

"What?" Her tone was sharper than she intended as she straightened her skirt beneath her. Hot air from the dash blew against her damp face.

"I'll leave my door open a minute 'til the truck cools." He sauntered back to the driver's side and swung himself onto the seat behind the wheel.

Lee plucked tacky hairs from her neck, closing her eyes as the air cooled. She held her arms perfectly still, willing herself to stop sweating. Tilting back her chin, she let the vents blast at her throat. *Ahhhhhhh.* Her pulse slowed as she swiveled her head to the right and left, relishing the cold draft lifting hair from her sticky skin. At the quiet click of his door shutting, she blinked open her eyes. Her heartbeat rocketed as her gaze lighted on hairs glistening from a golden triangle of skin under the unbuttoned collar of his shirt. Sitting upright, she averted her gaze and cleared her throat. "Kaleb seems to be adjusting well to preschool." She composed her face into what she hoped was an expression of professional neutrality.

Bricker leaned back, draping his left arm on the steering wheel and resting his other hand over the ball of the stick shift.

Her gaze drifted to the hairs on his wrist. They were darkened with sweat as the air conditioning flattened them against his skin.

"The staff has concerns. He doesn't eat much, and he doesn't participate in circle time." He tapped a button on the dash to adjust the intensity of the air flow.

A hint of stubble followed the angular cut of his jaw, but his throat, disappearing into a pale yellow polo shirt, was silky and bare. "He's probably just getting used to the place," Lee stammered. *Stop staring.* She turned to look out the windshield. "Kaleb's had a lot of changes in the past two weeks." Digging her nails into her palms, Lee forced herself to refocus on the image of Amber's tear-stained face. The girl's veins against the pallor of her skin looked like a topographical map. She was fragile. She needed a champion. Or at least an advocate. Lee's gaze, no longer wavering, returned to Bricker. "But he played with the bricks like a normal three-year-old."

"Yes, but in this place, no one yells at him for acting like a kid." Bricker's forehead wrinkled. Air from the vents fluttered his wavy, blond-brown hair at the temples.

Lee took a deep breath. *Time for the sales pitch.* "Kaleb's parents are young and inexperienced, but they're fully cooperating with DCF. For six months, Amber has been meeting with me for parenting education. I've been teaching her about appropriate expectations for a child Kaleb's age. I'd like to see her visitations increased while Kaleb's in custody." If the guardian ad litem was really so influential, maybe he could pull some strings.

Bricker frowned. "If you're asking me to recommend increased visitation, you should realize I disagree. The nursery school teachers report Kaleb is anxious while she's there and plucks out his hair when she leaves."

Great. I wonder if Amber knows and just didn't tell me. Lee hoped her face was impassive. "Sometimes kids act out when they're separated from a parent."

One eyebrow rose high, and the corners of Bricker's mouth lifted. "Yet he doesn't pull out his hair after his dad's visits."

The man seemed bent on disagreeing. Lowering her head, she ground her teeth, forcing a smile before she raised her gaze. "But his dad sees him more often than his mom does. If Kaleb visited with her more than once a week, he might be less traumatized when she left." Whether or not she spoke the truth, Lee hoped she at least sounded convincing.

Bricker scratched his chin. "Kaleb seems a lot more comfortable with men than women. A little unusual for a three year old, in my experience." He shook his head. "Makes me wonder what, exactly, goes on at home."

Low blow. Slapping her hands against her thighs, she fired a look of pure venom. "Are you a psychologist, too, Mr. Bartender?" she snapped. "Because your statement is pure speculation. If you *have* been trained as a guardian ad litem, you should know your job is not to psychoanalyze my client."

He raised an eyebrow. "And what exactly are *your*

credentials? Since you're diagnosing Kaleb with post-traumatic stress disorder."

Lee's pulse thumped in her throat. "For your information, I studied psychology. In a real college. Not Bartending School." The nasty words were out of her mouth before she could stop them. What was she doing?

He raised his palms, twisting his lips into a mocking smile. "A psychology major! I had no idea who I was dealing with," he drawled. "I most humbly beg your pardon. Maybe you can diagnose me next."

Lee scrabbled for the door handle with her right hand. If she didn't get out fast, she'd slap his arrogant face. Sliding off the seat, she jumped to the pavement. Staggering in her heels, she flung her palm against the side of the vehicle to steady herself. *Ow!* Burned by the sun-baked metal, she squeezed her fingers under her armpit. Why had she agreed to talk in his stupid truck? Tossing back her hair, she took a deep breath before looking up. "We'll discuss this another time, Mr. Kilbourn." Her tone was too sharp, turning her words into a rain of arrows. Losing her temper wouldn't help her client. But damn, she felt good putting him in his place.

"That's Mr. Bartender to you." Smirking, he gunned the engine.

She just had time to slam the door before he peeled away. Covered in a cloud of exhaust, she watched the truck squeal across the smoking blacktop and disappear down the street.

****

"Don't you ever work?" Bricker watched Austin shoulder his way into the bar, past a family of tourists heading out the door into the late afternoon swelter.

"Seventy-two hours off, pal. I'm telling ya, you should have gone to Fire Academy instead of law school. Great hours, great exercise, great perks." Austin settled himself sideways on a bar stool and saluted two attractive young women at a table near the window.

They waved back, giggling.

Bricker glanced at the women as he poured a draft beer and set it in front of his friend. After his run-in with Lee Cooper earlier that afternoon, he appreciated a woman smiling instead of sneering. "You met these girls on the job?"

"Nope." Austin took a long draught of his beer, swiping the back of his hand across his upper lip. "Sometimes girls can just *smell* hero on a guy." He glanced around the restaurant. "Pretty quiet in here for a Friday."

"It's early yet," Bricker said. "The seniors already came for the Early Bird specials, so we're in a lull before the dinner rush." He restocked the wine glasses, polishing each one with a damp rag before hanging it on a rack above his head.

"Glad you're back behind the bar where you have half a clue what you're doing. Don't want you chasing away the dinner clientele like you did the Asian girl yesterday at lunch." Austin's dimple burrowed into his cheek.

Bricker's hand stopped for a split second before he resumed wiping a glass. "What Asian girl?" Lee Cooper dismissing him as nothing more than a stupid bartender bothered him more than he wanted to admit. He sure as hell wouldn't acknowledge it to Austin.

"The only Asian in the restaurant yesterday."

Austin's mocking smile grew wider. "The girl you tried to impress, who looked at you like you were lower than a well in a California drought. Don't play games with me, bro." He waggled his finger. "I've known you too long. The girl got under your skin."

Bricker shrugged, keeping his expression stony.

"So make a play for her, dude. When's the last time you had to work up a sweat to get a girl's attention?" Austin's gaze swept the dining room, lingering on the two women shooting glances toward the bar.

Bricker shook his head. "She's involved with the family of a kid I've been assigned to as guardian."

"Oh, man." Austin propped his elbows on the bar, his biceps bulging from the weight of his shoulders. "Conflict of interest?"

Bricker grimaced. "Conflict, anyway. She slammed the door in my face when I left."

Austin snorted, raising his eyebrow. "What did you say?"

"I made fun of her psychology degree." Bricker fixed his gaze on the rag as he polished the wine glass.

"Why'd you do *that*?"

The moment dragged on until finally Bricker met Austin's puzzled gaze. "She called me 'Mr. Bartender.'"

Austin collapsed with laughter against the bar.

Gritting his teeth, Bricker continued hanging wine glasses.

"Dude." Austin paused for a breath. "Did you tell her you have a law degree? And graduated at the top of your class?"

"Why would I dredge up ancient history?" Bricker

scowled, wiping up Austin's spat-out beer. He forced a polite smile as a customer stepped up to order a drink.

Austin waited 'til the drink had been poured and the customer returned to his table. "Well, the details might help her understand why a bartender's moonlighting as a guardian ad litem."

Bricker shrugged. "What do I care what she thinks?"

"Oh, you care, dude. You care." Austin stroked his chin. "I haven't seen you worked up over a girl since you moved to the Virgin Islands."

His shoulders tensed. Austin was wading into dangerous waters. "I don't know what you're talking about, and neither do you." Bricker hoped his tone was warning enough.

"Oh yeah, you do." Austin wagged his finger. "Before everyone found out what you did, and you ran off to the islands."

Bricker slammed his hand on the bar. "Tell you what, pal." He packed his quiet voice with steel. "If I wanted to talk about my past, I'd hire a shrink." He picked up the empty glass rack and shoved open the door to the dish room. It banged against the wall.

Found out what I did. Bricker crashed the clean racks of bar glasses onto a cart. *Only three people in the world really know what I did. One of them's dead, and the other two aren't talking.* He loaded the dirty glasses into the dishwasher, grinding his teeth. Austin knew him too well. Since he'd graduated from law school, he'd kept his relationships with women strictly casual. Nothing but one-night stands with unattached local girls and a steady stream of tourists.

Why did he care about Lee Cooper's opinion,

anyway? Just because he liked her laugh? She sure didn't use it around him. He shook his head and started the dishwasher. Jets of water roared as he stepped back from the steam and leaned against the wall, waiting for the cycle to end.

Her condescending attitude and wicked temper should have doused his fire. But the way her eyes flashed when she defended her client... Most of the social workers he dealt with in custody cases had already made up their minds against the parents. Lee obviously intended to fight for Amber Maly. He respected her commitment, no matter what he thought of her client.

He hadn't meant for things to get so hostile in his truck, either. As soon as he stepped from the air-conditioned school into the sweltering heat, he noticed beads of sweat trickling down to the base of her throat. When he saw her lift a heavy curtain of hair from her neck, he knew he needed to get her out of the heat. Her waist had yielded beneath his hand as he helped her into the truck. When she stumbled into her seat, she'd seemed less haughty. More approachable.

By the time he'd climbed into his seat, he found Lee leaning back with her eyes closed, resting for a moment in the flow of cooling air. The dampness of her skin under the blast of air magnified the scent of her perfume. She smelled so good, like an armful of wildflowers. He craved a smile, just as he had when he'd first seen her on the beach. But when she opened her eyes, she was all business. And before he knew it, he was fighting her in the family services trenches again.

Rolling back his shoulders, he gave his head a hard

shake and hoisted clean glass racks from the dishwasher. Ignoring the steam, he stacked them shoulder-high to cool before returning to the bar.

Austin's glass was empty.

Bricker set a fresh beer in front of him. Peace offering, guy-style. "So what's your plan for tonight?" As he listened to Austin debate the pros and cons of familiar Bellamy hot spots, Bricker filled drink orders for the servers. He hoped they'd get a good crowd tonight to keep him busy. Anything to sweep Lee Cooper from his mind.

****

"Take a picture, Lee. I want to pretend I'm with you on the beach at sunset."

Lee sighed. "Hold on." Barefoot couples in front and behind her strolled the edges of the surf. The imprints of their feet filled with water and dissolved. Lee plodded onto the dry sand to avoid the foot traffic, snapping a quick picture of the sun setting over the Gulf and another of the stream of people strolling back and forth.

"Almost done," she muttered to her sister through the phone, attaching the photos to a blank text and hitting Send. Crouching, she clawed the sand into a hollow, turning to sink her bottom into it and dig her toes in the soft powder of Pomegranate Beach. She put the phone back to her ear.

"Beautiful." Lee heard a long, satisfied sigh. "Wow, you're around a lot of happy couples."

"Maybe they're happy," Lee said darkly. "Or maybe they're zombies."

"Always the cynic." Brett's voice was amused. "So why aren't you out on a Friday night?"

"Why aren't you?" Lee countered.

"Because I have two young children and a husband who's out of town. What's your excuse?"

Wriggling her toes deeper into the sand, she frowned. The truth was she'd wanted to clear her mind after her encounter with James "Bricker" Kilbourn today. She didn't know why he threw her so off-balance. Yes, he was disproportionately blessed with good looks. On the other hand, he was still tending bar at the age of thirty-something. Now, she wasn't usually such a snob. Heck, most of her friends worked in the restaurant business, funding their passions for art, acting, or writing. But she needed to find *something* to undercut her infuriating attraction. Just because he'd made an instant connection with Kaleb didn't mean he had the right to make fun of her awkwardness with kids. And okay, maybe she *had* acted like a fool by bragging about her psychology degree, but did he have to be so mean about it?

"Lee? Are you still there?"

Her sister's voice dragged her from her musings. "Yeah."

A mother with three young children had stopped, looking for a spot for her beach blanket.

Lee offered a brief smile, avoiding eye contact and drawing her arms around her knees. Bracing the phone with her shoulder, she faced the opposite direction. "Brett, do you think I'm cold and unapproachable?"

The phone was silent for a long moment. "Who is he?" her sister asked.

Lee winced. She hated when Brett used her all-knowing, superior tone of voice. "Who is who?"

"You're the opposite of 'cold and unapproachable'

unless you're attracted to someone."

"You're ridiculous, Brett!" Lee blew her hair from her eyes. "Why would anyone use hostility to get someone interested?"

"You tell me, little sister," Brett replied. "Your tactic works. And as soon as you've got the guy eating out of your hand, you drop him."

Lee's shoulders tensed. *Not fair.* Her siblings were amused by the many boyfriends she'd split up with over the years. "Black Widow," her brother Conrad called her. The wind picked up, and Lee pushed the bangs from her eyes. "Stick to your day job, Sis. You don't have a future as a therapist." She cast her mind back to Bricker's jeep. The hairs of his forearms painted gold by the sun, the muscles of his jaw clenching as he spoke... She had to admit, her nervous system *had* been on high alert.

"How are the kids?" Lee's voice was so bright, it almost squeaked. "Did Neil score any goals this week?" *How's* that *for being good with kids*? She congratulated herself as Brett listed the high points of her son's last soccer game. *Does a person who's* not natural with kids *know her nephew's weekly schedule*? She wished Bricker could see her now, keeping updated with little Neil's life despite the many miles between them.

The line was quiet.

"Are you even listening?" her sister's voice demanded.

"Yes!" Lee was indignant. "Give him a hug from Aunt Lee and tell him I'm proud of him."

"For kicking a little girl in the shins and being sidelined the rest of the game?" Brett asked drily.

Oops. Lee winced. "For being spunky!"

Brett tsked.

She wasn't buying it. Lee giggled, reburying her toes in the cool sand. "I really do miss your kids." Even though she was exhausted by her nephew's and niece's endless requests to play tag, hide-and-seek, and duck-duck-goose, watching them discover the world was fascinating. "Are they still awake?"

"Deeni's asleep, and Neil's settled into bed with a book. I'll tell them you said hi." Brett's voice became more brisk. "How's work?"

"Busy. I'm working with about twenty families now." Lee glanced over her shoulder as seagulls squawked overhead, vying for crackers scattered on the young family's beach blanket. She plugged a finger into her free ear. Talking about clients outside of the office was a no-no. But who could be hurt if she didn't mention names? Lee's sister lived a thousand miles away, after all. "One of the mothers I work with was charged with abuse and neglect. I'm working to get her more visitation with her son."

Brett's shudder was audible. "How can you defend someone who hurt her child?"

"Because I think there's more to the story than meets the eye. The mother's very young, and she had a really bad childhood. Her own mother was physically abusive." In her cold apartment, Amber had reminded Lee of an abandoned child, wrapping skinny arms around herself to stay warm.

"The cycle of abuse," Brett grated. "I see it all the time in my work at the family clinic. You'd think parents who were abused themselves as children would try harder with their own kids."

"Her life is complicated, Brett." Lee struggled to

hide her annoyance. "How does she learn to 'do better' by her own child if she's never had a role model?"

"I guess you have a point." Brett sighed. "Kids who don't bond with their parents when they're young are stuck with emotional issues the rest of their lives."

Lee rubbed her forehead, holding the phone close to her face. "I don't know about 'the rest of their lives.'" Her voice sounded scratchy, and she cleared her throat. "I think a person can be normal as long as they're shown love at some point." In the picture Brett had posted on social media, the whole family seemed poised to protect the wary orphan newly arrived from Korea. They'd surrounded her with care. Suffocated her with it, sometimes. She'd had as much love in her childhood as anyone else. She'd just started two years later.

"Hey." Brett's voice was tender. "Of course they can. I didn't mean anything, Lee-Lee."

Her old nickname. Lee relaxed, running her fingers through the cooling sand. "She wants me to get her more visitation with her son. So far, I haven't been much help." The memory of Bricker's face, sneering down from his truck before she slammed the door, made her chest tighten. He was the one person Amber most needed on her side. And Lee only made matters worse when she talked to him.

"Well, if anyone can help her, it's you." Brett's voice, so much like their mother's, was soothing. "I'm so proud of you for doing this work."

"Professional work." Lee completed her sister's sentence, making quotation marks with her free hand.

"Yes, professional work." Brett laughed. "After all those years of watching you search for your calling, I'm so glad you finally landed a respectable job."

"I guess," Lee agreed, her voice flat. She watched the youngest child lurch from the blanket and race into the gentle waves, his body wracked with giggles. "I just wish I had more time to do *other* things I like." Blank canvases leaned against the wall of her living room. Maybe she'd find time to paint this weekend. She hadn't picked up a brush since she moved to Pomegranate Key.

"You think you're busy now? Just wait 'til you have kids." Brett paused. "As if."

"Yeah, yeah, yeah," Lee muttered. The whole family teased her about settling down. Brett, Conrad, and even their parents had all married and started families right out of college. Lee, as usual, was the black sheep.

The sun dropped on the horizon, a glowing orange half-circle visible above the sea. "I'd better get going. The sun's going down, and I don't want to have to find my car in the dark. Give the kids a hug for me. Mom and Dad, too," she added.

"I will." Brett's voice dipped. "I'm looking into a conference in Orlando. Close enough to swing over and visit you afterward."

"I'd love to see you." Lee meant it. She missed the whole family, even if they treated her like the hapless heroine of their favorite sitcom. "Just email me the details." She stood and slid her phone into the pocket of her shorts. This time, the dry sand was cool. She hurried along a mile of beach to get back to her car, goaded by the sinking sun.

Chapter Four

Agency staff meetings happened every Friday, and Lee looked forward to them. She'd picked up a lot of useful knowledge from listening to the team of parent educators discuss, or "staff," their clients' problems. Three other co-workers had already finished when Lee saw Janna gazing at her from the head conference table. "Ready to update us on what's going on with Amber Maly?"

"Sure." Lee hesitated, hating to look like an amateur. Her coworkers had years of experience dealing with the Department of Children and Family Services. They'd let her know in a heartbeat if she was bungling her case. Speaking with more confidence than she felt, she summarized Amber's situation.

At the mention of Kaleb's placement with a foster mother, Shari, a seasoned home visitor, nodded. "I work with the mother of one of Gloria Marshall's foster kids. I've been to her house to do developmental screens on one of the babies. Gloria's great."

Lee nodded, fighting the urge to roll her eyes. "Most people agree with you. Anyway, Amber denies shaking Kaleb. She thinks Gloria Marshall's undermining her."

Shari snorted. "Who will believe her? Not after the way she whipped her son's butt with a race track."

A slow burn crept up the back of Lee's neck.

"Amber's husband, Daniel, told her to beat Kaleb, but somehow *Dad* is still allowed unsupervised visitation. Amber thinks Gloria's using her influence to protect him. She's been like a second mother to Daniel for years." Bristling at Shari's smirk, Lee pointed her gaze at Janna. "I don't understand why DCF is only targeting Amber."

Tapping her pencil against the table, Janna frowned. "Has Amber talked to the guardian ad litem?"

Lee shook her head, her pulse galloping. "I did, though. Actually, you met him, too. At lunch the other day."

Janna's response was a blank stare.

Her lips tight, Lee braced herself. "At Whistler's Grille. He was our server."

Recognition dawned on Janna's face. She threw back her head and laughed, shoulders shaking. Their co-workers stared back and forth between Janna and Lee in bemusement.

Wiping tears from her eyes, Janna shook her finger at Lee. "I *told* you, you should have been nicer!" Janna's face became serious. "If you really want to help your client, you'd better find a way to get the guardian to see what you see in her. Because nobody else is taking her side."

No kidding. Lee's shoulders sagged. "I met up with him at Kaleb's preschool, and I kind of…argued again. He already seemed to have his mind set against Amber."

Janna swept her papers into a neat pile and placed them in her workbag. "Maybe he's right." She sat back in her chair, her smile compassionate. "We never want to see the worst in our clients. Sometimes we get too close."

Lee clenched the seat cushion. Becoming emotional in a staff meeting was a sure way to lose the respect of her colleagues. "Maybe I *am* wrong. But you told me all I can do is testify to what I've seen. And what I see is a mom who really loves her son. Yes, she makes a lot of mistakes. But I see her wanting to be a better mother. And I hope she'll get the chance to prove herself." Heat built behind her eyes as she shifted her gaze to the floor.

"Then you know what you have to do, Toots."

When she heard a hint of laughter behind Janna's words, Lee raised her head.

"Make nice with the guardian ad litem." A wicked glint shined from Janna's eyes. "But not *too* nice. I wouldn't want one of my girls getting accused of trying to influence a court case."

Lee flushed. Janna's sense of humor sometimes leapt over the bounds of good taste. Ignoring the chuckles from around the room, Lee checked her calendar as the meeting ended. She had an hour free this afternoon. Enough time to try again with Bricker Kilbourn. Maybe this time she could maintain professionalism. For Amber's sake.

****

When she opened the door to Whistler's Bar and Grille at one o'clock, she was breathing a little faster than usual. *Just keep a smile on your face, and whatever he says, don't take the bait.* But when she saw a young woman behind the bar, her smile faltered. "I'm looking for Bricker Kilbourn. Is he working today?"

The young bartender shook her head, her high-set pony tail swinging to either side of her face. "Do you want me to call him?"

Lee slid her work bag off her shoulder onto a stool. "I don't know. Maybe I should come back another time."

The bartender raised her phone from her apron pocket. "Girls come in here all the time asking for Bricker. I'll just call him. What's your name?"

Lee's cheeks burned. "Lee Cooper. And I'm here on business." Bad enough that Bricker's co-worker had sized her up as just another lovesick girl. How much more humiliating if he refused to take her call.

Holding the phone to her ear, the bartender tapped black fingernails against the burnished wood of the bar. "Bricker." She stared at Lee. "Lee Cooper's here for you." She paused, her gaze never faltering. "Asian chick."

Lee narrowed her eyes, plucking the phone from the girl's hand and turning a cold shoulder as she spoke. "Um, hello." Lee strained to keep her tone polite. A loud pounding reverberated from the other end of the line. "I'm sorry to bother you. I was hoping we could talk for a few minutes."

"Can't hear you, darlin'." Bricker's voice hollered in her ear. "What'd you say?"

She moved the phone a few inches away. "This is Lee Cooper," she called, extending each word. "Can I talk to you for a minute?"

Only the din of the continued pounding assured her he was still on the line.

"Lee Cooper to your friends, as I recall," he finally answered. "I suppose if you're ready to be friendly, I'd better jump on it."

Lee flexed her fingers. *Smile*, she commanded

herself.

"What can I do for you, Lee?"

The sharp ring of a hammer against metal rang in her ears. "I wanted to talk again about my client, Amber Maly. Without arguing." Her laugh was tinny and nervous.

"Say again? It's pretty loud out here." He was almost shouting through the phone.

Releasing her breath, she strained to raise her voice over the racket. "I wanted to talk to you about Amber— Look," Lee interrupted herself. "Can you go somewhere else for a minute to talk?"

She heard Bricker call out, followed by the buzzing of sudden silence in her ears.

"I'm down at the dock today. Why don't you come over to the marina so we can talk face-to-face?"

She glanced at her watch. Her lunch hour was almost halfway over. "I hate to interrupt your work. I just wanted to tell you what Amber's been doing to become a better parent."

The banging resumed on the other end of the line, even louder than before.

"If you want to talk today, you'll have to come here. I've got a lot of work to do while I've got my friend around to help. Look for the *Tequila Mockingbird.*"

"But I—"

The call disconnected before she could finish. Handing back the phone to the bartender with a quick thanks, she calculated how much time she had. The marina wasn't far. If she left now, she'd have just enough time to talk to Bricker before her next appointment.

She trotted out to her car and slid behind the wheel, checking her face in the mirror. *Smile.* Obediently, her reflection broke into a wide grin. Satisfied, Lee cruised down Main Street and headed toward the harbor.

The marina was small, tucked out of the view of tourists for the use of local boat owners. Parking her car in the thin shade of a loblolly pine tree, she stepped onto the sandy berm of the access road. Her car engine, overheated and suddenly cooling, ticked into silence as she searched the boatyard. She crossed the road and listened for the sound of hammering, wandering past The Snack Shack, a ramshackle restaurant with a bait-and-tackle shed on the side. The salt air was tinged with an odor of decaying fish from the fishing boats lining the docks.

Hammering rang from the left. Shading her eyes with her hand, she squinted over the long dock stretched above the water, perpendicular to the shore. She stepped onto the wooden planks, unnerved by the creaking of old wood. Could her weight break a board? Despite the glare of the sun, she finally located the source of the pounding.

A man swung a hammer at the end of the dock by one of the largest boats.

She steered herself along the long wooden platform, her hesitant arrival cloaked by the noise. Not until her shadow fell across the planks in front of him did the man's face swivel toward her. She recognized him from the bar the day she and Janna stopped for lunch. With the grace of a cat, he jumped from a kneeling to a standing position, stretching his arms overhead and groaning despite his wide smile.

"Hi, I'm Lee Cooper." She put out her hand and

tried not to stare at the sweat pouring down his hairy, shirtless torso. "Is Bricker around?"

"Austin Stevenson. Pleasure to meet you." He jerked his head toward the back of the boat and shook her hand. His gray eyes twinkled against a sunburned face. "Bricker's working on the motor."

"Thanks." Shading her eyes with her hand to survey the boat, she gave a low whistle. White, sleek, and gleaming with polished metal, it looked like a mini yacht. Where did a bartender get the money for such a fancy boat? More to the point, where did she board? On her father's fish 'n ski boat, stepping over the side was easy. Here, she'd need to climb over the rails…and in these heels, she'd have a hard time keeping her balance. With the toes of the opposite foot, she pried off the straps at the back of her ankles and stepped onto the hot planks, wincing.

Austin placed his hands on her waist and lifted her off the dock, swinging her over the rail into the rear of the boat like a bag of groceries. Before she'd caught her breath, Austin winked and strolled down the dock toward shore with a luxurious roll of his muscled shoulders.

Lee clutched the rail, her gaze searching each corner of the boat. "Mr. Kilbourn—uh, Bricker?"

"Down here."

She craned her neck to peer around the motor. Was he in the water? She inched toward his voice, her hand sliding along hot fiberglass.

Bricker's head bobbed up to the left of the motors just as she sank onto the bench. "Afternoon." He nodded, grabbing a cleat on the floor and heaving himself out of the water. His bottom landed on the transom with a practiced side twist. Water coursed over his broad shoulders as he shook his hair like a wet dog, spraying Lee with a cold, salty shower.

She put up her hands in protest.

He opened his palms. "Sorry."

Don't act like a princess. Lee swallowed her annoyance. "No problem. A little water's refreshing on such a hot day."

He padded across the deck in his bare feet and reached over the seat for a white towel. Turning his back, he ran the towel over his head and neck, rubbing it against his face and down his chest. The muscles of his shoulder blades shimmied beneath golden skin. He wore a pair of cut-off jean shorts, sodden with water and sagging just enough to reveal a velvety V above his waistband. In the nick of time, she raised her gaze from the curve of his back when he swung around to face her.

"So—?"

With an effort, she dragged her attention back to her purpose. "I wanted to let you know what Amber and I have been working on these past six months. The parenting education, I mean."

Seagulls called in the air high overhead as the boat rocked among gently splashing waves. Bricker ran the towel over his biceps before draping it over the bucket seat. As he sat, his gaze locked with hers. "I think we've seen the effects of her parenting education."

His tone was dry. Lee's mouth snapped open to retort, but she forced a smile instead. "She had a lot to learn when I first met her. But she kept every appointment and asked lots of questions about child development. Amber isn't comfortable showing her emotions, but she loves her son."

"I'm willing to believe she does." Bricker shrugged, the tips of his hair curling in the warm air. "Doesn't mean he's safe with her."

Lee tapped her toes against the scratchy deck rug. She needed a different approach. "Look. Amber doesn't believe in corporal punishment. Do you know how exceptional that is among teenaged mothers in her circumstances? She told me from day one she'd never spank Kaleb. She blames her own anger problem on the abuse she suffered from her own mother while she was growing up."

His eyes wide, Bricker raked his fingers through wet hair on the crown of his head. "I agree. I saw the pictures of what she did to Kaleb."

Lee flushed. "But *she* didn't lose her temper that night. Her husband told her she needed to teach Kaleb a lesson. Daniel was afraid if Kaleb misbehaved, Gloria Marshall would make them leave the house. The water heater in their apartment was broken. They had nowhere else to go."

Bricker frowned. "The report says Mom struck Kaleb, not Dad. No one's documented concerns about Dad's behavior."

Here we go again. She narrowed her gaze, shaking her head. "The father keeps getting a pass, and the mother gets blamed for everything. How convenient."

Bricker acknowledged her point with a tip of his chin. "A year ago, the pediatrician raised concerns over Kaleb's failure to thrive. He reported the father was appropriate, but he didn't trust Amber's reactions to Kaleb. She didn't show affection. Her reactions were too harsh when Kaleb acted like a typical toddler. Even when Amber's not hitting her son, she may be doing damage."

"She's fighting against the cycle of abuse." Lee's voice sounded thin and desperate to her own ears.

"Breaking the cycle is hard," Bricker said. "Not without a lot of therapy and more support than she seems to have. And we can't allow Kaleb to be a guinea pig while she works out her own childhood traumas. Because the next time she shakes him could be his last."

"There's no proof she shook him." Lee clasped her hands on her lap to keep them from trembling. She was getting nowhere with the guardian. Again. "He didn't vomit, or have tremors, or have trouble staying awake. The doctor didn't even bother to order a CT scan."

"The ER doc wasn't a neurologist," Bricker reminded her. "On the other hand, Gloria Marshall is a court-mandated reporter of abuse. Are you implying she lied?"

"Maybe. Gloria thinks of Daniel like a son, and she doesn't like the girl he married," Lee snapped.

Bricker's eyebrows rose. "You really think Amber's the victim of a conspiracy?"

"I don't know." She threw up her hands. "I just don't think we should take away a young mother's child when no one ever taught her how to be a good parent. I think she should be given a chance, for God's sake!"

Bricker raised a calming palm. "Take it easy. I'm looking at all sides of the issue."

Lee snorted. "You're siding with the foster mom just because she works for the county. You're not objective!"

"Well, I'm not the one who's shouting."

Bricker's low voice held a warning. And damn it all, he was right. Every muscle in her body was clenched. Poised on the edge of her seat, she probably looked ready to fly at him with her fists at any second. Drawing a deep breath in and out, she forced her fingers to loosen. She tried to relax her shoulders and smile, but the best she could manage was an awkward twist of her lips. "Sorry. I just hate to see a child taken from his parents."

Propping an elbow on the arm of the chair, he rubbed his finger over his lip. Still gazing at her, he dipped his head. "She's lucky to have you in her corner. Someone who understands how tough parenting can be." He paused, squinting. "Do you have kids?"

"Ha! No." Brett would laugh at the very idea.

The skeptical eyebrow tilt was back. "Seems like a funny line of work to be in, telling parents how to raise their kids."

She thrust her shoulders back and glared. "I've spent plenty of time with children. I'm an aunt."

The corners of Bricker's mouth twitched.

Lee lifted her chin, pushing a strand of hair behind her ear. "I've been trained on the job, too. I know more about the stages of child development than most mothers, I'll bet."

He slid a palm over his mouth, but smile lines fanned out from the corners of his eyes, and a deep chuckle rumbled from his chest.

Her breath caught as she remembered his face, unreserved and lighthearted, when he'd steadied her at the beach concession. Since then, so many angry words had passed between them. But now, seeing him hide his smile behind his hand made her knees weak all over again.

At a call from down the dock, Bricker stood and waved his arm. "Austin's coming back. We'd better repair the rest of those planks before he has to leave for work."

Jolted from her daze, Lee rose to her feet. Swaying, she planted her feet wider and groped for the railing. "I appreciate you meeting me today. And I'm sorry for getting…all keyed up over Amber. I hope I haven't made matters worse." She shaded a hand over her eyes to find his face against the white-hot sun.

Shrugging his arms into a T-shirt, he paused.

Deep grooves cut the corners of his mouth. She'd never seen someone fight a smile so hard.

"'All keyed up,' huh? More like a boxer warming up in the ring." He threw out a hand to stop her protest. "I understand, okay? You're just protecting your client." He tugged the shirt over his head and chest. "No matter what I read in the reports, I do my best to stay objective when I meet the parents. Family reunification is always the goal, as long as the child is safe. But a lot of this decision rests on Kaleb. If he showed delayed development while he lived with his mother, but he hits the normal range in a foster family, then he might need a different home environment." He strode to the front of the boat, hopping over the side onto the dock.

Lee slid her way along the side of the boat again, ignoring the two pairs of eyes tracking her progress. "Can you let me know when you plan to meet with Amber?" Releasing the rail, Lee swayed, eyeing the dock below.

"So you can coach her? I don't think so." Bricker extended his arms to help her down.

Hesitating, she placed her hands in his large palms. Holding tight, she stepped over the railing and prepared to hop off.

He pushed his foot down hard on the bow to tilt it, and Lee tumbled off, falling against his sun-warmed chest. "Whoa, girl." He smiled down at her, his fingers still entwined with hers.

Her skin smoldering, she lurched back, her tender instep landing on the sharp heel of a shoe she'd shed on the dock. Lee winced, plucking her sandals off the boards. "I'll let you guys get back to work." She exited the dock faster than she'd arrived, more unbalanced by her fall against Bricker than the swell of the waves beneath the planks.

At least this time, their meeting had ended with a smile. A smile that would linger in her thoughts and quicken her heartbeat all day.

Chapter Five

Lee closed the front door of Jodi's beautiful Mediterranean house and made a mad dash for her car as the skies opened in a sudden afternoon shower. Her heavy work bag was stuffed with files and toddler toys. She flung it into the passenger seat and scuttled behind the wheel, slamming the door behind her.

To avoid the daily downpours of the Florida rainy season, she'd learned to end her work day right before four o'clock. But visiting Jodi was such a pleasure, her sessions often ran long. The mother of twins born fifteen weeks premature, Jodi and her husband had been married ten years and were financially secure. They'd requested a parenting educator to help them navigate the complex world of pediatric therapy providers. Astonishingly, at the age of two, Connor and Isabel were on track, showing no delays in language or motor skills. Lee had just completed their developmental screens and celebrated their progress with their mother.

Lee mopped at her brow with a napkin from the glove compartment. No sense driving until the rain let up. Might as well check her messages.

"This is Amber." In the week since Lee had last seen Amber, her voice sounded even flatter than usual. "We met with our lawyer today. He said Gloria started Kaleb in speech therapy and occupational therapy. She's claiming his development is delayed, which is more BS. I told the lawyer you test Kaleb all the time, and he's never shown any delays. He wants you to fax your test results to his office."

Frowning, Lee jotted down the fax number and dropped her phone in her purse. Kaleb's developmental screens were no more than six weeks old, and they showed he was on target in all areas. He couldn't have lapsed so much since his last assessment. And finding child therapists for new patients took months. How had Gloria managed the feat in a week? The whole situation was bizarre.

What had Bricker said last week as she got off his boat? Something about developmental delays as a factor in cases like Kaleb's. She'd thought Bricker was speaking in generalities. Had accusations been filed Lee didn't know about?

Her stomach knotted. What was Gloria Marshall up to?

The rain subsided into a steady drip. Fastening her seatbelt, she popped the key in the ignition. She'd get back to the office and fax Amber's attorney six months of proof that Kaleb's progress was typical. After rolling away from the curb, she accelerated through the street's flooded gutters. Synchronizing her phone to the car with a touch of a button, she dialed Bricker's number.

She didn't know she was holding her breath until it puffed from her lips at the sound of his voicemail. Maybe he was working tonight. *Or maybe he's screening your call.* She glanced at herself in the rearview mirror, giving her hair a little shake as she prepared to speak after the beep. "Hi, this is Lee Cooper. I've got something I think you'll want to see." She flushed, squelching an urge to giggle. "Something about Kaleb, I mean. It's important. I'd appreciate you calling me at your earliest convenience." She glanced back at the mirror as the call disconnected. Her client deserved to regain custody of her son. Delivering proof of Kaleb's progress was just the help Amber needed. Surely that accounted for the silly grin on her face.

Not the idea of seeing Bricker Kilbourn again.

****

He hopped up the step from the passenger cabin onto the helm deck, whistling. Leaning over the bow, he looked down the dock toward the shore. Nothing.

He returned to the cockpit in the back of the boat and opened a fold-away bench. He sat, stretching his arms on either side of him along the gunwale. The grill was fired up, and the mini fridge was stocked with vegetables and T-bone steaks for dinner. A six pack of a local craft beer chilled on the bottom shelf.

From the pocket of his khaki shorts he retrieved his phone. No new messages. He tucked it back in his pocket and then changed his mind, scanning through the messages he'd sent and received in the past hour.

He'd answered Lee's voicemail with a text on his way out the door of the restaurant. Even at five o'clock, the bar was getting loud. Phone conversations were impossible.

—*Meet me at the boat*—

Good grief, do you live on that boat?

He smiled at her response then punched onto the keyboard.

—*I wish. I'm taking her out tonight. Can you get here in a half hr?*—

She'd been quiet for so long, he gave up on hearing back. But his phone lit up again as he checked his oil and fuel levels.

I'll be there

That was over an hour ago. Where was she? And what was so important she needed to show him tonight? If he weren't so curious, he'd leave right now. If dedication to her client meant she was willing to work late on a Friday night, then she deserved to be heard. He tapped his fingers on the gunwale. She'd hung to this railing for dear life last week, like she couldn't wait to get back on dry land. Trotting down the dock, high heels swinging off the ends of two fingers, calf muscles pumping like two round apples under her tawny skin…

As if summoned by his thoughts, footsteps approached, a slapping of sandals against feet. She wore a high-waisted summer dress with halter straps and bright splashes of purple and turquoise blue.

Her wary smile made him want to pick her up and carry her onto the boat. She'd have none of his help, though; he knew. His chest expanded with held breath as she approached—small, but determined, like a miniature steam engine.

Her hand clutched a manila folder thick with papers. "Thanks for waiting." She sounded breathless. "The printer at work ran out of ink, and I had to figure out how to refill it. When I got home, I just had time to change and come over here. And then I forgot my phone at the house."

"No problem." He was glad she'd explained before he gave her a hard time about being late. For once, he'd like their conversation not to turn into an argument. He hopped from the side of the boat and extended his arm to help her up.

Sunlight reflected off her shiny black hair as she

shook her head. "Could I just show you my papers down here? I don't want to take too much of your time."

She wasn't even planning to get on the boat? *Great.* He could have been gone an hour ago if he hadn't stopped at the market to buy fixings for their dinner. Drumming his fingers against the railing, he frowned. "Are you afraid of the water?"

"No, I love the water. I'm just not crazy about boats." Large sunglasses masked her eyes.

She had to make this difficult, didn't she? He sighed. "Then we've got a problem." With those glasses on, her face was unreadable. All he'd wanted was to grill some dinner and try to get along. Why did every meeting turn into a battle of wills?

Licking her lips, she eyed the boat and took a deep breath. "All right." Her lips clamped into a thin line. "Did you ever think about buying a ladder? Climbing on the boat in a dress isn't easy."

"I'm not usually wearing one when I get on." He gritted his teeth. *Stop sparring with her. She's just nervous.* After their last meeting, when Lee had flared over Amber and unexpectedly backed down, he'd begun to suspect her sarcasm was a mask for insecurity. He needed to pacify her, not antagonize her. "I'm sorry. The thing is, I've got a grill up there. Steaks, vegetables, and some good local beer. I'd like to have dinner. And while I cook it, you can tell me all about what you've got in your hand."

After a long moment, she gave a tiny nod. "Can you give me a hand?"

Placing her folder on the weathered boards of the dock, she unstrapped her sandals and tossed them onto the boat. Hesitantly, she held out her hands.

With an encouraging smile, Bricker slid his palms under her forearms, tightening his grip and lifting her easily onto the deck. He hopped back to the dock to retrieve her folder, handing it up before swinging himself behind her on the bow.

Sliding her hand along the gunwale, she advanced into the cockpit and lowered herself onto the rear bench, her brow slick with perspiration.

He opened the refrigerator in the tiny kitchen area behind the front seats. "Beer?" He held out a bottle toward her, but she shook her head. He shrugged, flipping off the cap with an opener on his key ring and taking a long draught. As he lowered the bottle, he fixed his gaze on her. "Mind if I take this boat out on the water?"

From over the stern, Lee scanned the sky. "I love the ocean." Her fingers twisted the hairs escaping from the loose bun resting on her neck. "I've just got some bad memories of being on boats, of being more of a hostage than a passenger."

Bricker frowned. "A hostage?"

Lee shrugged. "My family loves to boat. But once they get you out on the water, they make all the decisions. They make you water ski whether you want to or not. They put you on a tube and spin you just to see if you can hold on. They don't stop the boat 'til *they're* ready." Her words rushed out.

If she'd just take off those sunglasses, so he could see her eyes. "Don't worry. We're not going tubing," he said. "I'd just like to take the boat out in the deeper water so we can watch the sun set while we talk and have dinner. We won't stay out any longer than you want to. I promise."

Mouth drawn tight, Lee swiveled her head to examine the length of the boat. "I don't even have a phone to call anyone. If I agree to this, I have to just trust you."

His heart beat a little faster. They were making progress. "I guess you do." He stepped into the helm station and returned with a life vest. "You want to wear this?"

She shook her head. "I'll help you cast off the lines."

"Okay." He hid his surprise as she crouched in the back left corner. Taking his seat at the helm, he pressed the button on the throttle handle to lower the twin motors into the water. He pushed the throttle forward and turned the key, easing back on the lever as the boat roared to life.

Lee had already untied the line. He hastened to the right side of the boat to unfasten the ropes.

She joined him up front, perching in the aft helm seat with her legs folded to the side under her sun dress. She tucked her paperwork under her legs.

He backed the boat straight out of the slip 'til the bow was clear of the last piling. Only then did he turn the steering wheel and accelerate away from the shore. He pointed at tall, white pencil buoys dotting the waters ahead. "Manatee safe zone," he called out.

With her face angled toward the water on her side of the boat, she nodded. "Do you ever see any?"

"Not this time of year. They head north during the summer, but in the spring, they come out of the canals and estuaries to find colder water. You're most likely to see them then."

Her palm over her forehead like a visor, she swiveled her head back to Bricker. "Don't they get attacked by alligators in the canals?"

He laughed. "You haven't been in Florida long, I guess. Manatees are too big to attack. Besides, they're herbivores. They're no competition for the alligators."

Her eyebrows arched above her sunglasses. "I never realized how full of predators Florida is. Alligators, snakes, fire ants, wild boar, poisonous spiders—all the wild life here can kill you. I'm glad at least the manatee is safe."

Bricker's lips twisted. "Except from humans. But I promise you, I give manatees a wide berth when I see them from my boat."

They coasted in silence until they passed the last of the buoys. The sun, a glowing ball casting golden light into a horizontal bank of clouds, had begun its descent toward the silvery ocean. Still two hours from sunset, Bricker calculated. He accelerated, watching Lee from the corner of his eye to gauge how fast he could go.

Leaning against the armrest, she gazed over the port side of the boat.

When he opened up the throttle, spray from the waves climbed up to half the height of the bow as he steered into a turn.

Lee's eyes were masked by her dark glasses, but her lips were relaxed.

Bricker slowed, the water sucking back against the boat as he faced Lee. "You want to drive?"

"No." She shook her head. "I've never been out on the ocean before. I'm just enjoying it."

For the first time since he'd seen her at the beach, she grinned. He caught his breath. After all their bickering, he'd forgotten how her smile had captivated him when he first spotted her with her friends. Her cheeks lifted, smooth and cinnamon-warm with curves like a ripened peach. Her lips, beaming upward and disappearing into deep dimples at the corners of her mouth, had shed their severity. If he could just see her eyes. He was tempted to remove her sunglasses himself.

"I can't believe how calm the waters are out here. How deep are we?" She swung her head to peer over the rail. Locks of black hair slipped from the bun, dangling long and sleek on either side of her face. She tossed back her head, disentangling an elastic band from her hair and sweeping her mane into her other palm in one smooth motion. She wrapped her hair into a higher, tidier roll.

He swallowed hard before glancing at the controls. "We're at a depth of about seven hundred feet. Deep water starts at twelve hundred." He glanced toward the shore. At this distance, the pine trees at the edge of the sand were a hazy green line. "Does this spot look good?"

"Yes, fine." She slid down in her seat 'til her head rested against the top of her chair. Tilting her chin to the sky, she sighed, holding out her inner arms to the warmth of the sun.

Bricker cut the motor, the familiar rumble in his ears vibrating to a sudden stop. Sea waters sloshed against the boat, rocking the vessel like a cradle.

"It's so peaceful out here, miles from anywhere. No wonder you spend all your time on this boat." She tilted her cheek against the seat leather to regard him, her lips curving. Golden-orange sunlight haloed her head, casting her face into shadow.

He lifted out of his seat and sprang across the fiberglass flooring to the galley behind him. *If she keeps smiling, I'll forget why we're out here.* He flipped open the grill and squatted in front of the refrigerator, retrieving two seasoned Porterhouse steaks and a platter of sliced zucchini, red onions, and asparagus. He glanced at Lee. If they were going to talk about work, he wanted to get it over with as quickly as possible. "Want to carry your folder back here and show me what all the excitement's about?"

Her smile faded as she plucked the papers from beneath her legs. She rose, placing a careful hand on the forward facing helm seat as she worked her way to the back of the cockpit. Settling herself on the bench, she placed the unopened folder on her lap. "What did you mean when you said 'if Kaleb's development has been delayed'?"

Her tone was all business again. Bricker wished he hadn't reminded her of the file. He brushed olive oil onto the hot metal bars before placing the steaks on the top rack. They sizzled as he nudged the thick flanks. "How do you like your steak?" he asked over his shoulder.

"Medium rare. Did you hear what I asked you?"

Her voice was edged with impatience. He sighed, dropping his chin to his chest. Detente had been too good to last. He lifted his head and pivoted to face her, holding out the tongs at an angle from his body. "Yes, ma'am. You asked what I meant by Kaleb's delays. The reports show Kaleb is delayed in gross motor skills, fine motor skills, and social-emotional development. Not necessarily proving his mother was abusive," he added, as Lee's mouth opened to interrupt. "But Amber gets another strike against her if his skills all jump into the normal range now, when he's out of her home."

"Who *says* Kaleb is delayed?" Lee's eyebrows huddled like a bank of storm clouds.

He waved small circles in the air with the tongs. He needed to get the vegetables cooking. "Gloria Marshall has her own—what do you call yourselves? Parent educators?—for the children she fosters. Her gal screened Kaleb and found multiple delays." Turning back to the grill, he prodded the steaks. Satisfied, he lifted the vegetables one by one onto the bottom rack.

"Was Kaleb even *there* when Gloria's 'gal' assessed him?"

Lee's voice behind him sounded incredulous. Bricker stiffened but continued arranging the vegetables in neat rows on the grill. "I'm sure he was."

"Don't be so sure," Lee shot back. "Lots of times you can't get a child to cooperate with the assessment. So you let the parents, or the temporary guardian in this case, answer the questions. You said yourself Kaleb doesn't seem comfortable with women. Imagine a complete stranger asking Kaleb to stack ten blocks or hop on one foot. Do *you* think he'd obey?"

Bricker paused. She had a point. He pivoted to find Lee on the edge of the bench, thrusting her folder toward him.

She swept her sunglasses onto the top of her head. Her gaze was searing. "I've screened Kaleb in person for the past six months, and he's *never* had a delay." She handed him the folder. "Gloria Marshall's worker doesn't know Kaleb. If he was too shy to cooperate, and Gloria told the worker he couldn't do what's on those tests, the worker would take her word. The parent's report carries the same weight as witnessing the child perform the activity."

Bricker flipped through Lee's tests. The squares following each question were filled with neat check marks in all the *Yes* columns. He glanced at the dates. The tests had been administered at two-month intervals starting in February.

"We do these questionnaires to identify developmental delays as early as possible. If we have a concern, we connect the child with a therapist." Lee's hands were clasped between her knees, her face upturned. "We try to help the parents, but our number one concern is *always* the child. And Kaleb Maly had *no* delays when I screened him."

Perplexed, Bricker raised and dropped his shoulders. "I don't think anyone would believe Gloria Marshall is lying about Kaleb's development. She takes care of special needs kids. She knows the developmental timelines as well as anyone."

Lee flopped back against the bench, her fingers thrumming the leather. "I know my argument sounds crazy. Gloria's got all the credibility in this case." She slapped the seat with the flat of her hand. "I've spent a lot of time with Kaleb over the past six months, though. A kid doesn't develop delays overnight. But you said yourself, the case against Amber gets stronger if her son's development lagged behind while he lived with her but improves as soon as he moves in with a new family." Lee drummed her fingers against the white leather. "I'll call Gloria Marshall's home visitor. She works for a different agency, but she can tell me the circumstances of Kaleb's assessment that day." She stopped, lifting her nose into the air. "Is something burning?"

Uh-oh. He'd been so wrapped up in their conversation, he'd forgotten how fast asparagus burned over an open flame. Grumbling, he swept the blackened stalks onto the platter.

"Don't worry." Lee moved to his left, holding on to the rail behind her. "I love charred vegetables. Really."

Way to go, burning her dinner like an amateur. He glanced up from the platter with a moody shrug of his shoulders.

The sinking sun caressed her from behind, warming to a dark caramel the long hairs framing her face. Her smile whipped across his heart. He fought the urge to drop the plate of burnt food and gather her in his arms, running his fingers over her sun-heated shoulders and tilting up those smiling lips to his…

Before his face betrayed him, he backed away, gripping the platter with white knuckles. What kind of sorcery did this woman cast? One smile, and he'd do anything she asked.

Setting the vegetables on the counter, he wiped his brow with the back of his hand. *Focus on the food.* He flipped the steaks, approving the black lines seared across the browned meat. Sprinkling kosher salt and coarse ground pepper over the top and bottom racks, he lowered the grill lid and cleared his throat. "They'll be done in a minute." Relieved to hear his voice sounded normal, he opened a drawer and removed heavy plastic plates. "I don't have a table up here. I hope you don't mind eating with your plate on your knee." He grabbed two sets of plastic cutlery and a handful of paper napkins and turned to face her.

"No, of course not." Lee's expression had clouded

again. "But aren't my tests evidence Amber could use in her case?" She picked up the folder he'd dropped on top of the sink.

She wasn't thinking about the dinner arrangements, that was clear. He shot her a warning glance. "Save your question for Amber's attorney, not me."

Lee winced, shamefaced. "Sorry. I know you're just a court volunteer. I shouldn't be asking you about legal matters."

He laughed, short and sharp. "Because I'm just a stupid bartender, right?" He raised his beer and took a long drink, careful to block his face from her gaze. He didn't want her seeing how much her opinion meant. Hell, he didn't know why he cared so much himself.

"No!"

She actually sounded contrite. Dropping the bottle in the recycling bin, he risked a glance at her face. Her cheeks were flushed pink.

"I didn't mean to insult you. I just meant I can't expect you to know how to advise me in a court case." She spread her hands, shrugging her shoulders upward.

"You can't ask me for legal advice because I represent Kaleb's best interests. I don't take sides." Even to his own ears, his tone was severe.

Lee shrank back with a guilty smile. "Okay. Sorry."

Seeing Lee's pained expression, he gave a dismissive wave. "Don't worry." He hesitated. Should he tell her? "I do know something about the courts. I went to law school."

Lee's eyes widened.

He snorted. "Don't look so surprised." He fiddled with the knobs on the grill to hide his embarrassment.

Why'd he tell her? He didn't have to prove himself.

"Law school. Pretty impressive." She paused. "I guess that explains how a bartender qualifies to be a guardian ad litem." She laughed, an unexpected, noisy burst of gaiety.

Was she mocking him? He spun to face her. Her eyes squeezed almost shut as she slapped her hand on the rail and giggled. The dimples at the upraised corners of her lips were deep enough to plant seeds. His chest seized with delight. This was the girl who'd charmed him on the beach, her boisterous laughter so at odds with her demure Asian face. *Am I being racist?* His neck grew hot. He'd bought into a stereotype. And she'd smashed it wide open.

"I'm kidding!" She smiled up at him, her gaze a question. She struggled to stop laughing, reaching her hand to his arm again.

Her fingers, as soft and small as a child's, closed over his wrist. After the barbs and insults of their past encounters, the kindness in her touch woke every nerve ending in his arm. Without thinking, he lifted his hand to touch her cheek.

Her expression flickered into confusion, and she drew back, reaching for the grab rail behind her.

Damn it. Why had he pushed? He dropped his hand to his side and forced a grin. "A mosquito landed on you." He waved his hand around her head. "I think I got it. You ready to eat?" He spun to open the grill, hoping she'd bought the excuse. The puff of smoky air as he lifted the lid reminded him how hungry he was. Maybe food would help him get a grip on his reactions. One thing was for sure—now she was finally relaxing, he couldn't afford to scare her away.

****

"Can I have another beer?" A warm breeze, redolent with seaweed and brine, stroked Lee's shoulders as the sun melted into the ocean.

Bricker popped the cap with a bottle opener and handed her the drink. A whisper of cold steam curled through the opened hole and evaporated in the humid air. She clinked the neck of her bottle against his as he settled back onto the bench beside her.

"When I first moved to Pomegranate Key and heard people making plans for where they were 'going to see the sunset,' I thought they were crazy. Now I understand." A panoply of colors crossed the undulating surface of the sea as the sun sank lower on the horizon. Lee closed her eyes. "I'm trying to remember this so I can paint it later."

"Most people just take a picture." Bricker's Southern drawl was as soft as the night air. "I didn't realize you were an artist."

Lee shook her head. "I could never be an artist. I just like to paint." She took a long drink from the bottle. At first, the beer had tasted bitter, but now, it flowed down her throat like chocolate milk.

Elbow braced on the back of the bench, Bricker faced her, cheek propped on a fist. With his hair tied back, he reminded her of a Mohican warrior she'd once seen in a painting.

She squinted at his eyes. Nope. Too blue.

"If you're a painter, you're an artist *de facto*." Although his words sounded like a challenge, his lips lifted at the corners.

"If you go to law school, are you a lawyer *de facto*? What's *de facto* mean, anyway?" Mimicking his posture, she propped her chin against her folded knuckles.

The humorous curve of his lips dropped into a severe line. "It means 'in reality.' And no, I'm not a lawyer."

She gave him a light slap on the knee. "Don't be so sensitive. Just getting my undergrad degree took me years. Did you graduate? From law school, I mean."

He leaned back against the bench, crossing his arms over his chest. His lime-green T-shirt glowed in the twilight. "Yup."

"Did you pass the bar exam?" Why was he so quiet all of a sudden? She had all kinds of questions.

He nodded, taking a long swig from his beer and looking over the side of the boat.

"But you never worked as an attorney," she prompted him.

A muscle twitched just under his jaw line.

He wasn't answering or even looking at her. But on the bright side, now was her chance to stare at him. She tilted her chin to the side. Was his hair sun-kissed chestnut? Or honey-kissed, with a few bold strokes of hazel? He'd have to untie it if she painted him. Hair like his needed to sweep over the shoulder. Swing, and show movement.

His voice interrupted her thoughts. "What are you doing?"

She froze, aware for the first time she'd been swinging her own chin back and forth as she imagined directing him to sit for a painting. With a giggle, she slapped her hand over her mouth. Her voice sounded high-pitched and squeaky. "I—nothing." What had they been talking about? Sitting up straight with sudden insight, she frowned. "You're like the opposite of me. I dropped out of three different schools and had six different majors. After ten years, I finally graduated and got a sensible job. *You* studied a serious profession, and after ten years, you gave it up to do the thing you loved: bartending!"

His eyebrow quirked. "Where'd you get the idea I love bartending?"

Puzzled, she drew back. "Why else would you give up being an attorney?"

He stared down at his hands before he spoke. "Let's just say I wasn't interested in following in my father's footsteps after all."

"Your father was a lawyer?" she asked.

He nodded.

The muscle under his jaw twitched again. She wanted to rub her finger over it. "Well, your name makes sense now. 'James Bricker and Kilbourn.' A good name for a law firm." She lifted her beer to her lips.

"That's not how you name a law firm. Listen"—he took the bottle from her hand—"maybe you've had enough beer."

What an insulting suggestion! She hadn't even finished her second bottle. Or was it the third? Let's see, she'd had the first beer to help Bricker relax after he burned the asparagus. And there was a second beer as they ate. She was on her second drink, right? She shook her head to get out the fuzz. She always had been a lightweight. "I'm fine!" She stood, swayed, and sat again hard on the seat. "So, don't you get along with your father?" She drew her knees onto the bench and curled toward him. With the sun now dipping under the horizon, the night sky was deepening into midnight blue.

He sighed, placing her bottle out of reach. "He's dead."

"I'm so sorry." Lee squeezed her hand over his. She'd summed up Bricker as a cocky, dumb playboy. But he had a law degree. And inside, he was just a little boy, hurting over the death of his father.

Bricker gave a brief, sharp laugh. "Don't be. I'm not." He dropped his hand to his side. "If it's all the same to you, I'd prefer not to talk about my father." His eyes were steely gray in the moonlight reflecting off the water.

"Why?" A whisper of conscience told her to respect his boundaries, but the voice of her curiosity was louder.

He stared straight ahead, twisting his fingers in his lap before he met her gaze. "He wasn't the hero everyone thought he was."

The warning look in his eyes silenced her. Stars speckled the darkening sky, looking nearer and brighter in the unpolluted atmosphere over the ocean. No wonder he spent so much time on this boat. The waters lapped gently at the sides as she studied his profile. The long nose had just a hint of crookedness. Maybe someone had punched him in the nose. His father? Her eyes widened. She'd love to find out more about his family dynamics, but she couldn't ask about his father again. She tapped her finger against her lip, thinking. Then she smiled. "Do you ever take your mother out here?"

He faced her again, his eyes narrowed. "You have a lot of questions about my family."

She shrugged. "I thought you might be close to your mom."

Folding his arms, he nodded. "She's not very…mobile anymore. She has MS—relapsing-remitting multiple sclerosis. She uses a walker to get around. You think *you* had a hard time getting on the boat."

"Oh, how sad," Lee breathed.

But he shook his head. "Nothing is sad about my mother. She's always been the backbone of our family. She helped put my father through law school when they were first married, and she helped him build his practice. She raised my sister and me almost single-handedly. Mom's always been the one you could count on." A smile flitted across his face. "Finding out she had MS didn't change anything. Most people would have had a real crisis. Not my mother. She volunteers at church and raises money for charities. And since she's a master gardener, she gives talks at local libraries and community gardens to teach people how to grow their own vegetables."

"She sounds amazing." Lee couldn't even keep a houseplant alive. "How does she manage her walker out in the garden?"

"The vegetable garden had to go. She's got a smaller container garden now—I think it's called a horizontal garden—so she can water and weed while she sits in a chair. Her main focus is her bromeliads. She's a collector."

With a quick gasp, Lee shot up straight in her chair. "I *love* bromeliads! They come in so many shapes and sizes. Did you know there are tree frogs who spend their entire lives in the pools of water collected by the bromeliad leaves?"

Bricker rubbed his chin with his knuckles, a mild crease between his eyes. "No. To tell the truth, I never even heard of bromeliads 'til my mother started collecting them."

"How many varieties does she have? Does she grow them outside or inside? How does she keep them from frying in the summer heat?" Lee scanned her mind for more questions about bromeliads.

He held up his palm. "Hold on, now. I don't know what she's got. She'd be thrilled to show them to someone who's interested, though."

Lee clapped her hands. "Yes! I'd love to meet your mom! Do you think she's still awake?"

Bricker laughed softly. "I think we'll wait 'til the sun's up."

His warm breath glided over her shoulder, raising goose flesh down her arms. She shivered. When had the air chilled?

The seat beside her lurched, a quick sucking of air releasing from the cushion as Bricker disappeared into the front of the boat. The space beside her was empty and cold. She squinted to draw his figure into focus as he reemerged from the dark, carrying something in his hands.

He sank back onto the bench.

A soft fabric slid over her shoulders. She shifted closer to his warmth.

"Try some water." He snapped off the lid and handed it to her.

She took a long drink, wiping her hand across her mouth to catch the drips left behind at the corners. "Thanks." He was right. Water was just what she needed. She drank from the bottle again, using her senses to ground her. The fuzziness at the edge of her vision subsided, and she heard the distant rumble of waves rolling onto the beach. The fleece blanket wrapped her shoulders in warmth. Her cheek rested against the leather seat back. Bricker's right shoulder was so close, she could touch it with her nose if she leaned in.

His T-shirt sleeve stretched tight against his crossed upper arms. Even at rest, his biceps were taut. Her gaze trailed down to the flat abdomen beneath his shirt. She'd never known anyone to have a six-pack, but this guy might. Funny, she'd always disparaged people who placed too much priority on working out. But if *this* was the result… Heat flared beneath the surface of her skin. She shivered again.

"Are you still cold?" He bent his head down to find her face in the shadows.

She raised her gaze to his and sucked in a quick breath. His movie-star handsome face showed concern for her. *Her.* With the salty, musky odor of his skin flooding her senses, and her pulse pounding against her throat, she lifted her hand to trace the outline of his jaw.

He caught her fingers before they touched his face. "I don't want you doing something you'll regret tomorrow." With a brief caress on the back of her knuckles, he placed her fingers on the neck of her water bottle.

His tone was as gentle as his touch. Goose flesh rose on her arms, and her breath quivered. She held her cheek against his, positioning her lips just in front of his ear. "Why don't you let me worry about that?" She arched her back to move closer, aching to feel her body against his. But he braced her shoulders instead, steering her back against the bench with a gentle but unyielding grip.

Before she could protest, he stood. "I've lost track of the time, but I think it's pretty late. We'd better get going now." He rubbed his palms over his forearms. "The wind will be cold on the ride back. Keep the blanket over you."

"Wait!" Lee jumped to her feet, catching the fleece before it hit the floor. "Who cares about the time? Today's Friday!" She trailed after him through the galley passage, clutching the blanket to her shoulders. She stopped, swaying. Her head felt funny. Taking a deep breath, she held it a few seconds and let it out. How much beer had she drunk? She swiveled her head at a sharp intake of breath from the steering area.

Bricker was flipping through messages on his phone. Its light cast a sickly green glow on his face. He tapped out a hurried message and slid the phone into his pocket. "Sit now. We've got to get back."

The engine roared to life, and Lee just had time to drop into the rear-facing seat before the front of the boat lurched high and headed straight to the shore. "What happened?" Lee called to Bricker over the drone of the engine.

He stared through the windshield, his mouth drawn into a grim line. Tendons stood out on his forearms as he gripped the steering wheel. "My mother collapsed. I have to get to the hospital."

Chapter Six

A sudden explosion of firecrackers outside the window blasted the silence of Lee's living room. Her brush, wet with paint, scrawled a livid green zigzag across the delicate outline of the flower's bloom. She cursed, throwing the brush against the wall and leaving a sticky trail of green all the way down to the carpet. She would regret that later.

And it wasn't all she'd regret from this weekend.

She'd bowed out of plans made with two single co-workers. Three weeks ago, a weekend of beach bonfires, bar-hopping, and fireworks over the water had sounded like just what she needed to enjoy the long Fourth of July weekend. But after her embarrassing behavior on Bricker's boat, she'd decided to keep a low profile for a few days.

Remembering how she'd snuggled up to him after the sun had gone down, she winced. A man she could barely tolerate! How could three bottles of beer cause her to abandon her good judgment and make a pass at a man like Bricker Kilbourn?

She paced between the kitchen and the bay window at the front of the house where she'd set her easel to take advantage of the morning sunlight. As she focused on blending two shades of paint, she'd submerged the nagging shame of her encounter with Bricker. But then the fireworks set off outside her window blew her embarrassment right back to the surface of her thoughts.

He'd drawn away that night. Sure, he'd made an excuse about not wanting her to do something she'd later regret. Very smooth. No doubt he had years of experience thwarting the unwanted advances of girls smitten with his good looks and perfect body.

With a strangled yell, she punched the windowsill. Why had she acted like some star-struck girl, helpless to resist the charms of the local playboy? She *never* fell for guys like him.

She leaned against the wall, rubbing the bruised side of her fist. Her gaze fell on the canvas. After texting Bricker for the second time about his mother's condition, she'd stayed up late, poring through online catalogs of bromeliads. Maybe a painting of Mrs. Kilbourn's favorite plant would cheer her. This morning, Lee had started to recreate one of the plants from memory. On an eleven-by-fourteen inch canvas, she'd painted a close-up aerial view of spiky leaves cradling a pink-tipped flower. She was just putting the last touches on the glossy, zebra-striped leaves when the firecracker shattered her focus. Now she dipped a damp paper towel in water to clean off the spattered paint, working with care to avoid smudging the silvery spines cutting through the center of each leaf.

A light knock at the door made her jump again. She hadn't even heard footsteps. Wiping her fingers on the oversized, acrylic-spattered oxford shirt she'd borrowed years ago from her dad, she hurried toward the kitchen and opened the door to a blast of hot air from the side porch.

Bricker was wearing the same green T-shirt he'd

worn on Friday. His face was pale in the sunshine as he glanced up from his phone.

Even with stubbled cheeks and lank hair escaping from a ponytail, he was swoon-worthy. A flood of adrenaline careened through Lee's system. "Hi. H-how's your mom?" Lee stuttered. She hoped Mrs. Kilbourn had stabilized. She also hoped his worrying had driven all memory of Lee's flirting from his mind.

"Doing better." He leaned his forearm on the door frame. "They let her go home this morning."

"I'm so glad!" She'd never met Bricker's mother, but after spending two days studying the details of the bromeliads, she sensed a woman who collected them would be a friend.

"I wanted to stop by on my way home to shower and apologize for how our night ended." Grabbing a fistful of his T-shirt near the collar, he mopped it across his brow, revealing a tanned and toned sliver of abdomen.

"Oh, I understand." Lee waved her hand to dismiss his apology. The scent of his cologne mingled with his sweat drifted to her nostrils. After two days, how could he still smell so good? "I'm just happy she's able to come home again. Will you need to stay with her?— I'm sorry, you must be roasting in this heat. Come inside." She opened the door wider and stepped back.

He hesitated before he came in, looking up at the elevated ceiling as he crossed the threshold. He followed Lee to the counter separating the living space from the kitchen space. "No, she's got a home companion who lives on site. But I'll head back over there after I get cleaned up and make sure she's settled in."

Lee handed Bricker a water bottle from the refrigerator.

Pressing it against his cheeks, he twisted off the plastic lid in one quick rip. Half the bottle was gone after one drink. He set the bottle on the counter, exhaling as he surveyed the living room.

Conscious of the bare, unfriendly walls of her bungalow, Lee fidgeted as his gaze explored her home. Why hadn't she taken time to unpack over the long weekend?

"I see you've been painting." He stared pointedly at the green paint skid trailing three feet down the white wall to the carpet.

"I had a little accident." Lee crossed her arms. "Kids were setting off fireworks, and they scared me."

"So you attacked them with your paint brush?" His expression was amused as he leaned over to retrieve the brush sticking to the carpet. With his foot, he nudged the canvases leaning against the couch as he handed back the brush. "You've got the artist mentality, all right."

"What do you mean?" Lee's shoulders stiffened as she snatched the brush and tossed it in the sink.

"You're kind of a slob." He took another drink from his bottle and placed the cap on top.

"I am not!" She gave a snort of irritation. "I just haven't had a chance to get moved in yet."

Between the couch and the bay window, he stopped to stare at the easel. Glancing her way, he jerked a thumb at the canvas. "Did you just paint this?"

Lee nodded, grinding her fingertips over her chin. Giving his mother a painting had seemed like a nice thing to do. On the other hand, maybe he'd think she was pandering for his approval. Well, too late now. "It's for your mother. To help her feel better."

One hand grasping his elbow, the other stroking his chin, Bricker studied the painting. "You really have an eye for color. This is amazing." He faced her, his smile wide and dazzling. "Mom will love it."

Lee bit down on her smile, hiding the flood of pleasure his approval evoked. "It's not quite dry, but if you're careful, the paint shouldn't smudge." She lifted the canvas along the wooden supports in back and extended it to Bricker.

But he shook his head, raising his palms. "You have to give it to her."

Lee thrust the unpainted edge of the canvas into his gut. "I don't even know her."

He harrumphed. "You sure wanted to meet her the night we were on the boat. You wanted me to turn the boat around and storm her house."

So he *hadn't* forgotten. Lee flushed, remembering her overblown enthusiasm about everything that night. "I was a little…tipsy."

"You're telling me." He gave a swift smile, and then he became serious. "She'll love your painting, and she'll want to meet the person who did it. Besides, meeting someone new is the perfect distraction for my mother right now. She's dealing with…a lot."

Lee bit her lip. "I'm not going like *this*." She swept her hand over her painter's smock.

Grinning, he backed toward the door. "I need to change, myself. Pick you up in an hour." With a wink, he slipped outside.

As she listened to his footsteps retreat from the porch, she caught her astonished reflection in the

97

hallway mirror. Would an hour be enough time to scrub the paint from her hands and make her hair look presentable? She sighed. Bricker had only to shake himself after a shower and he'd look like the cover of a men's health magazine. How many women who dated him could compete with his looks?

Straightening her shoulders, she pointed at the mirror. "This is *not* a date. You are visiting the man's invalid mother. Got it?" She forced her lips to settle into a frown before she searched her bedroom closet for a new summer dress.

****

"What a beautiful neighborhood your mom lives in," Lee remarked as Bricker's truck rolled to a stop in front of a white stucco home. A stamped concrete driveway curved like a cat's tail from the garage to the street. "All the houses are so different from each other." She glanced at Bricker. The stubble on his cheeks and throat was gone now, and his blond hair, swept back from his high forehead, gleamed in the sunlight. But for his reddened eyes, she'd never know he'd spent the past two nights sitting beside a hospital bed

He nodded. "Still has trees, too, unlike most of the housing developments around here. Hang on, and I'll help you down."

Unlatching the door, she waited on his assistance. She'd chosen wedge sandals because they complemented her dress, a short-skirted, sleeveless A-line in a salmon floral pattern. Its round collar made it the perfect combination of demure and flirty. But from the height of the jacked-up jeep, she was reconsidering the heels. They wouldn't make for an easy landing.

Bricker opened the door wider. "Swing your legs

around and give me your hands."

With a squeeze of her thighs to prevent the skirt from sliding any higher, she pivoted on the seat until her feet hung outside the vehicle. His hands closed around hers, making her heart gallop.

He pressed in closer, steering her heels onto the running board. He glanced at her face as she found her balance. "Ready?"

She nodded, bracing her hands against his as she lowered one hesitant foot after the other onto the pavement. As her nose brushed past his shoulder, it tingled with the clean scent of his aftershave. The man was sending her into sensory overload. She yanked back her hands and tugged down her skirt, mumbling her thanks.

Before he shut the door, he handed her the bromeliad painting from the dashboard. They trudged through the suffocating heat to the front entrance, passing a shiny silver convertible coupe in front of the garage. "Looks like you'll have the pleasure of meeting my sister today," he muttered.

Sheltering her eyes with her hand, Lee squinted up at him. He'd tensed beside her as he spun the doorknob, but his face was impassive. Whatever reservations he held about his sister, he wasn't going to share.

The home was as tasteful as she'd expected, with miles of tile leading into an open floor plan under elevated tray ceilings. To the left of the foyer was a formal dining area dominated by a glossy cherry table large enough to seat a dozen. The great room stretched in the opposite direction, decked out with soft leather sofas and mahogany end tables. A discreet TV niche was tucked in a recessed corner. Floor-to-ceiling glass windows overlooked a pool sheltered by exotic plants.

"We're out here," a voice called.

Bricker gestured to the right, leading her through the dining room to a long, seated bar dividing the kitchen from the great room. "Lee, this is my sister, Tatum."

His voice sounded wary. Lee followed him around the corner into the kitchen, eager to see the woman who could throw the suave bartender off his game.

Behind the granite countertop stood a young woman in an ivory midi-dress. The cap sleeves and notched neckline emphasized her cleavage to a degree just within the bounds of tasteful. Her hair, dark brown ombre with platinum tips, trailed over her shoulders in wavy layers. Squinting at a prescription bottle she held close to her eyes, she revealed tanned and toned upper arms.

Wow. The Kilbourn family must have won the genetic lottery. Aware of each chipped fingernail, Lee hesitantly extended her hand.

With an exasperated sigh, Tatum set the bottle on the counter. "Nice to meet you, Lee. I was just figuring out Mom's medication schedule so she doesn't accidentally overdose." A hint of a smile softened her green eyes as she shook Lee's hand.

"Drama queen." A voice called up from Tatum's side.

Bricker rounded the counter and emerged a moment later with a woman in a wheelchair.

Her face, drawn with fatigue around the eyes, was wreathed in a smile.

With the woman's high cheekbones and straight Roman nose, the family resemblance was unmistakable.

"So you're the bromeliad fan."

Her voice, courteous and low-pitched, carried a welcoming Southern lilt, putting Lee at ease in an instant. "I sure am." She nodded, holding out the small canvas to the older woman. "So nice to meet you, Mrs. Kilbourn. I'm glad you're back home and feeling better again."

Bricker's mother examined the painting. She lifted her gaze, wide and intelligent, to Lee. "A zebra bromeliad."

Locking her fingers together at her waist, Lee nodded. This woman knew flowers. She'd be a tougher critic than her son.

"Lee painted it herself," Bricker interrupted.

"Wow, you painted that yourself?" Tatum leaned over the bar to gaze at the bromeliad. "You're actually talented. What are you doing with a deadbeat like my brother?"

Tatum plays rough. Lee smiled awkwardly at Bricker.

The hard look was back in his eyes as he faced his sister. "Isn't it time you head back to the office? Your assistant must be wondering what happened to her five o'clock whipping."

Bricker's mother raised her hand between her children. "Is this any way to behave in front of a guest? If you two would just take your fangs out of each other, you'd give me a chance to thank Lee for this beautiful painting." She leveled a commanding gaze at Tatum, who smirked as she continued pouring pills into the medication dispenser.

Lee hastened to fill the awkward silence. "Bricker told me about your bromeliad collection. I love painting them because of the huge species variation. They're like the dogs of the plant kingdom. No two are alike."

"Exactly." His mother nodded, her gray eyes shining. "They grow from the ground, from rocks and trees—even telephone poles."

"Terrestrial, saxicolous, and epiphytic." Bricker listed the species in the voice of a pompous professor.

His mother shooed him with her hand. "Show off. My son always could memorize Latin like magic. His skill helped him in law school." She tilted a fond smile in his direction.

"A fat lot of good *that* did him." Tatum's words were spoken under her breath from behind the counter, and if her mother could hear them, she gave no indication.

Bricker, however, stared at his sister with stony dislike.

"Could I see your collection this afternoon, Mrs. Kilbourn?" Lee cut in. The poor woman had just gotten out of the hospital, and her children were fighting like cats. The garden had to be a more peaceful place, even at a hundred degrees.

"I'd be delighted to show you. And please, call me Corinne. You and I will be fast friends, I can tell." Securing the canvas on her lap, she gripped the wheels and pivoted toward the lanai.

Bricker put a restraining hand over his mother's. "Are you trying to get yourself sent back to the hospital?"

"Don't be silly." Corinne spoke with the authority of a woman unused to being questioned. "We're going to the lanai. The ceiling fans make the air quite comfortable. Your friend wants to see my collection—

don't you, Lee?"

Her face coloring, Lee nodded. She hadn't meant to cause an argument between Bricker and his mother.

He sighed. "Fine. But right after, you're getting back into bed. You're supposed to be resting today. And take your hands off the wheels. *I'll* push the chair, Mother."

For the next half hour, Lee wandered through gardens surrounding the kidney-shaped pool, asking questions about Corinne's lavish collection.

Bricker stood behind his mother's chair as she pointed out distinctive qualities of each plant.

Like a proud mother showing off her children, she encouraged Lee to snap pictures for use in future paintings. Posing beside a brilliant star-shaped flower, she fanned her neck with her hand.

With an abrupt pivot, Bricker steered the wheelchair toward the ramp in front of the glass doors. "Time to go in now."

Corinne raised her hand. "But I'm enjoying myself! Just five more minutes. Please?"

Bricker shook his head, a tiny smile dimpling his cheeks. "Five minutes and no more. And I'm getting you a glass of water." He glanced at Lee as she inspected a container garden. "Can I get you a drink?"

"Yes, thanks." She ran her fingers along the sharp spines of a rock-rooted bromeliad, feeling cool air gust onto the lanai as the glass door opened and shut. "Thank you so much for showing me your collection. I'm sorry if I've worn you out."

"Are you kidding? This is the most fun I've had in ages." Corinne trailed her hand over the glass of the door. "Speaking of fun—my son hasn't left my side all weekend. Could you talk him into going out tonight? He needs a break."

Lee opened her mouth, not sure how to respond. Did Corinne think she and Bricker were dating? "I think he'd feel better being here with you, making sure you're okay."

Corinne rolled the chair closer to Lee, her brow wrinkling. "I'm not an exotic hothouse orchid, and I don't need round-the-clock care. Once I settle in for the night, I'll be fine. You both should be out celebrating July Fourth."

Before Lee could reply, she noticed Bricker at the door with two tall glasses of water.

"Feels nice and cool inside. You ready to come back in, Mother?" He handed a glass to Corinne and passed the second glass to Lee.

She took a long drink, holding the cold surface against her hot cheeks.

"After I drink my water, dear." Corinne took a sip of water and brushed her fingers over her forehead. "Lee, Bricker tells me you moved to Pomegranate Key just a few months ago. So you haven't seen the fireworks over the Gulf yet. They're spectacular reflected over the water." She shifted in her chair and raised her face to her son. "You should take her out on your boat."

Lee gave a quick shake of her head, shooting a helpless look at Bricker. "He already took me on his boat."

"You did?" Corinne asked her son, delighted. "Well, there's no better night than tonight to be on the water, with fireworks exploding overhead."

"And clouds dumping buckets of rain. A weather

system's working in the Gulf," Bricker informed her.

"A weather system is always working in the Gulf. The county would have canceled the show if there were anything to worry about." She drew her lips into a firm line. "Tatum is staying with me. I don't need you tonight, and I certainly don't need to hear you and your sister bickering anymore today." She squeezed his hand. "You always loved taking the boat out for the fireworks show. Would it be so hard for you to repay Lee's kindness with a special trip beneath the stars?"

He gazed down on his mother with an unreadable expression.

Lee's heart sank. Was he making an excuse not to spend time with her?

"Mother's got our evening planned for us." His gaze met Lee's like a dare. "The night was cut a little short the last time we were out. Ready to try again?"

Lee fidgeted with a rock from the planter, her cheeks flushing deeper with the memory of her behavior with Bricker after she'd had a few drinks. The idea of getting back on the boat worried—and excited—her. She hesitated a moment longer, and then she gave a nonchalant shrug. "I'm not doing anything tonight."

Bricker's face broke into a slow smile, and he squeezed his mother's shoulder. "Sounds like a yes to me."

The electric charge of his gaze, still locked on Lee, rocked her back on her wedges. She gripped both hands around her melting glass of ice water and concentrated on maintaining a neutral expression. *Don't let him rattle you. He may be a model son, but he's still a playboy.*

"Good!" Corinne leaned against the backrest, smiling. "You should get going, then. The docks will be crowded. Lee, thank you so much for your visit and for this lovely painting. I know just where I'll ask Hector to hang it. You have fun tonight, and make sure my son brings you back for a visit soon."

Lee lingered on the lanai as Bricker steered his mother up the ramp into the cool house. Sweat trickled underneath the bodice of her dress. As hot and damp as she was now, she was afraid it would get even worse when they were alone on the boat.

****

Sliding his gaze over Lee's muscular calves as she unsteadily climbed the ladder to the roof, Bricker resisted the urge to step in behind her. She'd been game for sitting up high to get an unobstructed view of the show. She wouldn't appreciate him coddling her now. When he saw her feet step onto the hardtop, he followed her up the ladder.

Lee leaned on one hand, sitting with her knees tilted to the side and her feet tucked under her.

In the dimming light of dusk, he could just make out tendrils of hair blowing against her neck, escaping from the twist she'd worn all afternoon. The space was small, not much bigger than a picnic blanket. He'd anchored at a distance from the thick crowd of boats. Music drifted over the murmur of the waves. "Do you feel okay up here?" If she had a panic attack, he'd have himself to blame.

"I'm fine, as long as we don't get big waves."

A row of white teeth gleamed at him in the dark. She was smiling, then. So far, so good. "You sure you don't want something to drink?" He'd already offered to open a bottle of wine.

She shook her head, her chin tilting to look at the stars.

How would it feel to stroke one finger from the soft indentation under her chin to the hollow at the base of her neck? His throat thickened. *Knock it off.* He gave his head a swift shake. She'd push him off the roof if he tried anything. He lowered himself beside her, crossing his legs at the ankles and wrapping his arms around his knees.

"When do the fireworks start?" Against the whisper of the lapping ocean, her voice chirped as high and excited as a child's.

He smiled. "Soon. Just needs to get a little darker out here." He liked her anticipation. He'd been afraid seeing the fireworks would seem kind of corny.

Leaning back on both hands, elbows straight, she stretched out her legs. Against the white helm roof, her red toenail polish glimmered. "I loved your mom." She flexed her bare feet, pointing her toes.

Bricker exhaled against the tightened muscles in his chest. "She liked you, too."

"Your sister, though—wow."

Bricker's lips twisted, but he forced his mouth to relax. How could he explain the complications between him and Tatum?

Lee shook her head. "I get it. I've always been the black sheep of my family, too."

If that's what she wanted to think, it would probably be easier. Anyway, he'd much prefer to talk about her family than his own. "You? A black sheep?"

Lee tsked. "Compared to the golden family who adopted me when I was two, yes." She unlocked her phone and showed him a professional family photo. "Here's my mom and dad."

Dominating the shot was a stately middle-aged man with an imperious eyebrow raised. Elegant in a well-fitted gray suit, his right arm enclosed the waist of a tall, sturdy woman with silver hair. She leaned against him with a shy smile.

"There's my brother, Conrad, and my sister, Brett, is beside them."

The younger man, tall and blond like the others, gripped his mother's left shoulder, grinning. To his left stood a woman in her early thirties, her tawny hair clasped in a chic bun, her gaze steady and her cheekbones strong. In front of the group was Lee, her long black hair and short stature marking a stark contrast with her family. While her smile was as wide as everyone else's, she held herself aloof.

"A good-looking family. All of you," Bricker added as he handed back her phone. "Don't you get along with them?"

She gave a tiny shrug. "We get along." After unclasping her hair, she twisted it into a rope in front of her shoulder. In the moonlight, her gaze was far away. "As long as I do what I'm told." She fell silent.

He waited before prompting her. "Control freaks?"

Her nose wrinkled. "No. They just want what's best for me. Doing the right thing comes naturally to them. Conrad and Brett did great in school. He was the captain of the football team, and she was the homecoming queen. They graduated college and got great jobs. My parents expected the same thing from me."

"But...?" Bricker cued her when she trailed off

again.

She flicked her hair behind her shoulders and stared into the distance. "My grades were good. My dad wouldn't have let me out of the house if they weren't. It's just"—she shrugged, lifting her gaze to his—"they all seemed to know exactly what they wanted to do with their lives. They assumed I'd be the same way. But I didn't have a clue. Still don't, really." Her forehead settled into a frown.

"You've got a degree in psychology. They must be proud."

She snorted. "Not before I was suspended from two colleges. I settled on psychology only because the department accepted my low GPA. My family was just relieved to see me graduate."

Bricker leaned back against his hands. "So social services isn't your dream. What is?"

With a scowl, she jutted her chin. "I don't have one."

Sometimes, she reminded him of a defiant little girl. "Oh, come on. Everyone has a dream." He sounded like his own mother.

"Oh, yeah?" She gazed with eyebrows lifted. "What's *your* dream?"

He tugged her hair gently against her back. "Being on this boat with you, darlin'." His voice caught as he released her hair. Had he gone too far? Or could she accept a little harmless flirting?

With a dismissive wave, she drew her legs toward her chest and locked her arms around her knees, staring into the night sky. Water slapped against the keel. A rising murmur of voices from other boats in the distance carried on the wind emphasized Lee's silence.

"Come on, now," he prodded. "What about painting? You've got a lot of talent."

She sighed. "You can't make a living at art unless you're really great. And I'm not even close."

"I don't agree." Bricker leaned closer. He wished she would look at him. "You impressed the hell out of *us*. And my sister, at least, can be a pretty harsh critic."

Her gaze fixed above, Lee gave a short laugh. "I noticed."

Before Bricker could respond, a muffled explosion sounded in the distance. A single flame shot through the sky, travelling high overhead and igniting into a thousand spokes of red light showering down to the sea.

Lee gave a cry, bracing herself with her knees against her chest. She sat erect, her head thrown back, as if straining to get closer to the fire display spilling from the firmament. Detonations sounded in the distance, accelerating in speed as one blast succeeded the next. Her face was washed with manic circus hues, her gaze reveling in the chaos of colors erupting overhead. Against the backdrop of the wide, gray sea and the unending heights of the supercharged atmosphere, she was small but fearless. A sudden whip of wind flung her hair against his cheek, as fragrant as the first splash of brandy into a snifter, bathing him in the floral scent of her shampoo.

For a moment, he heard waves break against the shore. His own breathing, suspended, released in a shuddering exhale.

She rotated her head, her eyes wide, lips parted in a question, focusing on him again for the first time since the fireworks began.

Unable to stop himself, he reached for her face. His

hands stole into the curtains of her hair, drawing her closer as he gripped the silky tendrils. Before she could protest, he pressed his lips against her cheek, lingering over the dimple at the corner of her mouth.

He heard her gasp as another firework exploded above them. His fingers slid down to cup the delicate contours of her skull, his thumbs caressing the soft skin over her jaw. Her dark eyes shimmered, unreadable with reflected fire. Did she want him to continue? His mouth brushed the opposite corner of her lips then lighted on her temple. A hint of sea spray wafted from the soft baby hairs framing her face. The muscles of his hands tightened, and he trembled with the effort of restraining his eagerness. He wanted to hold her gently, not scare off this delicate, wild beauty who sighed beneath him. He drew his lips over her forehead, the exquisite bridge of her nose, over each buttery-soft eyelid. His breath was shallow, his heartbeat thumping in his ears, and all was black to him except her face lit by electrified rainbow shafts streaking through the sky. He could feel her hands gripping his shirt, and her breath was warm against his cheek as she opened her eyes and met his gaze. For the first time, he found no challenge there—just the deep, velvet enticement of her ebony eyes.

How he hungered for her sweet, full lips. Heat surged through his chest, every nerve ending lit with desire. Not yet, not yet. Still cradling her head under the luxurious canopy of her glossy hair, he tilted her head and lowered his mouth to her throat, gliding over skin as soft as satin. A vibration like the purr of a kitten tickled his lips, and his heart drummed faster. He dared to touch her leg, caressing first the soft knob of her knee before sliding his fingers to the warm hollow beneath. Her skin was creamy, like melted chocolate. He stroked a tentative finger down the back of her thigh, following the trail of taut muscle toward the hem of her skirt.

Her hand seized his wrist, and he froze.

Releasing him, she slid her hand under his collar to his shoulder.

The whisper of her soft fingertips on his bare skin flooded him with longing. God, how long had he dreamed of her skin against his? His mouth met hers, savoring the lush generosity of her full lips as they parted against his. He clenched the smooth underside of her thigh as his tongue, hesitant, touched hers.

Were fireworks in the sky or ricocheting through his skull? He clamped his mouth against hers, trying not to groan with the relief of surrendering to his wild desire. Conscious of only the shy dance of their tongues, needing to get closer and deeper into the kiss, he pulled her into his lap and tilted back her head. Her mouth was warm, inviting, as intoxicating as a shot of bourbon. Withdrawing just enough to tug the swell of her lower lip between his, he stroked his fingers down her throat.

Her body nestled against his chest and his thighs with the weight and softness of a kitten.

He wanted to touch every inch of her, rove his hands over her naked arms and the tempting swells peeking from the V line of her bodice. As he grazed his lips across hers, from under lowered lids he discerned her dress stretched tight across her hips, riding high up her thighs and granting a glimpse of her panties. His heart pounded in his ears. They needed to go below decks. He allowed his fingers to dip below her skirt and stroke the soft flesh of her inner thigh.

Her eyes huge and dark, she gazed up at him, shivering.

He leaned down to brush his cheek against hers. "Why don't we go down to the cabin?" he whispered. He held his breath as he waited for her answer.

A high-beamed white light burst against his eyes, and he slammed them shut. What the hell?

"Bricker." A voice was coming from the port side. From the water. "Get your pants on."

Lee scrambled off his lap while he squeezed one eye open. He could just make out the familiar outline of a Coast Guard vessel. Shading his eyes with his hand, he squinted at the boat.

"Harry?" He should stand, but he wasn't quite ready. He tugged on the sides of his shorts. "Could you kill the light, man?"

The beam of light swung to the lower decks. "We're calling back the boats. The storm's turning this way, and the last thing we need is it breaking while everyone's docking. Better safe than sorry."

Bricker's eyes adjusted to the light.

Her face averted from the spotlight, Lee sat huddled with her arms around her knees.

He rubbed his chin and breathed a short, angry exhale. A parade of boats was making its way toward the dock about a mile away. "Okay. We'll get right out of here. Thanks for letting me know."

"We announced it on the bullhorn when the fireworks ended. Had to come out here and find out which bonehead was ignoring the warning."

Harry's voice, a reedy tenor, rang with judgment.

Having sailed these waters his whole life, Bricker was acquainted with all the local Coast Guard officials. Just his luck—Harry, the most uptight of all, was on duty tonight. Bricker stood, swaying for a moment. "Sorry for your trouble, Harry. Like I said, I'll take her right back."

"Guess you had other things on your mind up there." Harry snickered.

Like an illicit hand, the spotlight stroked over Lee's hunched form. Bricker snapped his fingers and pointed to the starboard ladder in mute command.

She scurried around him on her knees, tugging at the hem of her dress before she lowered herself down the ladder.

He clenched his fists before answering. "I got your message, Harry. We'll be leaving now."

The spotlight blasted Bricker in the face one last time. "Make it quick."

Biting his lips between his teeth, he hastened down the ladder after Lee. His eyes adjusted to the dimness and found her sitting in the cockpit, facing the back of the boat. "Hey." He kept his voice low. "We've gotta head back. You want to come up front?"

Her hair swung as she shook her head, her back ramrod straight.

"I'm really sorry." He wanted to touch her, but he was warned away by the stiffness of her shoulders. "Harry's an asshole." An acrid smell of ashes drifted through the air. Burnt chunks of spent firework casings littered the deck. When had they fallen? He hadn't even noticed the fireworks ending.

"Could you just take me home?" Against the quiet susurration of the waves, her words fell like a bucket of ice. She sat like a ship's prow maidenhead—still as a statue, and every bit as likely to talk.

He sighed, running a frustrated hand through the hair on top of his head. "Sure." Taking his seat alone at the helm, he switched on the engine and headed for shore.

Chapter Seven

Bricker had been warned the woman was cool and detached. Cold fish was more like it.

As he left the community center, Bricker reviewed his mental notes on meeting Amber Maly. Since she was limited to supervised visitation, she'd agreed to meet with Kaleb's guardian ad litem during parenting classes. Each week she had one hour to spend with her son in the Play Lab. They could choose from an indoor jungle gym, a pint-sized kitchen, a quiet reading area, or an art center.

Other parents were lighthearted in the environment, chasing their children through a rainbow tunnel or waiting obediently at child-sized tables for their portions of plastic peas and chicken legs. Not Amber. She and Kaleb sat at a table near the entrance, their backs to the rest of the room. In front of him was a coloring book and an old pencil box filled with crayons.

After signing in, Bricker observed the pair before he introduced himself.

Kaleb's mother didn't resemble the dragon lady he'd come to expect from his reading of the case. She was a frail young girl, her collar bones jutting out beneath her thin purple T-shirt. Her skin was so pale, he could see a blue web of veins in the dark hollows beneath her eyes.

Her gaze was fixed on the book as she lowered her

head and spoke in a low voice to Kaleb.

The boy turned a questioning face to his mother and then nodded, selecting a new crayon from the box.

Bricker cleared his throat, trying not to startle them.

Kaleb glanced up, a shy smile lighting his face. Amber's head lifted with the wariness of a squirrel interrupted at a meal.

Grinning, Bricker extended his palm to Kaleb. "Nice to see you again, buddy."

Kaleb slapped his small hand over Bricker's and giggled when the tall man wrung his hand in pain.

Assuming a neutral expression, Bricker addressed Kaleb's mother. "I'm Bricker Kilbourn, Kaleb's guardian ad litem. We spoke on the phone."

Amber nodded, lowering her eyelids and fixing her gaze on the coloring book. The page displayed a Northern winter scene—a large snowman surrounded by children bundled in parkas, mittens, hoods, and boots.

Bricker scraped up a chair to the end of the table. "You're pretty good at staying in the lines," he complimented Kaleb.

The little boy smiled, his gaze still fixed on the snowman's scarf as he colored it bright red.

"I told you to trace it first." Amber's flat voice was tinged with exasperation as her hand closed over his wrist.

Shooting a stricken look at his mother, he waited 'til she released him and then began tracing a methodical outline around the scarf.

Leaning back in his chair, Bricker tapped his thumb against his chin. "Outlining is a pretty advanced skill to expect from a boy who's not yet three, don't you think, Mrs. Maly?"

Amber fidgeted a crayon between her bony fingers. "We work on his fine motor skills all the time. I know he's young to color in the lines, so I have him practice a lot."

He wondered if he could credit Lee with Amber's use of the parenting lingo. His jaw clenched as he remembered how silent Lee had been on the ride home, waving away his apologies for the embarrassment of the Coast Guard spotlight. Frustrated, he'd refused to let her out of his truck until she talked to him. Only then did she turn with eyes as cold as icicles.

"I'm sure you'll find another girl to take on your boat tomorrow. Heck, maybe you can get started later tonight." With that, she'd unlocked her door and slammed out of the truck.

He was too stunned to stop her. She escaped into her house without a backward glance.

With a fierce focus of will, he forced his attention back to the Malys. For close to an hour, he observed Amber interacting with her son. While Kaleb was engrossed in his drawings, his mother answered Bricker's questions about her past.

Her expression was emotionless as she recounted a childhood marked by divorce, neglect, and abuse. Lee was right about one thing—Amber had experienced a terrible role model in her own mother.

A grudging respect for Amber's determination to reject her parents' example took a stubborn toehold. No wonder Lee defended the girl. Pushing back from the table, he beckoned to Amber. Taking a position against the wall just out of Kaleb's earshot, with Amber facing him, he asked about the night she'd struck her son with the plastic track of a race car set.

For the first time, Amber's face registered emotion. Splotches of red swarmed to the surface of her cheeks, and the rims of her eyes swelled, pink and fevered. "I never should have done it. We were stuck at Gloria Marshall's house because we had no other place to go while our water heater was broken. She already had two special needs babies staying there, besides her two older kids. Daniel and I just wanted to keep out of the way. But when we caught Kaleb throwing a car and hitting one of the babies, we were scared she'd make us leave." Amber rubbed her eyes with her fist, leaving smudges of black on the delicate tissue under her lashes. "Daniel was the one who picked up the track and took off Kaleb's diaper. He said pain was the only lesson a toddler would understand. I grabbed the track and spanked Kaleb myself because I was afraid Daniel would hurt him. I didn't realize how delicate his skin was." Her voice shuddered, and tears spilled out the corners of her eyes. "I didn't think I hit him very hard. I just wanted to get it over with."

Out of the corner of his eye, Bricker noticed Kaleb frowning at his mother's back as her shoulders heaved. With a reassuring smile, Bricker took Amber by the elbow and steered her to the water fountain, careful to keep her back to her son. "Kaleb is watching. Get yourself together," he told her in a low voice.

Amber swiped an index finger under each of her eyes, the tears helping to wipe away the black smears of mascara. Leaning over the water fountain, she took a quick swallow and stood. As if on command, she'd resumed her usual impassive expression, only the puffiness around her red-rimmed eyes betraying her lapse in self-control.

They rejoined Kaleb at the table.

Checking his mother's face, he held up the coloring book. "All done, Mommy."

Amber's smile was faint, just exposing her small, uneven front teeth. "Good job," she told Kaleb as she sat beside him.

He grinned at his mother, his face alight with pride.

She grabbed him and placed him on her lap, burying her face in the crook of his shoulder and neck.

Mouth formed into an O, he giggled with delight, shying away from her ticklish breath and turning to face her.

She squashed her nose against his, and he giggled again, reaching for the dark curls framing her face. Her smile vanished. She leveled a stern look, removing his hands from her hair. "No, no. We don't pull hair." She lifted Kaleb back into his chair. "Put all the crayons back."

Bricker's heart clenched at Kaleb's upturned eyebrows and quivering lip, but Amber seemed unaffected. "Can you get my visitation increased?"

Helping Kaleb toss the remaining crayons into the box, Bricker took a moment to answer. He wasn't sure what to make of Amber's sudden tide of emotions and equally unexpected return to business as usual. "The judge decides visitation. You should talk to your attorney."

Amber scowled, wrapping thin arms across her chest. "And while I get to see my son for one hour a week, Gloria Marshall gets to cash a nice, fat check for fostering a kid she claims has delays. You've sat here with Kaleb for an hour. Have you seen any delays?"

Bricker shook his head. Other than being as shy as a baby deer, Kaleb seemed to have the skills of a typical two-and-a-half-year-old. More, even. "No. But then, I'm no expert on child development." Tousling Kaleb's hair in farewell, he handed Amber his card and told her when she could reach him if she had further questions. As he'd made his way to the front lobby of the community center, Amber's comment nagged at him. Foster parents who cared for special needs kids *did* get paid more by the state.

Was Gloria Marshall looking out for Kaleb Maly's best interests, or her own?

****

"Where have you been, little sister? I've been waiting for hours!"

Lee had noticed right away that her key cache, a large vase by the front door, had been disturbed. She hadn't told any friends on Pomegranate Key about her spare key, so who was inside her house? With trepidation, she'd unlocked the door, fearing the unheralded visit of a family member more than a break-in.

And there on the couch sat Brett, wearing her signature expression—a smile not quite hiding her exasperation. As usual, Brett was flawless, even after a day of travel in the hottest season of the year. Silvery blonde hair framed her face in an elegant bob, highlighting the arc of her well-groomed brows. How many hours had Lee wasted as a teen squeezing her mouth into fish lips, attempting to emulate Brett's sculpted beauty?

Lee stifled a sigh and shut the door behind her. "I

had to work late. Why didn't you tell me you were coming in today?" Brett rose, half a foot taller than Lee even without heels.

"I told you I was coming sometime over the summer. I wanted to surprise you. You really shouldn't leave your key in such an obvious place." She tucked a stray strand of hair behind Lee's ear. "The dress code must be pretty informal at your job." She hugged her sister close and drew back, her eyes shining. "I've missed you, Lee-Lee."

Lee painted on a smile, resisting the urge to roll her eyes at Brett's criticism of her clothing. Even though her sister's perfectionism was exhausting, she meant well.

Reaching for her designer purse on the couch, Brett spoke over her shoulder. "I'm starving. I noticed the cutest little bar when I drove through town. Whistler's, I think it was. I thought we could eat there."

Lee's heartbeat rocketed into her throat. Since the night on the boat, when she'd almost made the mistake of sleeping with Bricker Kilbourn, she'd blocked his phone calls and gone out of her way to avoid the places she might see him. She didn't trust herself to be near him. His devotion to his mother, his easy manner with Kaleb—those qualities had blurred her judgment. Not to mention the soft kisses he'd planted all over her face. She shivered. A man like that had the power to hurt her. A man who'd never had a committed relationship in his life. "The food's not very good there. I'll take you over to the mainland so we can find whatever you're hungry for."

"Back over the bridge?" asked Brett, her eyebrows an eloquent arch. "I can't wait so long to eat. I've been sitting here for hours now."

"Fifteen minutes, and we'll be at a nice restaurant in Bellamy, okay?" Lee would have liked to change out of her work clothes, but changing her sister's mind about eating at Whistler's was a higher priority.

Brett shook her finger. "I've spent half the day in a stuffy conference and two hours in a rental car to get here. I don't *want* to go to the mainland. I want to go right down the street and eat at the bar. I don't even care what the food is, as long as drinks are served."

The memory of Bricker carrying a tray high over his head, showing off for Janna at lunch, made her wince. If he worked tonight, the evening would be a disaster. Lee wet her lips. "I could order in for pizza."

Brett threw up her palms. "What the heck, Lee? I just want to go to the bar for a drink and grab a bite to eat. Am I asking too much, after I've come all this way to see you?" Not waiting for an answer, her sister marched to the porch.

Lee squeezed her eyes shut. Only divine intervention could stop Brett when she got an idea in her head. Well, maybe God would hear Lee's prayer and make sure Bricker wasn't on the schedule tonight. Squaring her shoulders, Lee followed her sister into the muggy evening air.

****

"What's the deal with all the canvases lying around your place?" Brett popped a spoonful of chowder into her mouth, her gaze landing on her sister like an anvil.

After fifteen minutes had gone by with no sign of Bricker in the crowded restaurant, Lee had begun to relax. But Brett's question put her back on guard. "I'm just painting. Better than watching TV after work, right?"

Brett nodded, her lips pursed. "They're all weird plants, though."

"Bromeliads," Lee corrected her. "I'm on a bromeliad kick." For a fleeting moment, she remembered Bricker's smile when she gave his mother a painting, but she forced the image from her mind. Better to keep the embarrassment of her night on the boat in the forefront of her mind, when the Coast Guard had called him out by name. By name! How many women had Bricker seduced on the high seas?

"Okay." She shot Lee a shrewd look. "I was afraid maybe you were putting together a portfolio to apply to another art school."

Lee's face slid into a mask of indifference. A long time ago she'd learned how to veil herself from her family's well-meaning prying. "No. I like my job. Painting's just a hobby. I'll never be good enough to make it my career."

Brett put down her spoon. "I don't agree you're not talented. I just know you can't make a living as an artist." She lifted her fork and pointed it.

Here it comes. Lee sighed.

But as Brett opened her mouth to speak, her gaze shifted above her sister's head.

Unable to stop herself, Lee glanced behind her shoulder, and her heartbeat slammed against her ribs.

Bricker stood above her in faded blue jeans and an airy linen shirt unbuttoned to the sternum. His hair swung over one cheekbone as he stared down, his chin tilted to the side. A sardonic smile slanted his lips. "Imagine seeing you here, after trying for a week to reach you on the phone."

His low voice, seasoned with the sweetness of his Southern accent, generated a feverish flutter in her chest. Clamping her hands together on her lap, Lee willed herself to speak without emotion. "I've been busy this week."

Brett's face lit with curiosity.

"Brett, this is Bricker. Bricker, this is my sister." She rushed the introductions, praying Brett wouldn't ask questions. Picking up her menu, she leaned forward to block Bricker from her view. "Are you ready to order?"

Her sister's eyebrows dipped, as she regarded first Lee and the man standing above her. "Aren't you going to invite your friend to join us?"

Before Bricker could respond, Lee replied, "Oh, no. He can't eat with us. He works here." A clatter of dropped silverware from inside the kitchen made her jump. Bricker's fingers squeezed into her shoulder.

"I'm off tonight. And I'd love to join you." Rotating a chair in one fluid movement of his hand, he flung his leg over the seat. Leaning his chest against the back, he rested his right forearm on the top rail.

His smile was so wide, Lee could see his molars.

"What are you drinking, ladies?" He signaled for a server. Over Lee's objections, he ordered them both a specialty drink of the house.

"So, how do you two know each other?" A faint smiled curled Brett's lips, but her eyebrows drew together in a line.

Bricker Kilbourn, flaunting his role as island playboy, was not the type of guy Brett would approve for her little sister. Lee shrugged. "I come here for lunch a lot."

"We're dating," Bricker chimed in, his white teeth dazzling as he grinned his toothy grin.

Like a wolf, Lee thought, frowning back at him. "No, we're not."

They were interrupted by the server returning with their drinks. The sisters ordered entrees, but Bricker declined. An awkward silence descended on the table as the server disappeared with their order.

"The menu looks great." Brett's hesitant words floated above the table. "Are you the manager?"

"Just the bartender." His gaze shifted to Lee. "In fact, around these parts, some people call me Mr. Bartender."

As she noticed Brett's uncertain smile struggle to hold, Lee glared at Bricker. Why couldn't he take a hint and leave her alone? Surely other women would be grateful for his attentions. She drew a breath against the heaviness in her chest. The night of the fireworks had been so perfect. He'd told her his dream was being with her on top of his boat, and she'd opened her heart like a naïve teenager. How could she have let herself trust him? Hadn't she seen his true colors the first day on the beach, as she witnessed him getting his head handed to him by not one, but two, women?

He cocked his eyebrow and gave an innocent shake of his head.

Sure, act like you don't know I want you to leave. He was clearly enjoying her discomfort.

He focused his attention back on her sister. "Are you here for a vacation, Brett? Lee tells me you're from the Northeast."

As the conversation resumed familiar boundaries, Brett's shoulders relaxed. "I'm attending a medical convention in central Florida, so I left a little early to come over to the Gulf side and check on my little sister."

"You're a doctor?" Bricker rested his chin against his forearm on the top of his chair.

"Family practice." Sipping her drink, a pink concoction in a hurricane glass, Brett nodded. "This is good, Lee. Try some."

In stony silence, Lee opened her straw and stabbed it into the ice. Her gaze glued to the table in front of her, she took one sip after another. Brett was right. This *was* good. She swished her straw and took a longer drink.

"Don't mind her." Brett laughed. "She's always been a little greedy at the dinner table."

Lee's head shot up, her mouth opening to retort. She followed Brett's pointed stare to the glass Lee was drinking from. Half of the tall drink was gone. She flushed, pushing it away.

"When she first arrived from the orphanage in Korea, she guarded her food with her hands whenever somebody passed behind the table. She was just two, but she'd already learned to protect her meals from being stolen." Brett smiled fondly at Lee. "She's always bolted her food and drinks."

Wondering how many times she'd heard this story repeated, Lee compressed her lips. Her family loved to talk about how exotic she'd seemed. All she'd wanted was to fit in with the family. But no matter how she tried, they cast a spotlight on her differences.

"Old habits die hard, I guess." Bricker rubbed his chin.

The playboy smile had vanished. He surprised Lee

by standing, rotating his chair and tucking it under the table.

"I'll leave you to your dinners. In fact, let me go check on your order."

An unexpected welt of loss grew in the pit of her stomach when he swung open the door to the kitchen and disappeared inside. Rubbing her forehead, she closed her eyes. Why couldn't she harden her heart against this guy? How had she allowed herself to become so vulnerable? She swallowed hard.

Here she was, on the verge of tears over a man who'd probably dated and discarded hundreds of women. Why would she be any different? Despair puddled in her gut. She'd gotten herself into a mess this time. And now she'd have Brett's questions to contend with. Taking a deep breath, she relaxed her cheeks into stillness. Her face expressionless, she dropped her hand.

Brett leaned forward, frowning. "Are you okay?"

Stretching her lips into a bright smile, Lee nodded. "Thought I had a headache coming on. I'll be glad when we get out of here," she hinted.

Leaning back against her chair, Brett analyzed her sister. "You need to eat more. You're looking a little peaked."

Leave it to Brett to diagnose Lee's headache. Unfortunately, all the food in the world wouldn't cure the pain gripping her heart. Still, she crumbled off a piece of bread and stuck it in her mouth.

An amused smile animated her sister's face. "Your friend sure left in a hurry."

Lee took her time chewing before she answered. "You probably made him feel guilty about keeping a hungry orphan waiting for food."

"Come on!" Brett gave a dismissive wave. "It's a cute story."

After a long day of work, Lee had wanted nothing more than to crawl into some comfortable clothes and lose herself in painting. Instead, she was having the most uncomfortable meal of her life in the one restaurant she'd wanted to avoid. Brett was being her usual domineering self. And Bricker—she'd blocked him all week. She'd tried to shut him out of her thoughts, too. Why did he keep pushing himself at her? Did he think she was playing hard to get? She forced another smile at her sister. "So how are the kids?"

"Oh no, you don't," Brett chided with a shake of her head. "What's the story with you and the bartender?"

Leaning an elbow on the table and resting a cheek against her fist, Lee huffed out a sigh. From the corner of her eye, she could see Bricker talking to a server, a pretty young blonde with a butterfly tattoo on her upper arm. *Wonder if she's ever been out on his boat.* A spasm passed through her chest, but Lee coughed into her hand 'til it passed. "He's nobody. Just some guy who likes to flirt."

"I don't buy it. He said he's been calling you all week."

Brett's dark eyebrows were arched over her smooth brow like Halloween cats. Lee fought back a smile. "He's exaggerating. He hits on everyone." To avoid eye contact with her sister, she allowed her gaze to drift to the man behind Brett as he rose from his chair. His head bobbed on broad shoulders as he talked to his dinner companions.

"Hmmn." Brett tapped her lips, her gaze locked on

Lee. "He didn't seem like he was just flirting. I think he's fallen for you. I've seen you break hearts before." She raised her voice as Lee objected. "Classic Lee Cooper. The minute a guy gets close, you crawl into your shell like a hermit crab 'til he gives up." Brett chuckled.

Pain seared the base of Lee's throat. Her family liked to call 'em as they saw 'em. She struggled to keep her expression neutral. Was she incapable of love, as her sister seemed to think? One thing was for sure—she wasn't about to confide in Brett. Swallowing hard, she met her sister's mocking gaze. "For my client's sake, I need him on my side. I wouldn't get serious with a guy like him."

"I hope that goes without saying." Brett gave a short laugh. "We have higher hopes for you than seeing you settle for a bartender."

The man behind Brett's chair left, making way for Bricker to lower a tray on the table next to Brett.

Horror dropped like a stone into Lee's stomach. Had he heard them talking about him? She was afraid to check his expression as he placed their entrees in front of them.

"I hope you enjoy your dinners. Your server will be by to make sure you have everything you need." Without making eye contact, he left the area before she could thank him.

Great. She shook her head, her furious gaze boring into her sister's skull while Brett spun pasta on her fork.

Brett lifted her head, her eyes widening. "What?" she asked, her mouth half-full of linguine.

Lee leaned forward over her plate. "I don't care if he's just a bartender. He works for a living. And he has a law degree, you know."

"Why's he working here, then?" Brett asked, dabbing at a pool of pesto sauce with a shred of French bread.

"Because…" *Good question.* Why bother telling her sister Bricker didn't want to follow in his father's footsteps? She was the last person who would understand. "He's got a mother with MS, and he takes care of her. He's a really good son."

Brett sniffed. "He must be a pretty bad lawyer, though, if he ended up here." Her mouth twitched beneath her perfect nostrils. She cast a quizzical look at Lee's cooling crab cakes. "Aren't you hungry?"

"Success isn't measured just by how much money you make, Brett," Lee shot back. "How you treat other people counts for something. And he treats other people with kindness. Unlike some people I know." She flattened her lower lip against her teeth to stop it from shaking.

Brett set down her fork, her head dipping to one side as she stared. "I thought you said you didn't like the guy."

"I don't!" Lee raised her palms, splaying her fingers. "I mean, I don't think he's a loser just because he's a bartender."

"Why *do* you think he's a loser, then? You sure acted like he was beneath your notice when he sat with us." Brett dropped her gaze to her fork as she wound pasta against a spoon.

Lee was grateful for the time Brett was allowing her to answer. "He's been with a lot of people."

"So have you." Brett pointed her fork at Lee. She tilted the fork tines back to her lips for a bite. "Maybe he just hasn't found the right girl."

Lee snorted. "And you think the right girl for him is me?" Her heart pounded as she waited for Brett to finish swallowing.

"I hope not," Brett finally answered. "I'd like to see you with a man who has real prospects. But"—she held up her hand as Lee opened her mouth to interrupt—"don't sell yourself short, Lee. The guy is gorgeous, and he likes you. I wouldn't blame you for wanting to have a little fun. Just don't let yourself get serious. Wait, who am I talking to?" Brett's laugh was merry as she sipped her tropical drink.

Lowering her eyelids to conceal the scorch of her glare, Lee yanked the straw from her drink and finished it in one gulp. The night with her sister would be a long one, and Lee had better be fortified with more than food.

Chapter Eight

Two mornings later, Lee sagged against the door when her sister finally left. She'd gritted her teeth through most of Brett's visit, counting the hours 'til she could have her house to herself. Not that her sister's company was so awful, she reminded herself, wading through a layer of discarded clothing items on her bedroom floor on her way to her laundry hamper. Brett was just...hard on the old self-esteem.

Humming, she collected her clothes off the floor and tossed them into the hamper. Some hadn't been worn for longer than the minute needed to try them on, look in the mirror, and decide against them. She'd meant to hang them up again. But the darn pile grew so quickly. Now, after a week of getting trod into the carpet, they could use a washing. She wanted to get over to the laundromat before it got crowded. Her overstuffed laundry bin threatened to fall over like a double-decker ice cream cone. This purge would take a while.

When she drove into Island Breeze Laundry fifteen minutes later, she counted two other cars in the lot. *Good.* Slipping on her wireless headphones and streaming music from her phone, she lugged her tower of laundry out of the car. She was more than ready to enjoy the simple pleasures of watching her clothing toss and tumble through the large windows of the dryers.

Somehow, her spirits were always a little brighter afterward, too.

While feeding coins into the five washers she'd claimed, she glanced at the open door to the rear of the building where a small wooden deck overlooked a canal. Hooking her purse over her wrist, she headed outside to her favorite spot while she waited for the wash cycle to complete.

In another hour, the air would be too hot. But as she'd hoped, a breeze stirred along the waterway. No chairs stood on the deck, so she sat against the wall, the wooden planks warming her legs. She removed one ear bud to enjoy the sound of the lapping water.

A snowy egret foraged for food in the shallow water along the bank. Shading her eyes from the sun, Lee scanned the canal for evidence of other wildlife. You never knew what you'd see in one of these little waterways. Snakes and alligators weren't uncommon. She'd even seen an otter float by once, and she'd rubbed her eyes in disbelief. Herons, spoonbills, osprey—just some of the bird names she'd learned since she'd moved to the island. She liked to imagine one day she'd spend her early mornings out on a dock, sketching the creatures she spied upon.

A manatee, though—the massive, gentle mammal was the *real* prize. Other than at the maritime museum, she'd never seen the huge, graceful creatures in the flesh. And from what Bricker had said, she wouldn't have much hope of seeing one pass through this canal until the winter months.

Bricker. She bit her lip. After the dinner at Whistler's, he'd stopped texting. Maybe it was for the best. Before Brett had arrived and made matters worse,

Lee had spent the week steeling herself to stay away from him. She wouldn't make a fool of herself over a "love 'em and leave 'em" guy like Bricker Kilbourne.

But she'd seen his livid face when he set their plates on the table. He'd been angry, sure; even more, he seemed hurt. Wounded. And no wonder, after Brett had dismissed him as "just a bartender."

As Lee herself had done when she first met him. She buried her face in her hands, her cheeks burning with shame. Maybe the guy *was* a playboy. She still didn't have the right to treat him with such contempt. Before she could second-guess herself, she punched in Bricker's number, sighing when voicemail picked up. She swiped over to messages. Her fingers hesitated over the letters, then she finally typed.

I'm so sorry about the other night

"*Anyoung.*"

Jerking up her chin, Lee stared at the young child standing at the door.

Chubby, with straight bangs and shiny black hair falling to her shoulders, a three- or four-year-old girl poked out her head from the doorway, grinning.

With a defeated sigh, Lee removed her second earbud and smiled at the little girl. "*Anyoung haseyo.*" Without fail, each time she visited the laundromat, one of the Koreans who owned the place talked to her in her native tongue. When she raised her palms and shook her head, they'd laugh. *Humiliating.* After the second incident, she'd found a video online to teach her a few basic pleasantries: *Hello; how are you; nice day, isn't it?* Only *hello* had stuck.

Still grinning, the girl ran to the railing and threw a cookie onto the bank. The egret squawked, lifting its heavy wings and flying across the water to the other side. Rising on her toes, the little girl grabbed the railing and bounced up and down, calling to the bird.

The girl was so small and stocky, Lee wanted to pick her up and squeeze her. She reminded Lee of Brett's daughter Dieneke, who could stand, enthralled, before the cage of a zoo animal for hours.

A voice called from inside the laundromat.

Still holding to the rail, the little girl glanced over her shoulder. As if she'd forgotten Lee, a happy smile spread over her face again. She chattered a string of words and stopped, looking back and forth from Lee to the water.

Here we go. Pantomiming her lack of comprehension, she glanced at the canal. The top of an alligator's head jutted from the surface of the water. Listening to the girl release a stream of unfamiliar words, she was relieved to see a young woman emerge onto the balcony. She'd already met this woman and explained through gestures she didn't understand Korean.

Barking a command at the child, the woman nodded pleasantly to Lee.

Feeling foolish, Lee waved back.

At the sound of the woman's voice, the child whipped her head around and released the railing. She ran to the woman's side, wrapping one arm around her leg and popping her finger into her own mouth. Straining her chin upward to gaze at the woman's face made her shiny black hair slide back from her round cheeks. *"Umma."*

Lee froze, watching the woman tap the child's chin and nod toward the laundromat.

The child raced inside the door, and the woman followed, smiling again at Lee as she left the balcony.

Lee's gaze was glued to the spot where the two had stood a moment before. Without making a sound, she formed the word the child had spoken. *Umma.* The forgotten name Lee had intoned over and over again in the one memory she'd retained from her time in the Korean orphanage. *Umma.* Mommy. A wave of longing washed over Lee. She hugged her hands against her chest, eyes filling with tears. Why had her birth mother given her away? What had happened to her? Was she even alive after all these years?

The chiming of bells from the phone on her lap made her jump. She checked the screen.

Bricker.

Her heart pounding, she swiped the corner of her eyes with the sleeve of her shirt. She cleared her throat, praying her voice wouldn't croak. "Thanks for calling me back."

Silence. "Yeah."

His word was tight with anger, like a firecracker needing only the flicker of a flame to erupt. Wrapping her arms around her bent knees, she trapped the phone between her ear and her shoulder. "I…I'm sorry about what my sister said. About you not being good enough for me." A hot flush of embarrassment stole up her neck to her face. "You obviously overheard her."

Bricker gave a short, jagged laugh. "You think I'm mad about what your sister said about me? I don't care what your sister thinks." His breath was rough and uneven through the phone. "But hearing *you* say you'd never get involved with a guy like me? Because you were using me to influence my opinion of your client?"

The words scratched from his throat like sandpaper. "At least now I know where I stand."

A gasp escaped, and Lee's eyes popped wide open. She hadn't even remembered saying those words. Lee's stomach flipped. "I didn't mean what I said to Brett." Her words rushed out. "I wanted to stop her questions. I had to shut her down."

"Shutting down people seems to be a habit of yours."

Blinking, she slumped her shoulders. "You don't understand," she whispered, gazing at the canal. Had the alligator inched closer to the egret? Her heart swelled with sympathy for the bird. A man who made her heart tremble; a critical sister; an ineradicable memory of losing her mother—sometimes Lee felt like prey, too.

"Then make me understand, Lee," Bricker urged. "Talk to me."

She closed her eyes. How to explain a lifetime of being the outcast, rejected by her birth family, and not quite fitting in her adopted home, either? "My sister. My family." The words caught in her throat. "They want me to be a person I'm not. I have to tell them what they want to hear. My sister expects me to act like a professional. Find a guy with good prospects. I let her believe what she wants. My life is easier when she thinks I agree." Holding the phone close to her ear, Lee ground her forehead against her knee. He'd never understand what living a lie was like.

"You have the right to be happy, Lee. Even if your idea of happiness is different than theirs."

His tone was soft now, all traces of anger vanished. She shook her head. "What kind of life would I have led if they hadn't adopted me? I owe them everything. I want to make them proud." Her throat seized on the last word.

"But what are you really doing?"

His voice was insistent but gentle. She shivered.

"You move halfway across the country to get away from them. You pretend to be someone you're not and tell them whatever they want to hear. Do you believe you're making them happy? Because you sure as hell don't seem to be making *yourself* happy."

Squeezing her eyes shut, she lifted her face to the sun. Tears burned the back of her throat. "You're right. When it comes to being the perfect daughter, I'm even a failure at faking."

"Lee."

The tenderness in his voice cut through her self-pity. She opened her eyes and sat up straight.

"If you're not making them happy by 'faking,' you may as well be truthful about who you are. Try being honest with how you feel. Tell them what you really want." He paused, his voice deeper. "You could practice with me."

Her breath caught as she sensed an invitation in the thickening of his voice. She slid her legs down to the sun-warmed planks of the balcony, pressing her hand over quaking knees. "What do you mean?"

"Tell me what you feel about me."

His voice purred through the phone like a sunbathing lion's. She ran her hand over the back of her damp neck. Every nerve ending in her body stood at alert. She eyed the alligator, as still as a boulder in the canal. Mere yards away, the egret remained oblivious to its stalker. Taking a deep breath, Lee pinched the bridge of her nose. "You have a lot of experience with women."

Bricker's soft laugh whispered through the phone. "That's what you think about me. Now tell me what you feel about me."

A spreading dampness through the seat of her shorts made Lee squirm into the thin shade of the potted palm to her right. She held the phone away from her mouth, afraid her hitched breathing would sound like panting. "I'm afraid of you." His answering chuckle, as soft as feathers, tickled her ear.

"Why would you be afraid? All I want is to get close to you."

His words caressed her like warm hands.

"Do you want to get close to me?"

His voice poured through the phone like melted chocolate. Tight as a coil ready to spring, Lee dug her fingers into her thigh. "I..." She couldn't force the words through her swollen throat.

"Lee. Tell me."

She swallowed hard. Sweat slid from her neck in great drops down into her T-shirt. "Yes," she whispered her answer into the expectant silence at the other end of the phone.

A violent splash of water from the canal, followed by an unearthly screech, shattered the stillness.

With a startled spasm, Lee dropped her phone on the deck. It clattered against the wood and shot across the surface to the railing, where a baluster block stopped it from careening over the edge. As she sprang to the rail to grab her phone, she saw the egret soar into the air, its great wings straining as it raced away over the canal.

The alligator stood motionless on the shore.

The line had disconnected, and her heart pounded. Sure, the alligator had scared the heck out of her. But the direction of their conversation was scaring her even more. Her message inbox lit up.

—*Where'd you go??*—

She wiped her hands over her shorts. Her fingers still trembled.

Holy crap. An alligator just attacked an egret right in front of me

She glanced at the bank. Inch by slow inch, the gator slid back into the water, submerged 'til just its eyes remained above the surface. Looking for the next unwary victim, no doubt.

Her phone buzzed.

—*Where are you? Want company?*—

Lee licked her lips, putting a hand to her dry throat. *Be smart, Lee. Be careful.* Her thumbs hovered over the letters.

Can't today. Maybe another time

Fidgeting her legs, she hovered her finger over Send before biting her lip and punching the button. As she gathered her purse from the floor of the deck, she glanced a final time at the lurking alligator before returning to the coolness of the laundromat.

****

Bricker parked by a small pavilion on Deep Gorge State Park. The bluest waters of the key islands sparkled against the white beach sand. He'd needed to clear his head after his conversation with Lee. First, he hit the highway, following it south on the mainland for an hour and a half before turning west to make his slow way back up the chain of islands to Pomegranate Key.

He squinted against the glare of the sun on the white sand. Tugging off his shirt, he tossed it on the front seat and headed to the water. He'd chosen a secluded spot, where the beach was narrow and a thick stand of trees protected it from the road. He kicked off his loafers and splashed into the water, scaring up a school of small tropical fish. In a swoosh of orange, they darted away.

This was a great place for snorkeling. When they were kids, he and Tatum would splash in the shallows while Corinne sat beneath an umbrella with a picnic basket. On any given day, they'd see crabs, skates, rays, turtles, and barracudas. He liked to pretend Deep Gorge was his own private island, deep in the jungle.

After splashing water over his shoulders and face, he relaxed onto the sand, his thoughts returning restlessly to Lee. He'd told himself to give up on her after hearing how she dismissed him to her sister. For the rest of the weekend, he'd stumbled through work on autopilot, cursing himself each time Lee's face floated through his mind.

This morning, he'd spotted her name on his phone, and his heart had almost pounded out of his chest. He forced himself not to pick up. But when he read her text, he couldn't resist ringing her. Her words were small and forlorn on his screen. He read them again now.

I'm so sorry about the other night

His memory flung him right back to the table at Whistler's. He'd been pissed at Lee for ignoring his calls all week, especially after the insult she'd tossed like a grenade before storming out of his truck the night of the fireworks. *Go find some other girl to spend the night with*, or words to that effect. All week he'd fumed over her jab. He couldn't deny the truth in what she said—until he met *her*. Since then, he'd thought of no one else.

When he'd stopped at Whistler's that night for a beer and caught sight of Lee hunched over her plate, clearly hoping she wouldn't find him there, he'd wanted to punish her. He'd unbuttoned his shirt and swaggered to her table, acting for all the world like the male stereotype she was accusing him of being. He'd relished Lee's discomfort as Brett's avid gaze passed between the two of them.

But then Brett had told the story about two-year-old Lee covering her hands over her food when she first arrived in America. How had Brett not noticed her sister's expression? The mixture of desolation, guilt, and dignity her face wore made Bricker want to protect Lee from the whole damned lot of her adopted "golden family." And no sooner had Bricker left the table, resolving to be kind to Lee at least while her sister was in town, then he'd witnessed Lee wave him off like a bad smell.

He collapsed all the way back into the sand, stretching his arms out to the side and closing his eyes against the burning sun. But today…today, she'd apologized. Claimed she was stopping her sister from butting into her business. And he believed her. Because he'd finally gotten her to admit she had feelings for him. A vibration of longing coursed through him as he remembered Lee's throaty voice whispering the one word he was straining to hear. *Yes.*

He sat up, shaking his hair and brushing the sand off his arms. Like a frightened deer, she ran away as soon as he came close. Lee Cooper was a straight mess, no doubt about it. As he remembered her throwing back her head and laughing on the deck of his boat, he let out a breath, his chest muscles clenching. If she could get out from under the influence of her family—if she could tear down those walls she used to protect herself... He stared across the ocean, his eyes unseeing.

Lee had a helluva temper. She could be pretty childish when she didn't get her way. And her ability to shut off all emotions when she was upset was nothing short of scary. Hell, she was even a slob. And yet...he stroked his hands over the warm sand, digging his fingers into the coolness beneath. The gift she'd painted for his mother before she even met Corinne. Her protectiveness for Amber Maly when no one else gave a damn about the girl. Her ringing, gurgling, bubbling laughter rising from her throat like a release of untapped joy. And her sweet, wide smile fading into astonishment as he kissed a path of desire from her eyes, to her chin, to her cheeks, and finally to her lips.

He was in love with the girl.

Jumping to his feet, he yanked off his shorts. Wearing only his boxers, he plunged into the ocean, swimming underwater 'til his lungs wanted to burst. After breaking the surface, he gulped air and gave a strangled laugh. He'd given up on love a long, long time ago. Live for the moment had been his motto. As long as he had his boat, his beer, his buddy Austin, and his bimbos, he'd thought he could be happy. Happy enough.

But he was wrong. Because now, nothing more in the world did he want than to spend the rest of his life with the infuriating, impossible, irresistible Lee Cooper.

Chapter Nine

Lee stretched, reveling in the luxury of a Sunday spent sleeping in. Even the neighborhood rooster hadn't roused her today.

She fitted on a bath cap and took a quick rinse in the shower. Slipping into a pair of shorts and a T-shirt, she glanced out the window. What a beautiful day. Too beautiful to be inside. She'd ride her bike downtown and drink a good cup of coffee at an outdoor café.

After slathering sunscreen over her face, arms, and legs, she strapped on her bike helmet. Tucking a ten dollar bill into her pocket, she grabbed her sunglasses and stepped onto the porch, using her spare porch key to lock the door. The air, a little cooler this morning, brushed against her legs. She hadn't ridden her bike since she first moved to Pomegranate Key.

She spent so much time in Florida running from one air-conditioned space to another, she'd almost forgotten the sweet liberation of air rushing over her face, blowing her hair over her shoulders as she pedaled through the modest neighborhoods of clapboard bungalows to the outskirts of the small downtown area. The last time she'd enjoyed the warm air so much was—well, the last time she'd been on Bricker's boat.

They hadn't talked all week. She wasn't sure if he was waiting for her to make the next move. But one fact she couldn't deny. She'd spent every spare moment reliving the sound of his voice in her ear, daring her to tell him she wanted him.

Her path approached Deacon Street. Bricker might be there early, getting set up for Sunday brunch. What if she stopped by and asked him to have coffee? Her cheeks flushed. Would she be chasing him if she asked him out? *Come on, Lee, this is the twenty-first century.* Clenching the brakes, she slowed to a stop in the middle of the sleepy road. No sign of his truck by Whistler's Bar. Disappointment coursed through her. She passed by the café, no longer interested in having coffee alone. If he wasn't at work, maybe he was over at his mother's place. The memory of Bricker steering Corinne's wheelchair through her bromeliad garden made Lee smile. He seemed like the type of guy to spend Sundays with his mother. She liked his old-fashioned devotion.

Choosing a street parallel to the main thoroughfare, she pushed harder, pedaling into Corinne Kilbourn's tonier neighborhood. Even the air smelled rich over here, perfumed by fluttering clusters of jasmine blooms and the headier scent of potted plumeria. She wondered if Bricker had grown up in this neighborhood. Come to think of it, she didn't know where he lived now. Apparently not on his boat, although a cabin lay under the deck. For a fleeting moment, as he'd kissed her beneath the fireworks display, she'd imagined their night would end below decks. A swell of longing made her heart race. He'd wanted her as much as she wanted him, she was sure. Maybe he acted the same way with all the girls he dated. Or maybe—she bit her lip. Just maybe Brett was right. After years of playing the field, could Bricker have fallen for her?

She shook her head hard as she drove onto Corinne's street. Never had he indicated he was interested in a relationship, and she wasn't foolish enough to pin her hopes on a man with a long history of playing the field. Still…she slowed to a coast as she approached Corinne's house at the end of the cul-de-sac. Considering the collection of men she'd dated and discarded over the years, who was she to act as judge and jury of his past? She'd seen his sweet side. He'd spent days caring for his wheelchair-bound mother, not leaving 'til she kicked him out. He'd earned shy Kaleb's trust in just one visit—and kids were hard to fool. Maybe she *should* stop assuming the worst of Bricker Kilbourn. Maybe the time had come to have a little faith.

Bumping over the stamped cement of Corinne's driveway, she steered past the silver convertible and dismounted by the garage door. So Tatum was here again. No sign of Bricker's truck, but just in case he was inside, she'd knock.

Tatum opened the door, bedraggled in a ripped T-shirt and shorts. Blonde hairs escaped from a red bandana covering her head. Flashing a smile, she wiped the back of her hand over her brow, leaving behind a brown smear. "You're just the person I need!" Grabbing Lee by the arm, she yanked her into the house. "I told Mom I'd prune her bromeliads while she's in St. Petersburg for a couple of days, but I have no idea what I'm doing." She turned and strode through the air-conditioned rooms to the doors of the lanai.

Leaving Lee no choice but to follow. "I was checking to see if Bricker might be here." She addressed the back of Tatum's head. "I wanted to invite him out for coffee."

"I don't know where Bricker is. Not here helping me." With a sweep of her hand, Tatum gestured to a cluster of bromeliads with flaming red spikes. "Mom said something about pruning the 'pups.' I can't tell a pup from a leaf."

Lee spread her hands wide. "Don't ask me! I just paint them."

Slapping her hand to her forehead, Tatum moaned. "The doctor thought getting away was a good idea for Mom. The one way I could convince her to let Hector take her out of town was to promise I'd take care of her garden. But I'm afraid I'll kill these plants."

Lee grinned. "I doubt your mom would have left you in charge of her plants if they were *that* fragile." She pulled her smart phone from her pocket. "Did you look on the Internet? I'm sure we can find a video to teach us how to prune."

Minutes later, both women were on their knees, slicing tender bromeliad upstarts from beneath the leaves of the mother plant. "I don't know why I didn't think of looking online," Tatum commented. "When I don't know how to do something, I usually just outsource the problem to my assistant."

Remembering Bricker's comment about his sister's whip-cracking at the office, Lee stifled a grin. "The Internet is the only assistant I can afford. Do you have pots to put the pups in?"

Tatum stood, brushing the dirt from her hands and scanning the shelves near the wall. "She's got a bunch of plastic containers."

"Grab some small ones. We don't want to mix the bromeliad types, so we'll need a pot for each plant. You should find some potting soil, too. I'm sure your mom has a bag somewhere." Continuing to cut the pups close to the mother plant, Lee heard plastic pots clatter to the floor beside her.

Returning a moment later with a bag of soil, Tatum heaved it onto a flagstone. She resumed pruning a few feet away and then glanced over her shoulder. "I don't know what I would have done if you hadn't shown up. I really appreciate your help."

Sweeping a strand of hair from her brow with the clean back of her hand, Lee smiled. "No problem. Who knew I'd actually enjoy gardening?"

"Well, I'm hating it. You're the one thing making this experience tolerable." Stretching her long legs to either side of the plant, she rolled back her shoulders. "How'd you meet my brother, anyway?"

Lee winced, recalling her first hostile introduction to Bricker as he served her lunch at Whistler's. Maybe she'd skip their first encounter. "I work in social services with mothers at risk for abuse or neglect. He's the guardian ad litem for a little boy whose mother is my client."

A dismissive sniff deflated Tatum's perfect nostrils. "Nice to know he's using his law school education for something."

Lee whistled under her breath. *And I thought I was hard on the guy.* "Actually, I'm impressed by the bond he's developed with my client's son. He takes his responsibility to protect the child's best interests very seriously."

"Now *that's* a good one!" Tatum snorted, swiveling her upper body toward Lee.

Her eyes narrowed, lips drawn against her teeth,

Tatum looked like she'd tasted something past its expiration date. Lee shrank back. How bad was the sibling rivalry in this family? Hoping to defuse Tatum's anger, Lee chose her words carefully. "I don't always get along with my older brother, either. But underneath it all, I know he loves me, and I love him."

Color rising high in her cheekbones, Tatum glared. "You try living with the shame of your brother's behavior in a small community, and we'll see how well you hold on to those loving feelings." With a violent shake of her head, Tatum grabbed a bromeliad, plunging a spade into the soil with enough force to uproot the whole plant.

Baffled by her sudden explosion of venom, Lee stared at Tatum's back. Was she really so embarrassed by her brother's job? Or did this have something to do with Bricker's reputation as a ladies' man? Either way, "shame" was a pretty strong word. Lee cleared her throat. "I was taught any work is honorable if it puts food on your table."

"Yeah? What'd they teach you about men who abandon their children?" Tatum's laugh scraped out of her throat like a snarl.

Lee froze, her eardrums pulsing with the whirring of ceiling fan blades overhead. Her gaze locked on Tatum's spade cleaving the center of a spotted bromeliad. Its stalk separated neatly, dropping its red leaves to the ground like two outstretched arms. "Be careful!" she croaked. Her pulse pounding against her throat, she wet her lips. "What are you talking about?"

Dropping the spade, Tatum rose and paced to the sink. She crossed her arms, dropping her chin and taking a long breath through her nose. Her lips were a pale line, bitten between her teeth. "I shouldn't have mentioned it. I apologize." She passed a shaky hand over her head, tugging her bandana into place.

Gripping the pruning knife with care, Lee stood. She was aware of each rise and fall of her chest as she forced herself to breathe. "You can't drop a bomb like that and not explain."

Avoiding Lee's gaze, Tatum waved her hand. "Forget I said anything." Lacking her usual composure, she shifted and stared at her feet.

"Tatum." Lee's voice brooked no argument.

Fingering the knot at the base of her skull, Tatum raised her head. Her blue eyes flinched when she met Lee's gaze.

"Tell me." Lee's heart hammered, drowning out the rotations of the ceiling fan. She held Tatum's wary gaze until she sensed the other woman's resolve crumble.

Tatum covered her face with her hands. "Bricker has a son he's never met." She blurted the words from behind her fingers. Shaking her head, she dropped her hands. "I don't have the right to tell you. But I like you." She wrapped her arms around her middle. "You deserve better than my brother."

Her blue eyes appealed for understanding. But Lee didn't understand. Her heart shuddered, vibrating distress between her lungs. She couldn't breathe. Leaning her hands against her knees, she forced in a gulp of air and shut her eyes against a whirling kaleidoscope of visions: rows of metal beds with thin white blankets; a ceiling fan squeaking overhead on each slow rotation; two chubby hands clasped in prayer—and behind the images, the rising wail of a child.

Tatum rushed to her side, gripping her hands on Lee's shoulders. "Are you okay? Do you need water?"

Mashing her lips together, Lee straightened and met Tatum's worried gaze. "Just tell me the whole story." The center of her chest felt bruised, like she'd been punched in the sternum.

"Okay, but first, will you put down the knife?"

At Tatum's faltering smile, Lee looked down at her hand. Her knuckles were white with the intensity of her grip. Loosening her fingers, she passed the knife handle onto Tatum's palm.

"Let's go inside." Dropping the knife to the floor, Tatum steered Lee through the lanai doors to a chair in the family room. She collapsed onto the couch opposite. "I had no idea you'd take the news so hard. I'm really sorry."

Lee sank onto the chair, the cool green leather absorbing the heat of her bare legs in a clammy hug. She fought to steady her breathing, forcing her words through trembling lips. "I have an issue with parents who abandon their children." Seeing Tatum's head tilt, Lee waved to forestall any more questions. "Can you just tell me everything?"

Tucking her feet beneath her, Tatum sighed. "This happened almost ten years ago, around the time Bricker graduated from law school. Dad had just bought him the boat." Her lips curled. "He was supposed to join Dad's law firm—Kilbourn, White, & Kilbourn." Her gaze drifted to a bookshelf against the wall. She rose, lifting a framed photo from the shelf and handing it to Lee.

His arms folded, wide blue eyes twinkling into the

camera, the man's confident smile dimpled his cheeks and chin. But for the wrinkles around his mouth and eyes and his short hair graying at the temples, he could have passed for Bricker's brother.

Tatum nodded. "Bricker was Dad's spitting image. But they didn't get along. Not since Bricker was a teenager. All Dad wanted was for his son to follow in his footsteps. And what did my brother do? He ruined the life of Dad's assistant. For once, even Dad couldn't forgive him." She took back the photo from Lee, stroking a finger over her father's smile before placing the frame on the shelf. She glanced at the clock and gave a shaky laugh. "I don't care how early it is. I need a drink. Can I get you something?"

"Just water," Lee answered. Tatum rustled in the kitchen behind her, and she stared at her hands in her lap. The optimism of pedaling her bike to find Bricker seemed like a lifetime ago. Dread seeped through her nerves as she waited for Tatum's story to resume.

"Her name was Veronica," Tatum continued, placing a glass of water in front of Lee.

Tatum, Lee noticed, had grabbed a bottle of scotch.

"For years she'd worked for my dad. We were all guests at her wedding when she married her high school sweetheart, Pete. They were like another part of our family, coming along on our vacations because they couldn't afford their own. Pete worshipped the ground she walked on. He was a little dorky, but he was sweet." Tatum sipped at her drink, grimacing. "Meanwhile, my brother came back from law school, all grown up and looking like—well, looking like he does now, except with shorter hair. He could have had any girl he wanted." Her eyes flashed. "But he pursued

Veronica. And he destroyed her marriage."

Lee fought a rising tide of nausea in the pit of her stomach. So Bricker had deliberately pursued a married woman, one who trusted the Kilbourns like they were her own family.

"I don't know how long the affair lasted. Maybe no one would have found out if she hadn't gotten pregnant." Tatum shook her glass, ice cubes clinking. "She and Pete had been trying to have a baby for a couple of years. Evidently, Pete had his sperm tested without telling Veronica. He found out he was shooting blanks and hadn't told her yet, because he didn't want to break her heart." She slipped the bandana off her hair, rotating her neck and scrubbing her fingers over her scalp. Two deep lines burrowed between her eyebrows. "Imagine his surprise when she told him she was pregnant. Pete was gullible, but even *he* didn't believe in Immaculate Conception. So on a night when he knew she was working late, he sat in a car outside the office building and waited for her to come out."

Tatum took another sip of her drink, leveling her gaze at Lee. "Guess who was with her?" She took a longer drink and set her glass on the table, running her finger along the rim. "He followed them to a motel outside of town. Poor Pete. I can't even imagine how he felt." She sighed, leaning back against the couch. "And then the shit hit the fan. When Pete left Veronica, she was three months pregnant. And the father of the baby? My brother? He refused to take responsibility. He'd had his fun, I guess." She gave a bitter little chuckle. "He took off for the Virgin Islands in his brand-new boat while Dad wrote a big, fat check for Veronica. For Mom's sake, Dad tried to keep the whole sordid affair quiet, but on this little island, news travels fast. Mom fell into the worst remission of her illness. I had to come home from college before the semester's end to help take care of her. Not 'had to,'" she amended with a shake of her head. "I wanted to."

No wonder Tatum had sneered at Bricker for hovering during their mother's most recent relapse. He was a caretaker just when the moment suited him. Lee passed a trembling hand over her face. She had a desperate desire to get away from this house. Gazing out the window, she viewed dark thunderclouds forming overhead. She lurched up from the couch. "I should go before it rains. I rode my bike here."

Tatum sprang to her feet, following Lee to the door. "I could give you a ride," she volunteered.

Her hand on the doorknob, Lee pivoted.

Tatum stood behind her, arms wrapped across her chest, chewing her lower lip.

She was having second thoughts about what she'd revealed, Lee supposed. *Too late*. "Thank you for being honest," she told Tatum. "You were right. I needed to know." Not waiting for Tatum to respond, Lee escaped through the door.

The heat of the afternoon was heavy with humidity, forcing her to pedal harder than ever. Already gray storm clouds roiled into menacing blackness. Lee lifted herself from the seat and used the weight of her body to ride faster, skidding around corners and pedaling with grim determination. No time to think about Tatum's revelations—just the thick bank of thunderclouds threatening to break overhead.

The first splash of rain hit as she rounded the corner to her street. Racing past the gate of her compound, she jumped from the bike and pushed it against a bush beside the porch. She'd put it away later. As rain slanted diagonally under the eaves, pounding onto the wooden deck like an unloosed bag of marbles, Lee bounded up the steps and fished frantically inside the vase for her key. Scraping her knuckles against the vase's rough finish, she fished out the key and stabbed it in the hole. With a twist of the knob, she stumbled into the bungalow, drenched right down to her underwear.

She kicked off her shoes and dripped her way across the cold tile floor, peeling off and tossing her sodden clothes behind her. Cranking the faucet all the way to the left, she stepped into the shower, sighing as steam rose in the square chamber. In the center of the pounding water, she closed her eyes, surrendering to the hot tears behind her eyes waiting for a safe place to spill. Against the thunder of the shower, her face seized and contorted with grief. Stretched in misery, her mouth gasped for air. She sucked in a ragged breath mingled with a sob.

Tatum's secret had ripped the scab off an old wound Lee had fought for years to hide. Why had her parents abandoned her? The years fled as the unmistakable gloom of the orphanage dormitory seeped into her, convincing her she didn't deserve a mother, or a father, or love. How could Bricker discard his own son?

For a split second, she was tempted to crouch on the shower floor and rock herself like a child. Instead, she whipped her wet hair across her cheek with a stinging slap. She was being ridiculous. If her birth mother hadn't given her up, she'd no doubt have lived a life of poverty. The best thing to happen to her was being placed in an orphanage and adopted by the prosperous American family who loved her.

Biting hard on her lip, Lee shut off the faucet and grabbed her towel, rubbing herself dry with grim determination. So she'd been right about Bricker Kilbourn all along. He cared about satisfying his own desires, and to hell with who got hurt.

She donned a clean pair of shorts and a soft terry shirt, wrapping her hair in a towel turban-style. She should call Bricker right now and tell him what a worthless piece of humanity he was. But even beneath her disgust, her heart surged at the idea of hearing his voice. She sank onto the bed and caught her reflection in the mirror. Scrubbed clean of makeup, with no hair framing her round cheeks, she looked as defenseless as a lost child. A child forsaken.

Drawing a deep breath, she squared her shoulders and frowned at her reflection without blinking. As she concentrated, her gaze emptied into detachment. The image of Bricker receded into the distance, and she welcomed the familiar numbness like an old friend.

A ring of her cell phone jolted her. A glance at the screen showed her the name of Gloria Marshall's service coordinator. Calling on a Sunday? She picked up the phone. Still observing her reflection, she forced a smile. "Lee Cooper speaking." A moment later, Lee's smile dropped like a curtain. Her face draining of color, she listened to the home visitor strike the death knell on Amber's chances to regain custody of her son.

Chapter Ten

"How was St. Petersburg?" Bricker called from the family room when he heard the front door creak open.

Corinne rolled her wheelchair around the corner. With a glance at her son's bare feet propped on the glass coffee table, she shook her head. "I had a marvelous time." She glanced up at Hector behind her chair. "I'm not sure if Hector would agree, though. I made him take me all around museums, parks, and gardens. The poor man must be exhausted."

With an easy smile, Hector parked Corinne across from her son and locked the chair's brake. "I had a nice vacation, too," he replied. "I'll go get your luggage from the car."

Bricker rose. "Let me help you there, man."

But Hector put up his hand. "I'll get the bags. You visit with your mother."

After leaning down to kiss her cheek, Bricker sat on the recliner. "You've got some nice color in your face, Mother. Glad you followed the doctor's advice to get away for a few days."

Corinne nodded. "I feel twenty years younger. Full of energy."

"Uh-oh." Bricker shook his finger. "Don't get any crazy ideas. You need to take it easy for a while."

Corinne dismissed his concerns with a wave. "Enough about me. What are you doing over here?"

He nodded toward the kitchen. "Figured you could use some dinner when you got home." He'd thrown together a chicken Caesar salad and left it chilling in the fridge. A pan of homemade croutons waited in the oven.

Corinne's smile widened. "I thought I smelled garlic. You're very sweet, Bricker. But shouldn't you be cooking for someone besides your mother?"

As he escaped into the kitchen, he sensed his mother's gaze on his back. "Who deserves a home-cooked meal more than the mother who raised me?" Keeping his face averted, he reached inside the refrigerator for the salad bowl. He knew exactly where this conversation was headed.

"As much as I appreciate your cooking, I imagine Lee would love to have someone cook her dinner after a long day at work."

His shoulders tensed. His mother was bound to grill him about the first girl he'd brought home in years. Too bad the relationship was over before it even began.

He'd gotten a text from Lee the night before.

You're not the man I thought you were. Please don't contact me again

So it went with Lee Cooper. One step forward, two steps back.

—What have I done now?—

I can't even comprehend the choices you've made. Please respect my decision and leave me alone

Stung, he'd dropped his phone. Was she talking about the women? Was she so insecure she couldn't tolerate the idea he'd been with anyone else? Or couldn't she believe a man like him could change?

Or—his heart froze in his chest. Had someone told

her about what happened ten years ago? He shook his head. The people close to him would never mention it. The people who weren't had forgotten the whole incident a long time ago. The gossip over Veronica and her baby had faded like yesterday's news, leaving the Kilbourn family to lick its wounds in private.

Who knew what Lee was spun up about now? He'd been crazy to think he could have a relationship with her. Turning off his phone, he'd cracked open a beer, drinking four more 'til he collapsed into the forgetfulness of sleep.

Hector's return through the garage door at the back of the kitchen spared Bricker from responding to his mother's hint. Ignoring the hollow feeling in the pit of his stomach, he busied himself with plating salads and quizzed his mother's home companion on the places they'd visited during their weekend away.

As usual, Corinne jumped in to finish Hector's sentences.

Grant Kilbourn had hired Hector shortly after Corinne was diagnosed with MS. Bricker wondered what his father would have made of his wife's relationship to Hector, who was now just another member of the family.

"When will Lee visit again?" Corinne returned to the subject of Lee as soon as they gathered around the table to eat. "I thought she was great."

Her long hair brushed back into a smooth ponytail, Corinne smiled, gray eyes sparkling above her rosy cheeks. He hadn't seen his mother look so lively in years. He stifled a sigh. Leave it to him to disappoint her again. Shrugging to feign indifference, he took a deliberate mouthful of salad, chewing slowly as he met his mother's gaze.

With an exasperated huff, she dropped her napkin and planted her hands on both sides of her plate. "Don't tell me you've broken up already?"

Bricker took a long drink of water. In the silence of the room, he could hear his Adam's apple sliding in his throat. He set the empty glass on the table and faced his mother. "Okay, I won't tell you." Seeing his mother's straight shoulders sag, he clenched his jaw. Why had he raised her hopes? He'd never have a normal life. When he sailed off to the Virgin Islands ten years ago, he'd sealed his fate.

"Oh, Bricker. Why? She seemed so nice. I could tell how much you liked each other." Corinne tilted her head, lips pursed.

He dropped his gaze to the napkin on his lap. Her compassion made him feel worse than her anger. "I guess she's looking for a guy with more prospects." He concentrated his attention on stretching the napkin between his thumbs and forefingers.

Corinne expelled a long sigh. "But you *do* have prospects! Or, at least, you could, if you'd just retake the bar exam."

Anger like a white-hot flame flared inside, and he smacked his palm on top of the table. Seeing his mother wince, he forced himself to put a calming hand over hers. "That dream is over, Mother. Let it die." He squeezed her hand to take the sting from his words. "Anyway, didn't someone say a man should be judged by the content of his character? We all know *that* won't help matters."

A strained silence followed.

Hector cleared his throat. "I hear the wahoo are

biting good out in the Gulf."

The gentle strains of the older man's Cuban accent calmed the tensions in the room. Grateful to discuss the safe topic of fishing, Bricker pretended not to notice his mother's deflated expression as they finished their dinners. He washed dishes as Hector guided Corinne into her bedroom and readied her for bed. Scrubbing plates with a soapy sponge, Bricker found his thoughts pivoting over and over to Lee. *Forget her.* He ground his teeth while he sprayed the sink clean and shut off the water. While he dried his hands on a dish towel, he remembered the words he'd overheard. *I'd never get serious about a guy like him. But my client needs him on her side.* Lee's tone, as indifferent as if she'd decided against a menu item, staggered him. Whatever childhood ordeals she was working through in her life, one thing was clear—she sure as hell didn't want *his* help. At the sound of his mother's bedroom door clicking shut from down the hall, Bricker was startled back into the present.

Hector padded across the tiles toward the kitchen.

"Hey." Bricker's voice was quiet. "Is she down for the night?"

His gaze focused like a laser on the younger man's face, Hector nodded. "She's reading in bed for a while." He stroked his fingers over his goatee. "I put on music in her room so you and I could talk freely."

Great. More talk. From behind the barrier of the kitchen counter, Bricker planted his feet shoulder width apart. "About what?"

"Don't get angry." Hector placed his palms against the marble. "I want to talk about the baby."

Bricker folded his arms across his chest. His pulse

pounded against his inner wrist. Struggling to keep his expression impassive, he shrugged. "Not interested."

Hector shook his head, his balding scalp glinting beneath the recessed ceiling lights. "You must stop punishing yourself. Let go of the past."

"I have." Bricker gave a strangled laugh. But Hector's gaze was locked on him.

"No."

Hector's one quiet word was a command more effective than any lecture.

"You have not moved on with your life. You bring sadness to your mother."

Bricker's throat clogged. "You know I never want to hurt her." Hector had been the person he leaned on when his life had fallen apart, the person who had helped him ready his boat to leave for the islands. He hadn't agreed with Bricker, but he'd supported his decision to leave.

Hector's dark eyes never wavered. "Your mother believes you have a chance for happiness with this young girl—Lee. You should tell her about your past. All of it."

Bricker clenched the edge of the marble counter with white knuckles. Hector's only motive was to see Corinne happy, but now he was crossing a line. "I'll make my own decisions, Hector. And I'll thank you to respect them." Half a head taller, he loomed over the older man.

As he absorbed Bricker's warning, Hector's face was still as a mask. The moment stretched until, with a faint sigh, he nodded.

Bricker relaxed, flexing his fingers. "Okay. I'll be heading out now." He hated the disappointment he saw in Hector's gaze. Especially after all the man had done for Corinne this weekend. He stuck out his hand over the counter. "Tell Mother good night."

Hector held his grip a long time. The corners of his mouth quavered when he released Bricker's hand. "Good night, my young friend."

Nodding, Bricker strode to the front door and stepped onto the portico. He closed the door, warm air enveloping him like the caress of soft hands. He shivered as his body adjusted to the sudden rise in temperature. So Hector thought Bricker should tell Lee about Veronica. Come clean. Lay the whole ugly story to rest.

He opened the door of his truck, gazing at the lit window on the far side of the house where his mother lay in bed. Reading to ignore the pain in her feet until exhaustion swept her under, he knew.

No good could come of rehashing the events of ten years ago. Despite what Hector believed, the one way to protect Corinne from more pain was to keep the door locked on the past.

****

Amber's eyes were tear-streaked and wild. "You have to believe me, Lee." She pointed a bony finger at the door as it closed. "They're setting me up!"

Lee had been fortunate to time her visit with the departure of Trish Nichols, Amber's caseworker, who'd confirmed the bad news passed on by Gloria Marshall's home visitor. Now, poised on the edge of the couch in Amber's frigid apartment, Lee gazed at the stained carpet and fought to control her queasiness.

An anonymous call to Children's Services alleged Amber had filmed live sex shows by webcam while her toddler was in the apartment. Amber's personal computer had been seized. While no evidence supported the caller's claim, an entirely new alarm had been sounded. Investigators traced hundreds of links to websites visited while her husband was at work. For three consecutive days in the past week, Amber had spent her mornings and afternoons visiting web pages connected with the murder of children by their own mothers.

A mixture of distrust and alarm lodged like a tumor in Lee's chest. Trish's expression of distaste as Amber signed paperwork had magnified Lee's dread. How could she have been so wrong about a client? She'd defended Amber Maly to everyone: to her boss and her co-workers, to the public defender, and to Bricker. But they'd been right all along. Her gaze slid to Amber's pinched face. Was the girl evil, or was she just sick?

Amber whimpered and shook her head, lank strips of hair lashing her face. "Don't believe them, Lee. You're the one person in my corner." Tears ran from the corners of her eyes, and she wiped her palm over her nose with a ragged sob.

As she clamped her cold hands between her legs, Lee searched for something to say. When she'd called her boss for advice this morning, Janna had told her to be supportive and stay neutral. "You're not the judge or jury. Your job is to help her make good parenting decisions unless and until the court terminates her parental rights."

Reaching in her purse, Lee handed Amber a tissue. "Why don't you sit, and we'll talk?"

Amber sank onto the couch and blew her nose. Her eyes, red-rimmed and swollen, were pressed deep into her bloodless face. She drew a shaky breath. "I would never hurt Kaleb." Her whisper was soft but fierce.

Lee trapped her hands between her thighs again. "I know," she reassured Amber. *I don't know anything.*

"I had a sinus infection last week. I waited an hour to see the doctor." Amber's voice had regained its habitual flatness.

Sociopaths tend to speak in a monotone. Lee shivered, clenching her hands tighter between her legs.

Amber gazed at the tissues squashed in her hand. "I picked up a magazine and read a story about a mother who drowned her kids in the bathtub a few years ago. I'd heard about the case before, but I didn't know the background story. I got called in to see the doctor before I could finish it, so the next day I researched the case on the computer." She shrugged her shoulders. "I was depressed, okay? My sinus infection made me feel like hell. I found the woman's story really sad, so I followed the links at the end of the article to other mothers who killed their children. I got kind of obsessed."

Sweeping her gaze over the dingy apartment, she grimaced. "With Kaleb gone, there's not much to do around here all day without a car. Dan told me reading those websites was making me more depressed. I stopped after a couple of days. But not before I ruined my chances of getting back my son." Amber's face crumpled, and she lifted a sodden tissue to her eyes.

Lee passed a fresh tissue. How many hours had she herself lost chasing links across the internet after her interest had been piqued? She bit her lip. Stories of mothers hurting their children sold copy. Surely not everyone who read about these tragic killings was a danger to society?

Racked with sobs, the younger woman drew her knees to her chest. Wrapping her thin arms around her folded legs, she dropped her cheek to her knees and turned from Lee.

If this was a performance, it was award-winning. *But then again, sociopaths are known to be great manipulators.* Lee squinted at the back of Amber's head. Janna had told her not to worry about the truth; to do her job, and support Amber as a parent. Lee waited until the girl lifted her head to blow her nose again. "Try not to worry too much. You've explained everything to your attorney, right?"

Amber nodded, sniffing.

"Then let him handle this. What you need to focus on is staying calm and working on the reunification plan. Don't miss any parenting classes or important appointments. Be early for visitation with Kaleb, and make sure you show him a lot of affection. Whatever you do, don't let him see how stressed you are."

When she heard Kaleb's name, Amber's lower lip quivered. "I just want my son back."

Staring into the younger girl's bruised eyes, Lee bit the inside of her cheek, her resistance wavering. Amber seemed so broken. Despite her misgivings, Lee still wanted to protect her. She chewed her lower lip and reminded herself again of Janna's advice. *Stay neutral.* The muscles in Lee's cheeks strained in an attempt at a smile. "At least Children's Services realized the webcam charges against you were bogus."

Amber flung her tissue onto the coffee table and glared. "You know who made the accusation, don't you?"

Lee shrugged and spread her hands. "Trish Nichols said the call was anonymous."

"Ha!" Amber spat. "No one else would have called but Gloria Marshall."

Again with the foster mother conspiracy. Lee rubbed her hands over her eyes.

Amber jumped from the couch and paced the worn carpet. "She's been filling Dan's head with lies every time he goes to her house to see Kaleb. She won't stop 'til she breaks us up. I'm serious." Thick cords bulged around the hollow of her throat, forming a T against the protrusion of her collarbone. Amber's body, always thin, was whittled down to knobs and angles.

"Hey." Lee softened her tone. "Have you been eating?"

"No, I haven't been eating! Who cares about eating?" Amber paced the living room, looking through the diamond-shaped window of the front door before stalking back to sit on the arm of the couch. "I met the guardian ad litem a couple of weeks ago."

"You did?" Pain stabbed through the center of Lee's chest. She took a deep breath. This was business, not personal. "How did it go?"

"Okay, I guess." Amber shrugged. "He wouldn't give me more visitation."

"No, he's just fact-finding—observing how Kaleb acts in different environments." Lee wondered whether the boy had been happy to see his mother during Bricker's visit. Had Amber shown her usual severity to her son? But asking such a question today would only rub salt in an open wound. "The guardian cares about Kaleb. I'm sure he's looking out for his best interests." As the words passed her lips, the difference between

Bricker's sense of responsibility to Kaleb compared to his own son rattled her. *How can I be sure of anything with Bricker Kilbourn?*

Amber stopped pacing and pivoted toward Lee. "Could you tell him the truth about those websites I visited? So he doesn't think I'm a psycho?"

Shaking her head against the hope in Amber's eyes, Lee leaned back. "I can't. I'm only supposed to talk with him about what I witness. Anyway, we've already met. He won't be calling me again."

Her memory vaulted to her first visit to Corinne's home, when Bricker had indulged his mother's desire to show off her bromeliad collection. When she'd observed his devotion, watching him steering Corinne's wheelchair from plant to plant, Lee had opened her heart for the first time. Two weeks later, on the same lanai, Tatum threw cold water on the dreams that had just begun to take shape.

With a grunt, Amber dropped onto the couch and pulled a tattered blanket from the back of the sofa. Draping it over her legs, she stared at the door. Her lips were drawn into a pale pink line.

Lee rose and hoisted her leather bag to her shoulder. She was more than happy to take Amber's hint and leave. "Everything's going to be okay."

Amber snorted.

I don't blame you. Lee closed the door behind her to face the withering heat of the afternoon. *Some things can't be fixed.*

Chapter Eleven

Gloria Marshall's home was a child's fantasy. Its wide top-floor balcony transformed into a big-wheel bike race track encircling the house. Tall windows commanded a view of the rectangular in-ground pool. A white pine play structure with adaptive swing seats and a wide, yellow slide sprawled on the other side of the drive. The woods surrounding the yard on all sides were as thick as a jungle, with white-pebbled paths snaking through the forest of live oaks and sabal palms.

Bricker had visited once before. He'd arranged to interview Daniel and Kaleb Maly while Gloria Marshall's family attended a Wednesday-night church service and potluck. The visit had been cut short when Gloria called Daniel to fetch his son there for a special blessing from the bishop.

Thunder murmured from a bank of thick gray clouds. The afternoon rainfall had stopped, but the portico was still dripping water. Bricker rang the doorbell, shaking a rogue trickle of water from his hair as he reviewed his first impressions of Daniel. The guy was built like a weightlifter, with short legs and a long trunk. He'd sat on the edge of the couch with hands folded in his lap, shooting nervous glances from Bricker to Kaleb as the boy played on the floor with a set of wooden logs. Most parents, forewarned by their attorneys to make a good impression, were ill at ease for their first interview with their child's guardian ad litem. But Daniel had been practically mute until Gloria Marshall's phone call abruptly ended the meeting.

A woman with short hair and round cheeks answered the door, a toddler balanced on her hip. "Welcome to our home! I'm Gloria Marshall, and this"—she dangled the little girl's limp wrist, while the child turned cloudy, unfocused eyes toward the light outside the door—"is Noemi."

Bricker brushed one finger over the soft skin of the girl's tiny hand and smiled when she swung her head toward his touch.

Gloria tinkled a merry laugh as she placed her palm under the toddler's chin to rest the girl's cheek against her shoulder. "Noemi is blind, aren't you, my little chick-pea?" She turned and called up the wide wooden steps to the second floor. "Daniel, sweetie? The guardian's here to see you."

Grimacing at the older woman's honeyed tones, Bricker shut the door behind him and followed her into the family room. Exposed wooden beams in a high-ceilinged great room drew his gaze to a balcony at the top of the stairs. Plush green carpet trailed down the stairs and covered the living area to the edge of the kitchen. Baby seats of different shapes and sizes stood along the wall. A widescreen TV, its volume low, played a cartoon for the empty room.

After she locked a baby gate at the exit to the foyer, Gloria hooked her foot around the leg of a frog-shaped child's seat and slid it near a rocking chair. She slipped Noemi, unresisting, inside.

Bricker sat on the couch. While he retrieved a notebook and pen from his briefcase, he observed

Gloria from the corner of his eye. Her short auburn hair was shot with gray at the temples, and a band of flesh swelled over the waistband of her shorts as she leaned over Noemi. He guessed her to be in her late forties.

She placed a fabric-covered child's book in the toddler's hand and swept her palm over the back of the little girl's head. Lowering herself into the rocker at Bricker's left, she cooed to the little girl.

A door creaked open upstairs. A moment later, Kaleb emerged from the hallway onto the balcony. As he squeezed his cheeks between the railings, he grinned at Bricker's upturned face.

"Hey, buddy," Bricker called, flooded with outsized happiness at the little boy's smile. He knew better than to get attached to the kids during the investigation, but something about Kaleb cracked his heart wide open.

"Hold onto the railing, Kaleb," Gloria cautioned as he stood at the top of the staircase. But Kaleb shook his head, descending the stairs one foot at a time. On the second-to-last step, he bounded off in a jump. When he landed firmly on two feet, he raised his small fists in the air.

Bricker clapped, but he caught Gloria shooting Kaleb a warning glance.

"No jumping off the stairs, Kaleb. You'll get hurt. Do you understand?"

Kaleb dropped his chin and stared at the floor, his victorious smile vanishing. One small hand lifted above his ear and clamped a hank of hair.

"No, no!" Gloria lunged from her seat to where the little boy stood. Kneeling, she teased his fingers out of his hair and wrapped him in her arms. "Grandma's not mad. Grandma just wants you to be safe."

Grandma? Bricker frowned. So Lee hadn't been exaggerating about Gloria considering herself Daniel's "adopted" mother. Well, Grandma or not, Kaleb sure had reacted with anxiety at her reprimand.

Kaleb peeked over Gloria's shoulder to Bricker, his expression anxious as Gloria hugged him. He peeled himself away, running past the adults to dive onto the floor in front of the TV.

Clucking, Gloria shook her head. "Pulling out his own hair. Thanks to having an m-o-m who y-e-l-l-s all the time. You get neurotic!" she sang, the middle syllable of her last word rising on a high note.

Bricker frowned at his papers. Bad-mouthing a parent, no matter how she disguised it, was always a strike in his book. "Where's your dad, buddy?" he asked Kaleb as the boy lay on the floor, already transfixed by a cartoon.

Gloria cut him off before Kaleb could answer. "Daniel will be just a minute. He needed to freshen up after work."

Did she plan on doing the talking for Daniel, too? Bricker never allowed relatives, no matter how well-meaning, to influence his interviews. He forced a polite smile. "Don't allow this meeting to hold you up, Mrs. Marshall. I'm sure you have a lot to do."

"Nothing as important as talking to Kaleb's guardian." She put her hand over her heart and widened her eyes. "We have to make sure Kaleb is safe and living in the right home environment." She brushed her hair behind her ear and gazed at Noemi. "I have to admit, taking care of so many children with special needs doesn't leave me much time for my older children, or my husband. I take care of another baby, too." She clasped her hands in her lap and lowered her gaze to her palms. "Angelica's mom was on crack. She was born three and a half months premature. Her grandparents have her this afternoon. I never get a break for more than an hour or two. But I wouldn't change a thing." Her gaze returned to Bricker's face.

She was waiting for a response. Was this the part where he was supposed to praise her selflessness? He didn't trust people who fished for compliments. And she seemed prepared to plant herself in the middle of his meeting with Daniel. Clamping his mouth shut, he returned her gaze.

Her smile faltered. At the sound of a door closing from the second floor, she turned away from Bricker and looked up at the landing. "Here he comes."

Daniel's dark hair, thick but trimmed close to his head, was combed and damp. His red polo shirt fit him like a second skin, exposing forearms as thick as small tree trunks. Bricker narrowed his eyes as he remembered Amber saying she'd smacked the race track on Kaleb's unprotected bottom only to protect him from his father. As he watched Daniel's short, powerful physique stride down the stairs into the living room, Bricker wondered if he'd been too quick to discount her claim.

Without a word, Daniel dropped into an easy chair next to Gloria and fixed his gaze on the television screen. *Like a kid called to the principal's office.* The guy could be described as handsome, maybe. He had an all-American football captain kind of look. But his eyes weren't right. They seemed blank. Hollow.

Gloria leaned forward, her hand on Daniel's arm.

Bricker spoke before she could. "Mr. Maly, a guardian was assigned to your son due to suspicions of abuse and neglect."

"By his mother!" Gloria interrupted.

Bricker held up his palm in her direction. "Marks were found on Kaleb's scrotum and buttocks. Can you tell me what happened?"

His gaze on Daniel, he noticed Gloria's knuckles whitening as she clenched Daniel's hand.

"We've already talked with the police and Children's Services—"

"Mrs. Marshall," he snapped. From the floor, he saw Kaleb shoot a look over his shoulder at the grownups. Bricker lowered his voice. "I'm here to speak with Mr. Maly. If you can't allow him to answer my questions, you'll be asked to leave the room."

Her jaw dropped, and her eyes widened. "This is my house!"

He squared his shoulders. "And you signed a document allowing Daniel to hold his guardian interview at your home. Do you need to see the paper?"

Snapping shut her mouth, Gloria shook her head. Her eyes glinted with anger.

Hesitating, Daniel glanced between Bricker and Gloria.

She nodded. "Go ahead, Daniel." Her lips were taut as she sat back and crossed her arms.

"Kaleb threw a toy at Noemi, so Amber spanked him."

Daniel's line sounded rehearsed. In his peripheral vision, Bricker noticed Gloria giving a tiny nod.

"Whose idea was it to spank Kaleb, Mr. Maly?"

Daniel shrugged his broad shoulders. "I dunno. I

don't remember."

His elbows on his knees, Bricker leaned forward. "Your wife says you wanted to give Kaleb a spanking *he'd* remember."

Gloria shifted on the rocker.

Bricker shot her a warning glance.

"Me and Amber were babysitting while Gloria and John went to a movie. I didn't want to make them mad." For the first time, Daniel lifted his gaze to Bricker. "Noemi had blood on her face." He glanced at Kaleb, swallowing hard. "Sometimes a parent has to spank a kid to make him mind."

"Daniel's parents were abusive. That's why I fostered him as a teenager." The pitch of Gloria's voice sharpened. "He doesn't know any better!"

Startled, Noemi let out a piercing wail.

Gloria jumped up to lift the child from her seat. She held the toddler close and stroked her hair, rocking and shushing while the little girl continued sobbing.

Bricker shot a glance at Kaleb.

With a young child's imperviousness to noise, the boy rested his head on his forearm, his eyelids heavy.

I'll never hear the truth from Daniel while Gloria's in the room. Bricker glanced first at his watch and then back to Noemi as she shuddered with sobs. "I only have a few minutes. I'm sorry the little girl is so upset. A bottle might help her calm down." Maybe Gloria would cave in and play the perfect foster mother to a crying child.

With her lips pinched between her teeth, she raised her eyebrows and shot Daniel a significant look before carrying the child into the kitchen.

Good. She took the bait. Bricker relaxed his

shoulders as he heard the refrigerator door open and close. The tap began to run. He glanced at Kaleb.

Lulled by the noise of the TV set, Kaleb had closed his eyes. His mouth sagged open as his chest rose and fell in steady breaths.

Bricker flexed his fingers, propping them in an A-shape under his chin. "Did Amber agree Kaleb should be spanked that night?"

Daniel shook his head. "She ran into the kitchen to wash the blood off Noemi's face. She told me to wait."

Suddenly the picture clicked into place—Amber holding a crying Noemi by the kitchen sink. Her husband ready to "make Kaleb mind." Bricker heard the hum of a microwave from the kitchen. Noemi had quieted. Gloria would be back any minute. "Why did she tell you to wait?" Bricker asked.

"Because I picked up the race track and went after him." Like buttons on the face of a cloth doll, Daniel's eyes were black and unblinking.

Bricker swept his hand over his face while he imagined Daniel swinging a chunky arm at his small son. Closing in on the terrified child, the cruel hiss of the track sizzling through the air. He inhaled, letting his breath slow his pulse. "Did you beat him?"

"No." Daniel rubbed his nose. "Amber said she'd do it. At first, she spanked him over his diaper, but I told her he needed it on his bare butt. She didn't hit him hard, but she left welts. The skin's pretty thin down there." He leaned back in his chair and glanced at the TV.

From Daniel's attitude, you'd think they were talking about the weather. Children's Services hadn't bothered to create a profile for Kaleb's dad. Bricker didn't know Daniel's IQ, but he suspected it wasn't high. "The reports don't mention your involvement with the spanking." From his briefcase, he lifted a manila file folder. "Did you tell the police or Children's Services the spanking was your idea?"

Daniel pouched his lips. "Gloria said the police didn't care whose idea it was. Only the person who hit him was in trouble. And that wasn't me."

Bricker choked back a shocked laugh. He'd scoffed at Lee's conspiracy theories about Gloria Marshall. But here was Daniel unwittingly exposing the county's prized foster mother for covering up information in a legal investigation. What else had she lied about?

Cradling Noemi with one arm while propping a bottle between the girl's little hands, Gloria returned to the living room. Easing the child into an activity seat near Kaleb's sleeping figure, she returned to the rocker. She cast an anxious glance at Daniel as he stared at the TV.

Swallowing his distaste, Bricker adopted a professional tone. "Daniel has just told me the race track spanking was his idea." Bricker's tone was polite and professional. He paused. "He also claims you told him not to admit that to Children's Services."

"No one has accused Daniel of *anything!*" Gloria sprang to the edge of her seat, her eyes narrowed to slits. "You're confusing Daniel and making him answer questions he doesn't understand. Now you interrogate him in *my* home while Amber's studying up on how to murder their child?"

Bricker threw an alarmed glance at Kaleb, but he could see the boy hadn't moved a muscle since he'd first fallen asleep. Good. Let the poor kid be spared the ugliness of this conversation. "I read the reports." With his pen, he tapped the file. Legally, the prosecutor had no leg to stand on. Visiting websites was no proof Amber was entering a psychotic state. "If the public didn't like to read about sensationalized murder cases, tabloids wouldn't be a billion-dollar industry." He thrust his chin toward Daniel. "Do you believe your wife wants to kill your son?"

Daniel swiveled his head to look at Gloria Marshall.

"Excuse me." Bricker snapped his fingers. "I'm not asking her. I'm asking you."

Daniel's gaze darted back. He ran his tongue over his lips.

"I think you should leave now, Mr. Kilbourn." Gloria stood and pointed to the door, her chest heaving with each breath.

Ignoring her, Bricker softened his tone. "We're talking about the mother of your child. Do you think she wants to hurt him?"

"Nah." Daniel rubbed his nose with the back of his finger. "Amber loves Kaleb. She cries every damn day, she misses him so much." He leaned back against the couch, relaxing as his gaze riveted on the TV screen.

With a snort, Gloria slapped her hands to her sides. "He's protecting her!"

He had the information he needed. "I'll be in touch." Shoving the file into his briefcase, Bricker rose. He glanced at Kaleb. Still asleep, his T-shirt was crushed against the floor and exposed his pale, rounded belly. Bricker's gut twisted. He wanted to pick up the child and run. Instead, Bricker stepped over the child gate into the foyer, not bothering to shake hands.

"Everybody knows Amber isn't a fit mother!" Gloria flung after him as he opened the door.

He shut the door on her shrill voice, readjusting his ears to the piercing calls of cicadas from the woods. Kaleb's hearing was now just a week away, and this visit had rocked everything he thought he knew. Absorbed in thought, he walked to the truck and opened the windows.

When the cicada drone cut off, silence buzzed in his ears. From deep within the wood, the ground rumbled and branches snapped. Wild boar. Around dusk, they'd head to the marshes for a drink. Often alligators lay in wait, hoping to catch a baby pig wandering away from the pack.

The squeal of a piglet seized between the jaws of a gator was a sound he'd never forget. And he didn't want to relive the memory tonight. He started the engine. What had Lee said the first time he'd taken her on the boat? Something about Florida being a predator state? He shot a hard look at the glossy wooden exterior of Gloria Marshall's home.

Not all predators lurked in forests and swamps.

****

"Over here." Beneath a cherry red octagonal umbrella, Janna waved to Lee from her table on the deck.

The Sea Hut—a wooden pagoda propped on stilts at the edge of the beach—was always the busiest restaurant on the mainland. The breeze off the water made sitting outside tolerable even in the heat of the day. Now, closing in on six o'clock, the deck was packed with patrons settling in for appetizers and a few cold cocktails.

Lee hooked her purse over the post of her wrought-iron chair and nodded at the pitcher of margaritas in the center of the table. "Put it on my bill," she told her boss as she poured herself a glass.

"You'd better believe I will. Dragging me to a family-style restaurant on a Friday night." Janna extracted the straw from her glass and licked the salt-encrusted rim. "I'm not complaining, though." She tossed her blonde curls. "I'm always here for one of my girls."

Her girls. With a sip from her margarita glass, Lee smiled at Janna. In a sleeveless blue handkerchief-hem dress, the neckline split low, Janna had dressed to draw the attention of any men in the area. Yet Lee and all her co-workers had faith their supervisor always had their backs. After a lifetime working in social services, Janna Wilson knew the system inside and out. She also understood the toll taken on her workers as they labored to help their disadvantaged clients become better parents.

Now her steady gaze rested on Lee. "So you go to court on Monday," she prompted.

With a glance at the appetizer menu, Lee sighed. "Right. And now I'm wondering if the mother I've gone to bat for is secretly plotting to…" She shuddered, raising her gaze to Janna, and gave a hopeless shrug. "Why am I even testifying?"

"Because you've been subpoenaed, Toots."

Lee's shoulders relaxed. Janna's pragmatism was exactly what she needed. No navel-gazing, no messy emotions. "What would you say if you were me?"

As she lifted her hand to signal a server, Janna's eyebrows tilted. "You're a witness. You want to have documentation on the times you've met with the parents. You should have copies of the developmental screens you've done for the boy. And then, just answer the questions to the best of your ability." She leaned forward. "You have no way of knowing what's going on inside the woman's head. If they ask you if you think Amber's a fit mother, which I doubt they will, just respond with the facts. 'She was there for all her appointments. I never witnessed her striking her child.' Her case won't be won or lost on your testimony, believe me."

Lee exhaled. Little by little, her shoulders relaxed. "I needed a little reassurance." She lifted her glass and tapped it against the older woman's. "Thanks, Janna."

After their appetizer order was taken, Janna unfolded her napkin and dropped it on her lap. "I wonder what the guardian ad litem's making of this case. Have you heard from him lately?"

Heat rose in Lee's cheeks. She bit down on the straw and took a long drink before she met Janna's gaze. She shook her head. "He had a lot of concerns about Amber's strictness with Kaleb. Those internet searches of hers might put the last nail in her coffin."

"Well, the investigation is out of your hands now." Janna swished the melting ice in her glass. "Did you ever figure out a way to get along with the guy? His name was Bricker, wasn't it? So hot," she murmured, sipping her drink.

The phantom of Bricker's face rose before Lee, his crooked nose and piercing blue eyes as his lips whispered over her face—her cheeks, her eyelids, her temples. She shivered. On top of his boat, he'd made her feel so desired. She'd felt safe, even cherished, in his arms. But Tatum's revelations about Bricker's past had collapsed her hopes. All week she'd fought to erase him from her mind. But the flip-flop her heart had taken at the mention of his name proved how far she was from forgetting.

She dragged her attention back to Janna's expectant face. "He didn't understand why I cared so much about Amber losing her custodial rights."

Janna shook her head. "Neither do I, to tell the truth. I've been to Gloria Marshall's house on nursing visits. She seems like a great mother. Kaleb might be better off in a stable family."

Those were just the words Lee had been told all her life. A stab of pain bloomed beneath her ribcage. "Having a nice middle-class life doesn't make up for losing your parent!" Lee's eyes filled with tears. Mortified, she swiped the corners of her eyes with a napkin and tried to smile.

Janna put her hand over Lee's. "I wondered if this case would open old wounds."

When she'd interviewed for the position, Lee had barely touched on her adoption. In fact, she'd pooh-poohed Janna's questions about childhood trauma.

Janna stared, her eyebrows knit together. "I should have realized why you were fighting so hard for this client. You didn't want Kaleb to lose his mother like you lost yours."

As she opened her mouth to protest, Lee hesitated. Was Janna right? Against her folded napkin, she slowly tapped her index finger. Kaleb's face loomed in her mind—his wide, anxious eyes and tremulous lips. She passed a shaking hand over her mouth. "Amber was a teen mom who'd been abused by all the people she trusted. When she had Kaleb, she didn't know how to bond with him. He was already two when I started working with her." *The same age I was when I was adopted.* "I believed she was making progress. That the damage done to him by not feeling love and affection from his mother would just...go away." An ache the size of a golf ball at the back of her throat stopped her.

"Oh, honey." Janna squeezed Lee's hand between both of hers. "You wanted to believe Kaleb would be okay even without parental bonding when he was a baby, because *you* didn't get to bond with *your* mother."

Tears slipped over Lee's cheeks as she lifted her gaze to Janna's sympathetic eyes. "I guess so," she croaked. "You may not realize it, but my life is kind of a mess." She dropped her hands to her lap as the server approached their table. As her focaccia was placed in front of her, she grabbed a tissue from her purse and wiped her face. She would not fall apart in a public place. She would not.

"Join the club, sweetheart!" Janna filled their glasses with margarita and raised hers in a toast. "Forty-eight-year-old woman looking for love in all the wrong places!" She widened her smile into a manic grin.

Drawing a wobbly breath and clinking her glass to Janna's, Lee giggled. "You and me both!" Thank God for Janna. She always knew how to break the tension.

They settled into a companionable silence as they started on their appetizers, watching the gentle waves of the Gulf of Mexico lap onto the beach. Barefooted children, released from the confinement of the dinner table, raced away from the surf, cackling each time the water licked their ankles.

"So." Janna leaned back from the table, scooping her last bite of artichoke dip onto a cracker. "Have you met anyone special since you moved to Florida?"

With a long draw on her straw, Lee stalled for time. What would Janna think if she learned just how far Lee had gotten into the guardian ad litem's "good graces?"

"I was dating someone for a little while, but we didn't work out." A sigh escaped her before she could stifle it.

"Sounds like you have regrets."

Janna doesn't miss a thing. Lee swished her straw in her glass 'til the last ice chip melted. Maybe the margarita was talking, or maybe she didn't feel like being glib. Not after what she'd already shared with her boss tonight. She faced Janna's gaze head on. "I really liked this guy."

"But?" Janna prompted.

"But he has…things…in his past. He's done things I just can't accept." The ache between her lungs whenever she thought of Bricker was back. She pressed her palm over the center of her chest.

Eyeing Lee's hand, Janna frowned. "Is he still doing these things?"

"Well, no…but the point is, I can't be with a man I don't respect." Glumly, Lee drained the contents of her glass.

Janna shrugged. "You're young. I guess you can afford to be choosy. But I'll tell you this, Lee—nobody gets through life without making mistakes. Sometimes serious ones."

Her eyebrows raised, Lee waited while the older woman paused.

"Everybody blames my husband for leaving me for a younger woman. But the truth is, I took him for granted for twenty years. By the time I realized I needed to make our marriage my main priority, he was already gone. He looks like the bad guy to the whole world, but he and I know the truth. He had his reasons for leaving."

In the shadow of the table umbrella, Janna's dark blue eyes looked bruised.

She twisted the white beads of her necklace between her fingers. "You obviously care about this guy. You say he's done things in the past. Unless he killed someone, for God's sake, maybe he deserves a second chance."

A collection of seagulls cawed overhead, tempted to shore by a wave of air heavy with the odor of fried food. Seagulls had circled the boat that night, before the fireworks started; before Bricker had tilted back her head and brushed his lips over her face, his hand sweeping back her hair as his kisses became more urgent. Remembering, Lee's breath hitched. He'd been so tender. And beforehand, at his mother's, pushing her patiently from bromeliad to bromeliad, his face lit with affection as she called each plant by its Latin name.

And his easy manner with Kaleb. Seeing Kaleb let down his guard with Bricker let her glimpse how, with lots of patience and love, the little boy might heal.

But what about his own son? Lee drew a deep breath, the pain between her lungs hardening like a stone. No. His abandonment of his own child was an act she could never understand.

Lee signaled for the server. She wasn't ready to go back to her empty bungalow. After unlocking the door on her feelings, she'd be haunted by the specter of Bricker chasing her from room to room. She flashed her brightest smile at her boss. "What say we blow this family restaurant and have a girl's night on the town?"

Janna raised her eyebrows. With a dubious shake of her head, she groped for her purse beside the chair leg. "No one's waiting for me at home." Her smile mischievous, she added, "We could go back to the cute little bar on the other end of the island. Let *me* have a crack at your guardian ad litem."

Feigning a chuckle, Lee pointed to the empty margarita pitcher. "Unless we're calling for a driver, we'd better just mosey down the beach to the cantina." With one last glance at the children splashing at the edge of the water, she lifted the hem of her skirt and trod through the sand, fixing her gaze on the neon welcome of the bar.

Chapter Twelve

"Take a seat." The court clerk, scrutinizing Lee from over the rims of her gold bifocals, nodded to the right. "You'll be called if you're needed."

"Okay," Lee whispered, swallowing hard. "Thank you," she said, louder, as she scanned the waiting room for a secluded spot. Lines of black plastic chairs against the walls were already filled. Fabric panels short enough for her to see over divided the room into four semi-private areas.

A young man and woman, their arms and necks crowded with tattoos, rose from a sofa and followed a suited older man down a hallway.

Racing to their vacated cubicle, Lee sank onto the brown plaid loveseat and placed her briefcase on the cushion next to her. *If you're needed.* Janna said plenty of the staff had gotten subpoenaed over the years but just a few ever had to testify. Lee had slept fitfully the night before, anxious about her day in court. Not being called would be a relief. Still, who else would stand up for Amber Maly?

She took a deep breath, counting to five before she released it. As her pulse slowed, she checked her briefcase for the hundredth time. She had all the documentation she needed: a log of her visits with Amber; Kaleb's developmental screens; copies of releases allowing Lee to talk to people involved in the case. All there.

She glanced at the hallway leading to the courtroom. Had they started already? The clerk behind the desk hadn't been the type to encourage questions. Better to just wait and be called, like the woman said.

With hands folded, she stared at the coffee table. Not even one magazine. She blew out a breath to settle her stomach. She could sit here in a state of nervous anticipation, or she could get some work done. From her briefcase, she retrieved her tablet, powered it up, and absorbed herself in transcribing a new client's oral history into the data entry system.

The squeaking approach of a pair of loafers penetrated her attention. A low murmur of voices rose from the clerk's desk. She lifted her gaze from her tablet, and her heart vaulted inside her ribcage.

Bricker, tall and elegant in a pale khaki suit with a blue-and-white-checked shirt, lounged against the sign-in desk. The clerk who'd seemed so forbidding to Lee now raised her chin to smile at Bricker, turning a framed photo in his direction and grinning at his response.

Lee shrank back against the cushion. She'd known he'd be at the hearing, of course; but she'd imagined sitting behind him in the kind of courtroom she'd seen on TV, with rows of chairs separating them. What was the big deal about talking with him, anyway? Just because for a minute, she'd hoped he might be the right guy?

Her heart raced as she peeked at him talking to the clerk. He'd slid his hand into the pocket of his pants, one knee bent with the casual grace of a man comfortable in any situation. When he threw back his head and laughed, the sight of his bare throat made the hollow at the center of her chest ache.

She passed a trembling hand over her lips. If he noticed her now, he'd know exactly the effect he had on her. *Pull yourself together, Lee.* Obeying a primal instinct to run away, she ducked her head and darted to the chair on the other side of the coffee table. Flattened as she was against the cushion, she prayed she was hidden from his line of vision by the partition at her back. The contents of her briefcase were scattered over the love seat. She clamped her lips against a hysterical desire to giggle. *Very mature, Lee, hiding behind a wall. Real classy.*

With any luck, he'd head down the hallway to the courtroom. He obviously knew his way around the place. Her breath suspended, she waited for the squeak of his shoes retreating.

But they weren't retreating. They were headed her way.

Her feet made a loud slap against the linoleum as she sat up straight and affected an attitude of nonchalance. With her chin lowered, she could only slide her gaze to the right as she heard him approach her cubicle.

His chin swiveled toward the loveseat, but he continued past.

Afraid to breathe, Lee leaned and followed him with her gaze as he strode to the hallway and lowered his head to the water fountain. Dashing back to the loveseat, she bent over her tablet and blindly punched numbers into the household income screen.

Squeak. Squeak. Squeak. Getting closer. She hunched her shoulders. Could she shrivel into invisibility?

From the corner of her eye, she saw his khaki pants pass by the cubicle opening. *Just keep walking. Please.* The squeaking suddenly stopped. Peeking out from under her bangs, Lee glimpsed shiny Italian loafers pivot back in her direction. Her heart hammered in her chest.

"Lee Anya Cooper."

She lifted her chin.

He stared at her, confusion furrowing his forehead.

After all these weeks of driving him from her mind, the reality of his presence made her dizzy. Behind her ear she tucked an invisible hair and donned a bright smile. "Hi!"

"Were you here a minute ago?" He rubbed his chin between his thumb and forefinger, puzzled.

"I was in the bathroom," she blurted. The sign for the restroom was posted beside the fountain he'd just drank from. As she saw his brows slant together, she changed the subject. "I guess you're here for Kaleb Maly."

With a nod to a police officer passing down the aisle toward the restrooms, Bricker stepped inside the cubicle. "I guess we both are."

His hair was cut shorter, swept off his high forehead and neatly combed over his ears so the golden curls along the sides of his neck were just visible. The breadth of his shoulders in his tailored jacket made her imagine the soft cotton of his shirt straining over his muscled chest. When he rested an arm on top of the partition panel, the scent of cardamom and rosemary rippled from his skin.

Lee wet her lips. Disowning Bricker Kilbourn had

been all too easy until he stood in front of her, his sea-blue eyes trained on hers. "I"—she fumbled for something to say—"I'm so nervous about testifying. I've never been in a courtroom before."

The lines around his mouth relaxed. "Don't be. Reality isn't nearly as exciting as what you see on TV. You'll probably just be asked to confirm your client met with you regularly. Her attorney will try to establish she's following her case plan."

"My supervisor said the same thing." She was relieved to hear Bricker say so, though. Unlike her, he knew what to expect from the morning's proceedings. Law school had prepared him well for this role. He was so comfortable, so at ease as he waited to be called into court. She hesitated. "You look like you belong here. In a courthouse, I mean."

He raised his eyebrows, lifting one corner of his mouth. "Pretty good for a bartender, huh?"

Lee flushed. She really *had* made some obnoxious comments. And he hadn't even mentioned the last angry text she'd sent. She had to give him credit for rising above bad blood between them. "I agree with your mom. You *should* retake the bar exam."

His eyes crinkled as he rubbed his hand over the back of his neck. He tilted his head, and a hint of dimples appeared at the corners of his mouth. "Speaking of my mother. She'd love to see you again. Added a prize bromeliad to her collection and doesn't think any of us appreciate it like you would."

Lee could just imagine Corinne's enthusiasm, her kind gray eyes wide with excitement as she named the qualities of her latest find. But what kind of message would Lee send Bricker if she visited his mother?

Bricker raised his hand toward the hallway. "Time to play ball." With a nod to Lee, he strode toward the clerk's desk to shake hands with a woman in a cream linen suit before he disappeared down the hall.

I could be called next. Lee drew a shaky breath as she slid her tablet and files back into the briefcase and snapped it shut. No point doing paperwork. Her concentration was shot. With her thumbs pressed to her temples, she revisited the moment when Bricker leveled his lopsided smile at her. A flush rolled through her, blistering every nerve-ending from her toes to the tips of her ears like they'd been touched by a match. Her brain had fought to extinguish her feelings for Bricker Kilbourn, but her heart had other ideas.

So he'd turned his back on his own child. Yes, it was terrible; but what if she could persuade him to reunite with his son? What if she'd been placed in Bricker Kilbourn's path just to help him fix the mess he'd made of his life? To heal the whole family, to repair his relationship with Tatum, and allow Bricker's mother to meet the grandchild she'd been missing all these years?

The flashing of her muted phone from within her purse interrupted her musings. She didn't recognize the number. Probably the new client Janna had just assigned her. "Hello?" Mindful of protecting a client's privacy in a public space, she kept her voice low.

"Hi, Lee, this is Corinne Kilbourn."

For a moment, Lee had the crazy idea Bricker's mother had read her mind. "Hi, Mrs. Kilbourn. I mean, Corinne," she corrected herself.

"My son gave me your number. I hope you don't mind."

The older woman's soft southern tones were a balm to Lee's nerves. "Not at all. How are you feeling?"

Corinne made a dismissive noise. "As strong as an ox. Now, the reason I called is because I've just found a beautiful bromeliad, with the most intense pinks and blues. It's so bright, you'd think it was plugged into an electrical outlet." She gave a throaty chuckle. "Anyway, the community garden fundraiser is coming up, and I thought what a wonderful donation I could make to the auction if I asked you to paint my bromeliad onto a canvas."

"For an auction?" Lee pinched the bridge of her nose. "I don't know. I paint just for fun."

"Don't sell yourself short, my dear! I've gotten all kinds of compliments on the painting you gave me. I'm sure you could sell anything. Once we frame it, we'll get lots of bids. I'll pay you for your work, of course."

"Hmmn." Lee stood and paced the cubicle. Being asked to put her artwork before the public eye was as scary as it was flattering.

"The auction supports a good cause," Corinne wheedled. "We're digging new gardens in sections of Bellamy where fresh vegetables are hard to buy. The auction is how we raise money to help members of the community plant their own gardens."

Good cause or no, she wasn't sure she could bear having her painting under the critical gaze of strangers. "Let me think about it."

"Why don't you come over this weekend and take a look at the plant? We'll have lunch and get caught up. Just us girls."

Corinne's voice was a compelling mixture of

command and appeal. No wonder Bricker had a hard time telling her no. "Okay." Lee's voice quavered as she made plans to meet Corinne at one o'clock Saturday afternoon. As she put her phone away, she sighed. Corinne's eagerness to see her son date Lee had been obvious a few weeks ago, but she'd made no mention of inviting him. Classifying the get-together as a 'girl's lunch' was Corinne's tactful way of demonstrating she understood Bricker's and Lee's relationship had changed.

A telephone rang at the front desk. The clerk picked up the receiver, nodded, and hung up. Frowning, she resumed her crossword.

Lee checked the wall clock. She'd been here nearly an hour. When would they call her? She stifled her impatience by imagining how agonizing this decision was for Amber. How many witnesses had they lined up to testify against her? Goosebumps rose on Lee's arms as she imagined the computer forensics expert listing the websites Amber had visited. Could the young woman be trusted with her son? Or had her own childhood history of abuse and neglect permanently warped her?

Lee shivered. As she balanced on the edge of the sofa, she stared into her hands. Amber's face had been so pale and heartbroken at her last home visit. No matter what mistakes Amber had made with her son, more than anything in the world, she wanted a second chance. She *deserved* a second chance. And Kaleb deserved to be raised by a mother who loved him.

Alerted by a rising buzz of voices from the front of the waiting room, Lee scanned the hallway. Trish Nichols was talking to a young man in an oversized suit, his tie off-centered and flapping at the bottom. From the briefcase he carried, Lee pegged him as the public defender she'd spoken with on the phone. Was the hearing over, then?

Amber and Daniel appeared behind them. Daniel stared at his shoes as Amber craned her neck toward a young woman wearing a badge.

After scribbling a note on the back of a business card, the woman handed it to Amber. A moment later, she bustled past the desk clerk and out of the waiting room.

Lee stood on her tiptoes, giving a little wave. "Amber!" She had to call the girl's name twice before Amber's gaze located her.

A smile broke across Amber's face. Seizing Daniel's wrist, she wound her way through the aisle to Lee's cubicle. With a loud sigh, she collapsed on the couch.

Taking his phone from his pocket, Daniel sank onto the cushion beside his wife and scrolled his thick fingers across the screen.

"So? What happened?" Lee asked. Amber had smiled. The hearing must have gone better than expected.

"We're working on a reunification plan. I get to see Kaleb two times a week at daycare, and we get him at home, unsupervised, for the whole day on Saturdays." Amber's chipped teeth, leaning in on each other like pencils jammed into a cup, peeked from behind her lips. She was too happy to hide them behind her hand.

"Oh my gosh." Lee's shoulders sagged with relief. "How wonderful!"

Amber nodded, her face transformed by her smile.

"I know. I figured I was doomed after the whole stupid internet thing." She waved her hand, dismissing the memory. "But the guardian ad litem came through for me. He told the magistrate I've been working with you on how to be a better parent, and I've attended all my child development workshops and classes at the community center."

"Really," Lee marveled. Well, how about that? After all the arguments Bricker had made against Amber, he'd pointed out to the court how hard she was working. Looks like he'd been listening to Lee after all.

"Yeah. And, get this." Amber bounced on the edge of the couch, her eyes alive with glee. "He said he believed the county's faith in Gloria Marshall's reputation had led to an unfair investigation of me. He reported Kaleb isn't showing any signs of delays. He's actually *advanced* in some ways. The guardian was impressed Kaleb could go down the stairs one foot at a time. We worked on that skill all the time." She tossed her head, flicking her hair over her shoulder. "He said Gloria was driving a wedge in our marriage. Dan's not supposed to see Kaleb at Gloria's house anymore. He has to visit him at daycare, like I do. And Dan has to take the parenting classes, too, now." She aimed a smug smile in her husband's direction.

Daniel shrugged. He pushed back his bangs and glanced at Lee. "Fine with me. I was getting tired of Gloria always complaining about Amber. I just want Kaleb home again so life can go back to normal."

Lee leaned back against the cushion. *Wow.* She'd never have predicted this outcome in a million years. Bricker had come to the same conclusions she had. She shook her head. "So, once you and Daniel complete the parenting classes, Kaleb comes home?"

Amber's smile faded. "We have to start counseling, too. I already set up an appointment with a woman from Southwest Behavioral Health. She testified about the psych eval she performed on me after the first hearing. The guardian wants her to evaluate Dan now."

"Seems fair." Lee raised one eyebrow toward Daniel and shrugged.

Amber giggled, digging the toe of her pumps into her husband's shoe.

With a roll of his eyes, Daniel returned his gaze to the phone on his lap.

Smothering a snicker, Lee dug inside her briefcase for a pen. Daniel Maly wasn't anyone's idea of a romantic hero, but maybe with some counseling—*and without the influence of Gloria Marshall*—, he could learn to be a better husband and father. Pulling out an appointment calendar, she was about to schedule her next visit with Amber when raised voices from the hallway interrupted her.

A middle-aged woman in a floral print dress shook her finger at Bricker while the man at her side laid a restraining hand on her elbow. "Come on now, Gloria. It's over."

"You've made a big mistake, Mr. Kilbourn. If anything happens to that little boy, you'll be responsible." She glowered at Bricker as she fought to free her arm.

Fascinated, Lee stared at the cords straining from the woman's throat. Her mouth had fallen open into a pant, and hostility radiated from her gaze. So this was Mangrove County's finest foster mother. Funny. She looked to Lee like a rabid dog.

The waiting room fell silent.

Across from Lee, hidden from Gloria's view by the fabric partition, Amber and Daniel froze.

Gloria yanked her arm away from her husband. With one last spiteful look at Bricker, she pivoted on her heel and left the waiting room.

Her eyes wide, Lee gazed at Bricker.

He wore a tiny smile as he watched the Marshalls leave. Glancing back to Lee's cubicle, he shrugged, his smile widening.

Flooded with happiness, she grinned, waving her fists in a victory salute as Bricker joined them. "Amber told me the good news."

Bricker composed his face into a mask of professionalism as he shook hands with Amber and Daniel.

Lee nodded encouragement to Amber.

The young girl couldn't quite look in the guardian's eyes. "Thanks for giving us another chance."

Bricker's gaze was serious. "Kaleb's a very special little boy. He deserves a safe, loving home with his parents. But you've got to stop coming down so hard on him. Both of you." His gaze swept over Daniel, then back to Amber. "He's your son. He needs your unconditional love more than anything in the world."

More than anything in the world. Kaleb flinching away from his mother's severity. A little girl huddled in the center of a thin mattress, crying for a mother who never answered. Children begging for the shelter of their parents' arms. And what of Bricker's son? What pain lodged itself inside a little boy whose father washed his hands of him? Lee pressed her hand over her abdomen. An ache at the pit of her stomach grew, strong enough to double her over. She scrabbled to her feet, slinging her purse over her shoulder and grabbing her briefcase.

Amber's gaze was fixed on the carpet like a repentant teen's. "We have to go now, Dan."

Standing back from the entrance, Bricker waited for the couple to pass before he turned to Lee.

Her cheeks were flushed. "I should get going now, too." In her haste, she wobbled off her heel and stopped to slide her shoe back on her foot.

Bricker steadied her with a hand to her elbow.

She jerked her arm away as if his touch burned her skin, raising her gaze to his.

At her wretched expression, he flinched, raising his palms in front of his chest. "What?"

Through the buzzing between her ears, she fought to answer. "Quite a speech, coming from you." She passed around him, avoiding any contact as she reached the front desk, her gaze glued to the exit sign on the door. Her pulse pounded her temples. *Just get to the door.*

"Excuse me?" In just a few long strides, he caught up to her and grabbed her arm.

Her purse slipped from her shoulder as she snatched back her hand. The leather clutch tumbled to the ground, and tissues, mints, and cosmetics spilled across the stained beige carpet. She crouched to sweep her belongings into the handbag as tears clouded her vision. When she noticed him bob down to help her, she clambered to her feet.

"Wait!"

Her purse clasped to her chest, she lifted her head, blinking back tears.

He shook his head, his forehead lined like trenches over the burning intensity of his eyes. "Lee, what's wrong?" His voice cracked on her name.

She slid her briefcase to the floor and reached a shaking hand into her purse. Her heart thumping, she gazed at him as she wiped her wet cheeks with a tissue. "You abandoned your own son, you son of a bitch." Her breath was a ragged gasp. "How could you?"

His head jerked as if she'd struck him.

For a moment, Lee hoped he would deny everything. Maybe Tatum had lied. Maybe there was more to the story.

She saw the moment recognition dawned—how his eyebrows collapsed, and his pupils shrank into a circle of blue. But even as his eyes acknowledged his shame, his lips stiffened and his jaw clenched. With a minute shake of his head, he held Lee's gaze without a word of defense.

So it was true. Pain blistered the back of Lee's throat. She shook her head wildly and grabbed her briefcase from the floor. Her chest shielded by leather, she flung herself against the exit door and escaped into the dank air of the stairwell.

****

The football spiraled against the blue sky, gaining speed and falling in a graceful arc. Bricker leaped into the air, his head twisted to the side and his hands cupped. But the ball glanced off his knuckles and shot onto the towel, knocking over a bottle of beer before wobbling to a halt.

Bricker raced to the towel, but a dark wet stain had already seeped through the terry cloth. He raised the bottle to his mouth. Practically empty.

"Dude!" Austin trotted toward him, kicking up a spray of sand with each step. "How could you drop it? My pass was perfect."

Shrugging, Bricker sank onto a dry corner of the towel and lifted another beer from the mini cooler. Twisting off the cap and flipping it into the cooler, he swigged before answering. "Out of practice, I guess." He leaned his elbows against his thighs, dangling the bottle between his knees.

"Old man," Austin teased, grabbing a beer and dropping onto a towel beside his friend.

Slapping at his ankle, Bricker stared out at the bay. He'd chosen Hyde Beach because of its solitude. A mangrove stand provided a natural barrier and a decent amount of shade, but the midges swarmed at dusk. Still, better than being surrounded by tourists. At least here, he could relax and toss a football with Austin with no one watching. Without anyone making judgments.

He closed his eyes against the image of Lee fleeing down the stairs at the courthouse. Running from *him*. Someone had told her about his past. From the way she stood almost on tiptoes, choking on a mouthful of air as if her next breath depended on his answer, he could tell she was hoping she'd heard wrong, and he'd deny having a son he'd abandoned.

But he couldn't. The choices he'd made ten years ago, when he found out Veronica was pregnant, had blown him off course from the dreams he'd worked toward in law school. His father had conceived the idea of writing a settlement check to pay for raising a boy the Kilbourn family would never see or acknowledge. "For your mother's sake, we need to put this behind us." She'd considered Veronica a second daughter. The pay-off was intended to keep Corinne in the dark about the father of the young woman's baby. But Pete, Veronica's estranged husband, had leaked the whole ugly story. Corinne's relapse put her in the hospital for several weeks. Bricker's father asked him to stay away. Two years would pass before he'd return home, to a mother whose forehead was etched with lines of sadness. To a sister who condemned him. And his father, who'd hatched the whole scheme, had died of a sudden heart attack, leaving Bricker to shoulder the consequences alone.

"You remember how we used to come here when we were kids?" Austin's voice tore through the gloom of Bricker's thoughts. "Best place on the island for finding conch shells and sea stars."

Bricker gazed at the sun creeping toward the horizon. Seagulls circled a spot of foam not far from the gentle waves lapping the beach. "Tatum used to scream at us for taking live animals from their habitat." He smiled. His sister had grown up to be a ruthless businesswoman, but every now and again, she still showed traces of the tender-hearted girl she'd once been. "She was right, too."

He wished he could go back to those times, when his greatest conflict with Tatum was over her dumping his bucket of sand dollars back in the sea. Not like now, when contempt for her older brother curled her lip and hardened her gaze into granite.

Austin leaned back on his elbows, relaxing his legs and crossing his ankles. "I've got vacation coming up at the end of August. Want to make a week of it? Head to Ybor City for some Cuban food and cigars? You bring the boat, I'll bring the beer."

Grunting, Bricker gave a restless shake of his head, staring at the circling seagulls.

"What's wrong with you, man?" Austin asked. "You haven't gone out in a month."

Tipping the bottle, Bricker took a long swig and balanced it in the sand. A muscle at the corner of his eye twitched again. He cursed softly.

"Is it a girl? Hey, what happened with the Asian chick?"

Dumping the remains of his beer over Austin's left leg, he watched with cold amusement as Austin jumped up and shook his foot. "What's the matter with you, dumbass?"

Bricker shrugged. He knew Austin didn't mean any harm, but he didn't like hearing Lee reduced to her ethnic background. Bricker had no right to defend her, of course. He'd recognized the disappointment bleeding from her gaze when she confronted him at the courthouse. His own mother had looked at him with the same brokenhearted eyes. Somehow, he managed to hurt the people he cared about most. "I'm going back to the Virgin Islands." He surprised himself with the words as they left his lips. "For good."

Hopping over the sand, Austin swiveled his head back to his friend. "You want to move there?" He slapped bay water on his shin then returned to the towels and sat down heavily. "Why?"

"Nothing for me here, man." Bricker tugged his crumpled T-shirt over his head and chest. The sun's corona dipped into the ocean, casting a gold glow all the way to shore. "Everyone on this island knows me for what I've done. I'm tired of living like I'm on probation." He brushed his sandal with the palm of his hand and squeezed it on, grunting as sandy grit rubbed the tender skin on top of his foot. "I want to take the bar exam again. Do the work I trained to do."

Austin snorted. "I've been telling you the same thing for ten years, dude. But you can take the test in Bellamy. The past is the past. No one cares anymore."

The seagulls circling near shore suddenly shot off in separate directions. A moment later, a pelican dive-bombed the surface of the water, emerging with a wriggling silver fish clamped in its bill. Tipping its head to the sky, the pelican swallowed the fish, gargling it from its pouch to the back of its throat.

Predator state, Lee had said the first evening on the boat as she stood watch for threats from the water. She'd been afraid of the unknown. But somehow she'd let down her guard. As the sky had darkened from a backlit gray into velvety night, he'd listened to her talk about her uneasy place in an adoptive family. His heart had beaten faster every time she smiled. And God, her laugh—so joyful, like the promise of every childhood dream fulfilled. His stomach tightened now as he remembered how she'd curled herself against his side. Trusting him.

She didn't have to explain what child abandonment meant. He'd seen ghosts flit across her troubled face as Brett joked about the past. She'd been damaged in the orphanage, and the news of Bricker's abandoned son forced the trauma back to the surface. She'd staggered from the courthouse hallway like a woman fleeing a burning building.

And her anguish was his fault.

Lurching to his feet, he caught the towel by the corner and gave it an expert shake behind him.

Austin stared up at him, brow wrinkled.

Bricker extended his hand, pulling Austin to his feet. He'd miss this guy, no doubt. But his days of partying and living like there was no tomorrow were over. He was as sure of the fact as if God had parted the skies and told him so personally.

He had to start over. Pomegranate Key held too many memories.

Chapter Thirteen

Hector opened the door, a mild smile softening his weather-beaten face. "Welcome. She's so pleased you agreed to come."

Ignoring the butterflies in her stomach, Lee handed him a bottle of white wine she'd decorated with Spanish moss and lantana blooms. "I'm so happy she invited me," she lied.

In truth, she'd dreaded this brunch more and more as each day passed. What if Corinne asked her about Bricker? Should she tell what she'd learned? No, reliving the past would be too painful for his mother. But how else could she explain why she refused to see Corinne's son? She'd hopped on her bike this morning, wine strapped to the rear rack, praying Corinne's sense of discretion would keep her from asking about her son's relationship.

She followed Hector through the house to the lanai where Corinne was seated at the end of the table. "You made it!" She beamed, her eyes crinkling as Lee sat beside her.

"Of course." Lee squeezed the older woman's hand. "It's not every day I get commissioned for a painting, you know."

Corinne clapped her hands together in front of her chest. "Well, this will be just the start, my dear! When the auctioning starts for your bromeliad painting, we'll have a bidding war on our hands. I'm sure of it."

Chuckling, Lee shook her head. "You're pretty confident about a piece I haven't even painted yet." She couldn't help but glow with Corinne's praise. *Imagine being raised by a mother who encouraged my artistic abilities instead of telling me to settle for something more practical.*

"I've seen your work, and I know what you're capable of. The bromeliad you'll paint is breathtaking. Hector, can you carry it to the table?"

Lee obediently made a space among the plates, glasses, and cutlery for Hector to place the pot. Her eyes widened when he set it before her. Those colors really *were* electric. Without realizing, she stood and peered into the plant from a bird's eye view. An explosion of fuchsia petals, cobalt blue at the very tips as if they'd been dipped in paint. Golden yellow stamens waved from the center. Waxy, succulent leaves formed a green basin to cup the flower in all its vivid glory.

"*Bilberia pyramidalis*. Grows on the bark of trees. I've had this species before, but never one so bright. I want to capture its beauty before the bloom fades." Corinne chuckled. "Or, rather, I want *you* to capture its beauty."

"Like a firework exploding against the sky," Lee breathed, hardly paying attention to Corinne. "The colors of the flower make the leaves seem even richer. I can't wait to paint this."

"Wonderful! I was prepared to plead with you to agree, but I'm happy to see you appreciate this little plant as much as I do."

"I'm kind of surprised myself," Lee admitted,

sitting back in her chair. "I just hope I do it justice." She was already calculating which colors to blend to mimic the plant's deep, dewy leaves and radiant blooms.

Corinne's smile was frank and appreciative. "You're a true artist, Lee. You're blessed to see in a whole different way than the rest of us. And like any great artist, you're insecure about your talent." She gave a light laugh. "I'm lucky to be investing in you at the start of your career. In ten years, I'm sure I won't be able to afford you."

Blushing, Lee shook her head. "I'm a total amateur. But I'll do my best." She placed her palms on the table to the sides of her plate, determined to change the subject. "What a beautiful spot for lunch."

As if on cue, Hector vanished through the lanai doors and returned a moment later with a salad bowl in one hand and a platter of sliced fruits and berries in the other. Sliding the bromeliad to the end of the table, he placed the food in front of the women.

"Thank you, Hector." Corinne smiled her appreciation as he poured ice water into their glasses. "You'll eat with us, won't you? He prepared the whole meal," she told Lee.

Helping herself to the food, Lee thanked him as he lowered himself onto a bench opposite Corinne. "I smell something delicious cooking on the grill."

"Oh, yes. Hector's blackened fish is his specialty. Bricker caught it this morning. What kind is it?" Corinne asked Hector.

"The usual. Red snapper. It's done cooking. Ready whenever you are."

"Would you like some fish now, Lee?" Corinne bit

into a slice of mango, gazing at her guest.

"Sure." Lee forced the word past her lips, fighting to calm the pounding of her heart after the mention of Bricker's name. She needed to keep her cool. If his mother sensed distress, she was bound to start asking questions. "You're a great cook, Hector." She blurted the first pleasantry that came to mind. "I can't imagine my father preparing a meal like this. *Any* meal, really."

"Neither would my husband. Hector is a prince among men." She smiled fondly as he placed a portion of fish on the plate next to her salad. "Although I must say, Bricker is quite a cook, too. Did he ever make you a meal?" Corinne sipped at her drink, cocking her head as she waited for Lee's reply.

Dread twisted like a snake inside Lee's gut. She attempted a smile. "No." She opened her mouth, and then closed it. In desperation, she nudged her napkin off her lap and dove under the table to retrieve it, her face burning with embarrassment. She couldn't talk about Bricker to his mother. She just couldn't.

"Is the fish cooked to your liking?" Hector asked.

Relief flooded through her. From his kindly expression, she knew he'd changed the subject for her sake. She flaked a piece of fish with her fork and popped it in her mouth, nodding. "It's delicious."

A door slammed inside the house. Corinne darted a glance at Hector. "Must be one of the kids," she told Lee with artificial cheerfulness. "They're the only ones who have keys."

Lee's heart plummeted. Corinne must have mentioned their lunch to Bricker when he stopped by with the fish. Surely after the wretchedness of their last meeting in the courthouse, he wouldn't stop by.

The clicking of high heels across the tiles signaled the arrival of a different Kilbourn. Tatum popped her head through the door. Her eyes widened as she surveyed the table. "Hey! Throwing a lunch party and no one invited me?" Crossing her arms, she gave Lee an uncertain smile. "How are you doing, Lee?"

Before Lee could answer, Corinne interrupted. "I thought you worked Saturdays."

"Just 'til noon. Thought I'd come over here and check on my old Ma. I didn't realize you had company." She glanced around her, her eyes narrowed. "Is Bricker here?"

"Nope. Just us girls," Corinne answered with an anxious glance at Lee. "And Hector. Join us."

Dropping into the seat opposite Lee, Tatum sighed, her thick gold bangles gleaming against her tanned wrists. Taking a plastic plate from the stack, she helped herself to salad and fruit while Hector offered her a piece of fish. Tatum lifted an eyebrow. "Red snapper? You said Bricker wasn't here."

Lee pretended not to notice the warning in Corinne's eyes as she met her daughter's gaze.

"He's not here, Tatum. And considering the way you two argue, I should think you'd be happy." Corinne's words were clipped and tense.

Her lips tight, Tatum sat back in her seat. "And I suppose it's my fault he's not here, right? Because I blew up his relationship with Lee."

Choking on a mouthful of water, Lee wagged her head back and forth, raising her hand to halt the concerns of her companions. "I'm fine," she gasped, putting all the force of her will into a wide-eyed gaze at Tatum. *No.*

Frowning, Tatum tore off a piece of bread and shoved it into her mouth.

Corinne observed her daughter, eyes narrowed into slits. "What do you mean, you blew up their relationship?"

Don't answer. Please. Lee prayed her gaze was forceful enough to convince the girl to keep her secret.

But like a young child, Tatum wilted under her mother's glare. She covered her eyes with her palm. "I told Lee about Bricker's baby." Her throat rose and fell in a labored gulp.

"You *what*?" Corinne sank back in her chair, her face drained of color.

Hector rose and stood behind her, one firm hand planted on her shoulder.

Harsh red splotches appeared on Tatum's neck and face. She nodded, her mouth pinched. "I know. I'm sorry."

"You're *sorry*?" Corinne gasped. Her hand gripped the edge of the table. "What gave you the right to tell something so private about your brother? Something he would have found a way to tell Lee when the time was right?"

Tatum shook her head, avoiding her mother's glare. "I didn't mean to say it. The words just…popped out."

Her heart galloping, Lee observed Corinne from beneath lowered eyelids. The older woman's hands trembled. Why wouldn't Tatum let sleeping dogs lie? How could she reopen wounds that had taken years for Corinne to heal?

"Do you really hate your brother so much, you had to ruin his chance for happiness? Even after all these years, you just can't forgive him." Tears slid over the sides of Corinne's nose. "I don't know why you have so much anger. He never hurt you. He hurt himself."

Scraping back her chair from the table, Tatum rose and flung her napkin onto the plate. Her eyes were vivid with pain. "He hurt us *all,* Mother. Me, you. Dad especially. Do you think Dad would've had a heart attack if his son hadn't ripped a hole in our lives and left Dad to repair it? I don't." Her wild gaze settled on Lee. "I really am sorry I told you. But one thing's for sure—you're better off without my brother in your life. I speak from experience."

Corinne moaned, reaching her hand to Hector's.

He clasped it tightly, his eyebrows furrowed as Tatum stormed from the lanai.

Frozen to her chair, Lee closed her eyes and took a few deep breaths to wash the ugliness of Tatum's words from her mind. Her hand stiff, she groped for the water pitcher to pour Corinne a glass. "Would you like a drink?" she whispered.

Rubbing her napkin to her eyes, Corinne sniffed. When she removed the cloth, a smile trembled on her lips. "Thank you, dear." She nodded to Hector at her shoulder.

His expression reluctant, he took his seat across from her, his gaze never leaving her face.

Corinne spun the wheels of her chair so she could face Lee. Although her face was still pale, her expression was determined. "Bricker has always been a wonderful son, despite what his sister thinks. He'd make an excellent husband, too." She put up her hand. "I know. This is your decision, not mine. But after hearing the terrible things Tatum said about her brother, you deserve to hear the other side of the story."

Her eyes wide with dread, Lee sank back in her chair. Why did Corinne have to put herself through this? Nothing would change for Lee.

"He was the kind of son every parent dreams of. Kind, smart, strong. He always watched out for everyone else. He could be playing football with his friends, but he never failed to come running if I needed help carrying in the groceries, or if he caught me taking out the garbage. Maybe because his father worked such long hours, Bricker made himself my protector." Her lips stiffened. "He was good to Tatum, too. No matter how much she teased and tormented him, as little sisters will do, he always let her hang out with his friends. He forced them to watch their language around her." Corinne's fingers glided over the embroidery of her napkin, her gaze unfocused. "When we allowed him to start dating, I was proud to see he showed his girlfriends the same courtesies—opening doors, complimenting them, buying them flowers. Little things make a girl feel special."

Lee's chest clenched. She'd seen this side of Bricker in his loving, protective manner around Corinne. In the way he'd placed a blanket over her own shoulders the night on the boat when beer made her woozy. He'd been a perfect gentleman, even though she'd practically invited him to take advantage of her.

"When I found out Veronica was pregnant, I couldn't believe Bricker was the father. I *wouldn't* have believed if I hadn't heard it from his own lips. To have an affair with a married woman—nothing could have been more out of character. For all those years when my husband was working long hours at the office,

Bricker was my right arm. He took his father to task for not being home and taking care of me." Corinne shook her head. "No one respected women more than my son. How he allowed himself to get involved with a married woman, I'll never know. He'd had a crush on her as a teenager, when she first worked for Grant. I suppose the allure of the forbidden was strong." Her eyes winced. "He was just twenty-four years old. His whole life was ahead of him. He made one foolish mistake, and he can't forgive himself."

Twisting her napkin in her lap, Lee bit down on her bottom lip. She hated to cause Corinne any more pain. She cleared her throat. "What I don't understand is why he wouldn't take responsibility for the child." As she spoke, the buzzing began in her ears, and a vision of the orphanage dormitory swam into focus. *Not now.* Putting her hand over her chest to still her heartbeat, she sipped from her glass of water until her vision cleared.

Sighing, Corinne sagged against the arm of her chair. "My husband made a mess of things."

Lee was struck by the bitterness in Corinne's voice. Had her relationship with Grant Kilbourn been as difficult as Bricker's own?

"He didn't want me to find out about the pregnancy. He was protecting me." Corinne gave a hollow laugh. "At least, he thought he was. I'd only recently been diagnosed with MS, and Grant decided the news would send me into some kind of nervous breakdown. Maybe if he'd spent more time with me over the years, he would have known how strong I am when my children need me." She lifted her gaze to Hector, who nodded with a trace of a smile. Corinne's cheeks were regaining some color.

He's in love with her, Lee realized suddenly. *And I think she loves him, too.*

"Paying off Veronica so she'd disappear forever was Grant's idea. He didn't bargain on losing his son, though." Corinne's lips twisted. "Bricker couldn't live a lie. He couldn't practice law in his father's firm, where Veronica had worked all those years, knowing she'd lost her job because of him. My husband may have been capable of carrying out the farce, but my son wasn't."

She brushed a hair away from her face, her eyes narrowed and glittering. "I didn't know any of this at the time, of course. All I knew was my son was packing his bags and moving to the islands in the new boat his father bought him. I assumed he was just taking a break from responsibilities after the demands of law school. But when I finally learned the truth, I realized my son had run away because he couldn't face himself for being less than perfect."

In Lee's cramped palm, the napkin was damp with perspiration. Taking a breath, she forced herself to relax her grasp. She could only imagine Corinne's anger at discovering the lies told for "her own good."

Shaking her head, Corinne clenched the arms of her wheelchair. "If I'd known what they were doing to protect me, I promise you, Lee, I'd have done everything in my power to make my son accept his responsibilities with his child. But I learned the truth too late. Bricker stayed in the islands for two years. And when he moved back, after Grant died, he'd changed. He'd sealed himself from me." She raised her hands to her lips, her fingertips steepled in a prayer position.

"I understand," Lee said slowly. Bricker hadn't turned his back on his child because he didn't care. He'd been forced into a lie by his father, and the lie had broken him. Sympathy stirred in her chest. She knew the shame of backing down to well-intentioned but domineering parents. "He's punishing himself. He doesn't think he deserves to be happy."

"Exactly." Corinne leaned forward and covered Lee's hand with her own. "He let go of his dreams. He acted like a party-boy. Like he was perfectly happy to be a bartender, living off his boat for the rest of his life. I was starting to think he'd have no better future, 'til you showed up at my door." Smiling, she squeezed Lee's hand.

Her hand was clammy and stiff under the older woman's warm touch.

"But with you, the *old* Bricker was back for the first time in years. Happy. Open. He'd let down his guard." She covered Lee's hands with both of hers. "I know he would have told you about his son, in time. I'm hoping it's not too late for you to give Bricker another chance."

Lee shut her eyes. She couldn't bear the hope shining from his mother's face. Lifting her hands from under Corinne's, she opened her eyes and forced herself to meet Corinne's gaze. "Everyone makes mistakes. And I know you want Bricker to be happy." A rattling sigh escaped her lips. *Just say it. Put the poor woman out of her misery.* "But I'm not the right girl for Bricker." *Because no matter what his reason, I could never be with a man who dumped his own child.*

For a brief moment, Corinne's face crumpled.

Lee's breath froze, and she put a hand out to the

older woman. Across the table, she heard a rumble from deep in Hector's throat.

But then Corinne straightened her shoulders, waving off Lee's hand. "I appreciate you listening, dear." The corners of her mouth lifted into a sad smile. "Bricker would have a fit if he knew I was interfering."

Lee shook her head, her throat clogged with emotion. "I'm glad you told me the whole story. I hope Bricker finds peace someday."

Corinne stared across the table at Hector, her shoulders slumped. "I'm sure he will."

The woman's voice was as mechanical as a robot's. Guilt weighed on Lee's limbs like cement, but she forced herself to stand. "Thank you so much for this wonderful lunch. I really should be going. I rode my bike, and I want to get home before the afternoon rains."

"But how will you get the bromeliad home on your bike? It'll bloom for just a little while longer. I was hoping you could get started painting it right away." Corinne's brow furrowed as she gazed at Lee.

She'd forgotten the bromeliad, but she'd be damned if she disappointed Bricker's mother one more time today. Lee straightened her shoulders. She'd balance the plant on top of her head if she had to.

Before she could respond, Hector rose from the table. "I'll drive you home. Your bike can go in the bed of my truck." He strode to the back of Corinne's chair and rolled her to the door of the lanai. "I'll meet you in the driveway."

Corinne smiled at Lee from her chair, a slight slumping of her shoulders the one concession to her disappointment. "Thank you, Lee. Call me if you need anything with the painting."

After lifting the pot, Lee slung her purse over her shoulder. Her sandals slapping against her feet were the only sound as she crossed the tiles to the front entrance. How quiet and empty the house seemed. Once more, Corinne's hopes for a brighter future had been disappointed. Her heart squeezing, Lee gently closed the door behind her. If she could just say the words Corinne wanted to hear. She waited on the sidewalk as the garage door opened and a small red truck backed out.

Hector hopped from behind the wheel and opened her door, holding the pot until she'd fastened her seatbelt. After he'd shut her inside, he lifted her bike into the truck bed and climbed into his seat. He nodded when Lee gave him her address, backing out of the long driveway onto the street.

An uncomfortable silence followed as Hector drove slowly through the neighborhood. Lee cleared her throat. "I'm sorry if I upset Corinne. I never wanted to." Afraid to see his expression, Lee squinted out the window at sidewalks painted a blinding white by the afternoon sun.

After a long pause, Hector replied. "Corinne is strong. Strong enough to handle the truth."

Lee chewed her inner lip. "But I hated to see her reliving the pain. I wish I hadn't come today." She should have known better. Her presence was only a reminder to Corinne of all her son had lost.

"She didn't tell you the whole story."

Lee faced Hector, her brow wrinkling.

A muscle twitched at Hector's temple. "Corinne doesn't *know* the whole story."

Sitting back against the leather seat, Lee stared at the older man. Indecision flitted across his face as he coasted to a stop at the intersection.

He nodded, turning the wheel to the left as he headed toward downtown. "Bricker looks just like his father. Have you seen pictures?"

"Tatum showed me a photograph." Where was he going with this?

Hector dipped his chin in acknowledgement. "I was a landscaper for Grant Kilbourn's firm when he hired me to be a man about the house, after his wife's illness was first diagnosed. I'd lost my own wife to MS years ago, in Cuba. I could anticipate how Corinne's illness would likely progress, and what she would need." His temple twitched again. "I took care of the yard work, did the cooking, and drove her to activities. Mostly, I was her companion, since her husband was always at work."

She was getting the idea Grant Kilbourn was not an ideal husband. But what that had to do with Bricker's affair, she had no idea.

"One night, a year or so after I'd first come to work for the family, I received a phone call from Mr. Kilbourn. He was stinking drunk." Hector shook his head, his weathered face grim. "He needed a ride home. Corinne was already asleep. I headed to the mainland and found him at a bar around the corner from his office. I had to drag him into my truck. He was sobbing, holding his head in his hands." His lip curled. "When he told me the reason, I didn't blame him for crying." As he waited for pedestrians to cross the street at the light, Hector fell silent.

Lee gave a little shake of her shoulders. She wasn't

sure she could bear a new perspective on the night Bricker fell from grace. "He'd just found out about Veronica's pregnancy, I guess."

Hector's laugh was sour. "Yes. And the news would rock his wife's world."

"Because Corinne was so proud of Bricker, and she'd be so disappointed in him." Lee had to stop herself from adding *Yada yada yada.*

Frowning, Hector put a firm hand on Lee's arm, shaking his head. "Because Grant knew the baby was his."

Uncomprehending, Lee stared at Hector, her face screwed into a question. What was he saying? Grant and Bricker had had an affair with the same woman? A knot balled her stomach. Her hand flew over her mouth. *Oh, my God.* No wonder Bricker hated his father.

"He'd been having an affair with Veronica for years. I suspected as much, after coming along on the last family trip. Every evening, Veronica would go to bed early, and Grant made one excuse or another about needing to work on a case." A noise of revulsion growled from the back of his throat. "He was so drunk in my truck, he confessed to everything. He'd been with Veronica at a hotel the night before. But this time, her husband followed in his car when they left the office. That was all the proof Pete needed of who the father was."

Bewildered, Lee shook her head. Her pulse raced. "Wait a minute. I thought—"

"Let me finish, please." Hector's tone brooked no argument.

Collapsing back against her seat, Lee clamped her mouth shut, hope flaring in her breast. Maybe Bricker had known the baby couldn't be his. Maybe he refused to see the boy because he didn't believe he was the father.

"Bricker heard me dragging his father to the guest room. I wanted to give Corinne one more night of sleep before the bastard blew up her life." The vein at his temple throbbed harder. "I handed Grant over to his son and tried to get some sleep, dreading the moment Corinne would hear the news. But days passed, and nothing seemed to have changed. The next thing I know, Bricker is moving to the Virgin Islands. After he'd planned for years to join his father's firm. I had a bad feeling. I was afraid of what he was about to do." He paused, easing his truck into Lee's driveway.

"What was he about to do?" She shouldn't interrupt, but her head was whirling. This story was a far cry from what she'd heard from Tatum and her mother. Bricker's father was unfaithful. He had an affair with the same woman his son had fallen in love with. And the woman became pregnant.

Hector shut off the engine, and the truck settled into silence. "Bricker decided to take the fall for his dad."

Lee shook her head again. How was Veronica sure which man was the father?

Suddenly, Lee's eyes flew open. *Listen to what Hector's saying.* She clung to the pot with cramped fingers, hardly daring to breathe. "Bricker never had an affair with Veronica."

Hector shook his head in a slow arc.

The way he stood behind his mother's chair like a sentinel, guarding her from any possible harm. Lee's lips moved, as if saying the words would make the truth more real. "He pretended the baby was his to protect his mother from his father's infidelity."

His hands gripping the steering wheel, Hector bowed his head once. "He didn't think Corinne could endure the truth." He paused. "And he was probably right."

Placing the pot on the dashboard, Lee massaged her temples. "But Veronica's husband followed them. He *knew* who was in the car."

"No, he *thought* he knew. As a 'favor'"—Hector's jaw clenched—"sometimes Grant let Bricker drive his luxury car, and he'd drive Bricker's truck. Only later did I understand—Grant drove Bricker's truck on the nights he 'worked' 'til after midnight. In case anyone caught him sneaking out with his secretary. When Veronica's husband saw his wife enter the hotel with Bricker, he really was seeing Grant Kilbourn."

Her body stiffened, and Lee's jaw dropped. "How...*slimy*. What kind of father could do such a thing to his son?"

Tapping his fingers against the wheel, Hector gave a half smile. "The type of father who buys his son a state-of-the-art boat for his troubles." His voice was laced with bitterness.

"But his mother thought he had an affair with a married woman—! And the whole world thinks he walked away from his son. And Tatum *hates* him." Lee was breathless at the scope of injustices Bricker had endured.

Hector nodded. "And Bricker has tolerated all of these wrongs. But losing you is the one blow he won't recover from."

Memories tumbled through her thoughts. Lee

clasped her palm over her mouth, appalled. What she'd said to Bricker at the courthouse—she'd crucified him. And he'd stood there and taken it. Just like he'd done for ten years. Stricken, she returned her guilty gaze back to Hector. "Why didn't you tell the truth?" she whispered.

He splayed his hands wide. "He wouldn't let me. He was afraid the truth would be too much for his mother. I was, too." He sighed. "Over the years, I've asked him to come clean. But he bound me in a promise to keep his secret." Hector put his hand over Lee's and gave it a shake. "I've broken his promise. But I can't bear to see him unhappy any longer."

Lee lifted an eyebrow. "Or Corinne." Lee had underestimated Hector's faithfulness to the Kilbourns. He'd been bound to a secret that was slowly tearing apart the family. What a terrible burden he'd born for the sake of the woman he loved.

A wide smile split his face. "Or Corinne." He circled the hood of the truck and opened Lee's door. Leaning her bike against the fence, he climbed back in the truck and started the engine. Rolling down the passenger window, he leaned across the seat. "If you want to talk to him, you'd better act fast. He's moving back to the islands tomorrow."

Her front door key in hand, she froze, her wide-eyed gaze locked on Hector's. If Bricker left tomorrow, she'd lose him forever.

With a salute, Hector backed the truck out of the drive and disappeared down the street.

Her hand shaking, she twisted the key into the lock and pushed open her door with her shoulder. The white walls of her silent bungalow greeted her. She placed the bromeliad on the kitchen counter. The one bright spot in a home she'd never bothered to make her own.

For her whole life, she'd protected herself from getting hurt. She'd fled every relationship before it had a chance to bloom. No one would abandon her like her mother had. And where had all her efforts led? To the bare walls of this room, where the only mark she'd left was the fits and starts of canvases left unfinished and unhung.

She couldn't let fear rule her life any longer. Time to stop running from what she feared and run toward the man she loved.

Chapter Fourteen

The Gulf waters were turbulent, rolling toward the shore like the underwater shrug of a giant's shoulders. Diffuse orange light lit the sky, brightening to a manic yellow as the sun settled into the horizon.

A storm was coming.

Wind whipped her hair into her eyes as she started down the long dock toward Bricker's boat. Against the darkening sky at the end of the dock, she could just make out the silhouette of the *Tequila Mockingbird*. With each wobbly step, she fought the nylon skirt clinging to her legs like a drowning man to a mast.

Steady.

Heart pounding, she forced herself onward, arms held out to her sides for balance. A wave washed the lip of wooden planks and growled away like a dog straining at the end of its leash. She stopped, paralyzed. What if the waters washed over the dock? She'd drown in this surf.

She sank to her knees, gripping the dock cleats at the plank edges with fingers as cold as bones. To her left, the sky was charcoal gray, bleeding into blackness. White light pulsated from behind the dark clouds. Lightning. How long before it struck overhead?

Squeezing her eyes shut, she stifled the urge to scream for help. The wind was howling. He wouldn't hear her. Why hadn't he answered his phone? She should run back to the safety of her car, now, before the waves washed her off the dock. She glanced over her shoulder. Her car was across the road, solid, secure, and dry. If she went back now, she could reach the car before the clouds opened up overhead.

But if she turned back, she'd never see Bricker Kilbourn again.

With a strangled cry, she wrenched herself upright and staggered forward. Gusts of air blew her hair into her eyes, and she shook her head like a wet dog. Thunder rumbled from far over the ocean. Streaks of lightning scorched the skies above Bricker's boat. Heart pounding, she rocked back on her heels as the walkway swelled beneath her. The waves were growing stronger. If she didn't get off this dock soon, she really might die out here.

Ripping off her sandals, Lee lunged in the direction of the horizon, forcing her feet into a lumbering jog. Black clouds swarmed in from the left, squeezing out the dying orange rays of the sun. She'd covered half the distance when the walkway rose up, hanging for a moment on top of a wave before sinking into a nauseating drop that knocked her to her knees. Water poured over the boards. She screamed, scrabbling for a handhold as her body slid toward the edge. Jamming her fingers around a rusted metal cleat, she strained to hold on until the dock reemerged from the waters.

Cold rain pelted her back. Pulse pounding in her throat, she ground her teeth together and rose to her knees. Blinded by the storm, she lowered her chin to her chest and stretched out her arms. She'd crawl the rest of the way if she had to. She was getting on the damn boat.

"My God! What are you doing?" Strong hands around the waist lifted her, tossing her in mid-air like a sack of potatoes until she was cradled against a wall of solid human flesh.

Relief surged through every pore. *Bricker*.

He staggered against the force of the wind, hands clamped around her shoulder and thigh, drawing her into the protection of his arms.

She buried her face against his wet shirt, eyes screwed shut as the storm raged around them. She could feel his heart pound against her cheek as he ploughed forward into a sheet of rain.

Staggering to a halt in front of the boat, he shifted her to her feet. "Step up!"

She scrabbled for a handhold as he hoisted her from behind. Knocking her nose against the gunwale, she tumbled inside the bow.

Bricker was at her side in an instant, dragging her under the helm and throwing open a short door inside the cockpit. He guided her down steps to the cabin, and then rushed past her, taking the stairs in two leaps to shut the cockpit door.

The roar of the storm vanished, leaving her ears ringing in the sudden stillness. Dazed, she stood in the center of a tiny room.

He guided her to a U-shaped dinette, nudging her to sit on the cushioned seats. Dripping water from his T-shirt to his shorts, he yanked open a closet near the stairs and returned with a stack of towels. Draping one over her shoulders, he placed another over her lap, tucking the ends beneath her thighs. With a third towel, he squeezed the ends of Lee's hair, coaxing them back from her face.

His touch was as gentle as a mother's. Shivering, she stared into his eyes, happy just to look at him.

Gazing at her mouth, he made a noise in the back of his throat. "You're bleeding." He wiped an edge of the towel over the corner of her lips.

She ran the tip of her tongue inside of her mouth and tasted iron in her saliva. "I guess I bit my lip." She winced, drawing her fingers up to her face to feel for the damage.

He caught her hand, turning it over tenderly in his own.

Her knuckles seeped blood. "Must have been when I was holding onto the dock for dear life." A laugh scraped against her throat. "Looks like I broke my nails, too."

He shook his head, his blue eyes dark and humorless. He left her again, disappearing into a room to the left.

She heard a drawer squeaking open then sounds of rummaging around. Running water in the sink. She closed her eyes, grateful to be inside, in a warm, safe place. Grateful to be with him.

When he returned, he carried a wet washcloth, a tube of ointment, and a roll of gauze. Kneeling at her feet, he placed the warm cloth over her knuckles, pressing with exquisite gentleness. After a few seconds, he unscrewed the lid from the ointment and squeezed it onto a strip of the gauze. Carefully removing the wash cloth, he placed the gauze over her torn knuckles and began wrapping her fingers together.

With his concentration fixed on her hand, she was free to study his face. Lines furrowed his brow. Water droplets coursed from his hair over his forehead. He shook the water from his eyes, his gaze never leaving her hand.

With a corner of her towel, she wiped the water from his temples.

Tearing the gauze with his fingers, he tucked the end securely and dropped his hands to his side. His gaze slid up to meet hers. "Lee." His voice was hoarse. "What were you thinking?"

His face, tilted to look up at her, was ashen. She swallowed hard. She hadn't been the only one scared out there on the dock. "Hector told me you were leaving. I had to talk to you."

"In the middle of a storm?" His Adam's apple pulsed up and down. "You could have drowned. If I hadn't heard you scream..." He shook his head, wiping his hand over his brow. "I can't believe you'd do something so stupid."

She'd risked her life to see him and didn't need to be scolded. Lee jutted out her chin. "Well, maybe if you'd answered your phone, I wouldn't have had to come out here and find you."

Bricker's jaw dropped. "And what if I hadn't been here? What would you have done then?"

Tugging the towel close around her shoulders, she winced at the sting of her cut knuckles. "I hadn't thought that far ahead."

A smile quirked the corner of Bricker's mouth. Standing, he took the last towel from the pile and ran it over his head. A flurry of curls haloed his face as he rubbed the towel over his shoulders, arms, and legs. Tossing the towel to the stairs, he sat again in front of her, locking one hand over his wrist in front of his bent knees. "What was so important you risked your neck to see me?"

When she'd jumped in the car, determined to find Bricker and apologize, she hadn't considered how she'd explain her knowledge of his past. Hector had been sworn to secrecy. He'd broken Bricker's trust. How would Bricker react?

He waited, his lips set into a thin line.

Squirming, she tried to cross her legs, but the flesh of her thighs stuck to the damp cushion. She shook her hair off her face. "You can't move to the islands."

He cocked an eyebrow. "Says who?"

"Says me!" Blowing on her bandaged fingers, she averted her face. Heat flooded up from her neck like a radiator switched on inside her chest.

A sigh whispered from deep in his throat. "I've had to live with the things I've done. You never could. We both know it."

Her heart aching at the sadness in his voice, she brought her gaze back to him.

His shoulders were tight, the tendons standing out in his neck as he hugged his arms around his knees, but he didn't flinch.

Wetting her lips, she tried a smile then gave up. *Here goes.* "I know about your dad. How you covered for him when he got Veronica pregnant."

His head rocked back, the black circle of his pupils dilating until just a rim of blue was visible. His mouth struggled soundlessly. "How?" he whispered.

Lee caught his hands. They were shaking. "Hector told me. He didn't want you to leave again and break your mother's heart."

Yanking back his hands, Bricker jumped to his feet, pacing across the small floor to the porthole.

Leaning his forearm against the wall, he pressed his face into his elbow. His wet shirt clung to the rigid muscles of his shoulders. He twisted his head to look back at Lee, his eyes glittering. "Did he tell my mother?"

Spreading her hands wide, she shook her head. "I don't think so. He just told me."

Bricker stared out the round window. Suddenly, he pounded his fist against the wall, bouncing a framed picture. It swung into a wide arc before settling, askew. He slumped onto the other end of the U-shaped bench and buried his head in his hands.

His head was bent so close to her knees. She yearned to reach her fingers into his hair and comfort him.

He lifted his face, resting his chin on two fists. Tension streamed from the corners of his eyes in fine lines. "Why did he tell you?"

Gripping the edge of the seat with her wounded hand, she ignored the pain flaming from her scraped knuckles. "He believed I had a right to know you weren't the kind of man who would abandon his own son."

Shaking his head back and forth in a long, slow arch, Bricker bit down hard on his lips. "He had no right. He promised me."

Does that really matter? Lee made an impatient noise. "He cares about you."

Bricker snorted. "He doesn't need to worry about me. He needs to worry about my mother."

Lee threw up her hands. "He's in *love* with your mother! He wants nothing more than to make her happy. And he knows as long as *you're* miserable, she is, too."

Straightening, Bricker frowned. "Did he *say* he's in love with my mom?"

Lee gave a dismissive wave of her hand. "He didn't need to. I could tell."

His eyes narrowed, and his lips twisted. "So now you're a mind reader."

The same cynical expression he'd worn every time they'd argued. The look that sent her straight up a roof. She jumped to her feet, ready to retort. A sudden flash of lightning outside the window was followed by a deafening crack of thunder. She staggered, knocking her head against Bricker's as he rose to steady her. "Ow!" She squeezed her hand over her nose, staring at Bricker reproachfully.

"Sorry." He rubbed his hand over his jaw. "Your nose was already a little swollen. Do you want some ice?"

Great. She was soaking wet, her mouth and hand were bleeding, and now her nose was swollen. She'd come out here to use all her persuasive powers to convince Bricker not to leave, and she was as enticing as a boxer beaten in the ring.

An irrepressible urge to laugh rose in her chest. She pounded her palm over her heart to stop the impulse, but a gurgle escaped through her throat. Her shoulders shook up and down. She clasped her hands over her mouth, but laughter bubbled between her fingertips. She couldn't breathe. Dropping her hands to her stomach, she succumbed, her gut spasming as peals of laughter bounced off the walls of the tiny room. *Oh God*. She could hear herself chortling and sniffing. Tears streamed from the corners of her eyes. She was humiliated. And it only made her laugh louder.

She heard Bricker try to speak, but she waved him away. Leaning over, she took a few deep, wavering breaths. A giggle or two broke through her lips before the hilarity subsided. She wiped her hand across her dripping nose. Could she look any less appealing? Steeling herself, she straightened and faced him.

Far from looking disgusted, he gazed at her with naked longing. His expression, so vulnerable and tender, catapulted her back to the moment on the boat, when fireworks had burst overhead and he'd brushed soft kisses over her eyes, her nose, her cheeks...

Her heart erupting with sudden courage, she grabbed his hand and brought it to her chest. "I'm sorry I seem like a lunatic. I was just thinking I was crazy to be fighting with you again when I came all the way out here, looking like a drowned rat, just to tell you I love you. Don't go." She held his hand with the force of all her bottled-up yearning, her heart hammering against her ribs.

His gaze softened, trailing down to her lips. Sliding his hands to her shoulders, he drew her toward him, cupping the back of her head in his palms. Stroking his thumb over her cheek, he lowered his mouth, breathing a kiss onto her tender, sore lips.

Heat roared through her veins. She leaned closer to sink into his kiss, inhaling the musky odor of desire beneath the tang of salt water.

Pulling away, he cradled her face with one hand, tracing a finger from her cheek to her chin. "I don't want to hurt you," he whispered.

She shook her head in mute appeal.

In response, he lifted her injured hand, kissing each

fingertip, his gaze never leaving hers.

She closed her eyes against the emotion swelling her chest. A moment later, his lips touched her eyelids, as light as a feather. Reaching under his soggy shirt, she ran her hands over the gooseflesh of his stomach and slid her hands to his back. Leaning into him, she stroked his cold skin. "You're freezing."

He nuzzled his face against her hair. "We both are. I'd suggest a hot shower, but until the storm passes, I think it's a bad idea." He drew away, shushing her when she protested. "We need to get you into some warm clothes before we add pneumonia to your list of ailments." Turning to a chest of drawers, he retrieved a thermal shirt and a pair of sweatpants. "Take them into the bathroom and change. I'll make us some hot tea."

When Lee emerged minutes later, her sleeves were rolled and the bottoms of Bricker's sweatpants dragged under her feet. She sank onto the blankets and pillows he'd tossed on the cushions.

After opening the microwave over the sink near the stairs, he carried two mugs of tea to the dinette.

"You look better in your clothes than I do." Lee lifted her arms to her sides and flopped them down.

"I don't think so," Bricker replied, planting a kiss on top of her head as he sat beside her.

In a soft brown jersey and a pair of running pants, his golden hair curling up against his neck, Bricker was nothing short of delicious. She had to swallow a cautious mouthful of tea to stop herself from kissing him again.

The wind was still howling outside. The sounds of the storm—clinking metal, the groaning of the dock as it lurched beneath the waves, tarps snapping against gusts of air—lent a melancholy soundtrack to the evening. The boat rose and fell with the swell of the tide. But inside the cabin, snuggled up against Bricker, she'd never felt so safe. Lowering her mug to her lap, she touched her torn lip with a careful fingertip. Why'd she have to go and bite her lip on a night like this? She gave a deep sigh.

Bricker raised his eyebrow. "Such a sorrowful sound. What's wrong?"

Staring at the ceiling, she raised her shoulders in an exaggerated shrug. "I had big plans for my lips tonight." Stealing a glance to the side, she was delighted to see his mouth curve into the lazy smile she loved.

He placed his hand over his heart. "Darlin', you're killing me." He wound his fingers into her long hair and gave a gentle tug.

She'd never felt such complete happiness. She wanted to revel in this moment forever. But underneath her contentment, a question nagged. Swallowing hard, she lifted her chin toward him. "Can I ask you a question?"

His fingers played down the length of her hair. "Sure."

She shivered when his knuckle brushed her cheek. *Focus, Lee.* "Why did you let everyone believe you were a bad guy?"

Feeling his hand go still, she stiffened, her heart plummeting. Maybe he'd never be ready to talk about his father. She'd broken the spell. He'd retreated again.

He stared across the cabin, his gaze unfocused. A moment later, his hand again stroked her hair.

Relaxing against his touch, she sighed with relief.

He raised his shoulders in an almost imperceptible shrug. "You've got to take care of your family." He spoke slowly, his gaze fixed on the wall. "A lesson my mother taught me. My father had been messing around with Veronica for years." He looked back at Lee, his eyebrows lowered. "I wish I'd told Mother when I first caught them together on the beach, before she was diagnosed with MS. But who knows? Maybe telling her would have triggered her illness earlier." He wound a strand of Lee's hair over his forefinger.

His words were deliberate, as if he were dredging up memories and sifting through them. She hated to make him relive the unhappiness and uncertainty of those years. Too much responsibility for any son to bear.

"That night, when Hector dumped Dad in the guest room, we were afraid the news would kill my mother. Her body was weak then. We had to find a way to keep her from finding out."

"But weren't you outraged when your dad asked you to be his fall guy? I'm furious just thinking about it." Lee twisted the blanket with her hand, wincing as the skin of her knuckles split.

Bricker kissed the inside of her wrist and laid her hand on his lap. "No. I'd have agreed to anything to make sure my mother never found out how her husband repaid her loyalty." He gazed at the floor, his eyes as gray as flint. "I got all the details before he passed out. While he snored in a drunken stupor beside me, I drew up the legal documents—a big, fat bribe to stop Veronica from talking and keep the child financially secure for the rest of his life."

Lee shook her head, a long sigh escaping. "I

understand why you wanted to protect your mother, and I think you're a saint for doing it." She put her fingers over his mouth to silence him. "But I don't understand why you've kept the secret so long, when it's done so much damage to your relationship with your sister."

He bent his elbow and leaned his face against his hand. "Tatum was Daddy's little girl. I was almost as worried about how crushed she'd be as I was about Mom. But I admit, when I took the blame, I didn't realize she'd hold a lifelong grudge." Rubbing Lee's earlobe between his fingers, he exhaled. "When I moved back to Florida after Dad died, I knew what everyone thought of me. Grant Kilbourn's son was worthless." He was silent for a long moment. "I believed I'd done the right thing, even if nobody besides Hector and Veronica would ever know. If the whole island wanted to call me a loser, then fine, I'd be a loser." He ran a finger over his lip, gazing meditatively at Lee. "So now one more person knows the truth."

Placing her mug on the table, Lee straightened, gazing with the full weight of her willpower. "Oh, no. You have to tell your mother."

Bricker sat upright, dropping his hands to his lap, his expression hardening. "*No.*"

"Oh, yes." Lee poked her finger into his chest. "You've been underestimating your mother all along. I talked to her today. She told me she would have more easily believed your *father* messed around with Veronica than you had. The hurt in her eyes when she talked about your life over these past ten years… You being unhappy is what's killing her!" She slapped her hand against Bricker's thigh, and pain splintered from her knuckles. "Ouch!"

"Stop hurting yourself," Bricker grumbled, covering her hand lightly with his own.

"And did you ever see her face when you and Tatum argue? Believe me, your mother can handle learning the truth about her husband. He's part of her past. Her kids are her future." She bobbed her head. "Yeah, she'll be upset for all you've gone through. *And* for being lied to. But once she sees we're together, she'll just be happy the truth is finally out."

The corners of his eyes crinkled and his mouth lifted into a mocking grin. "Oh, yeah? All I need is you on my arm to make everything right with the world?"

She couldn't stand to be apart one second longer. Climbing into his lap, she wrapped her arms around his chest and snuggled her head against his shoulder. "Everything will be right in *my* world, anyway."

He tipped her chin, dropping a gentle kiss onto the center of her lips. "What about *your* family? Your sister didn't seem too keen on the idea of you dating a bartender."

Placing her small palm against his, she shook her head. "Don't take what Brett said personally. She—"

"—means well," he finished, lacing his fingers through hers.

Beneath the words, Lee detected an edge of bitterness. "I know. I make excuses." She squeezed his hand. "But I owe my family so much. Who knows what would have happened if I'd stayed in Korea?" She bit her lip. "The thing is, I've been living between two worlds. For whatever reason, my parents in Korea didn't keep me. My parents in America wanted me to be just like them. But I'm not. I'm not a high achiever, and I don't care about having a job with good benefits and great pay. I'm just me. I like to paint. I'm messy. I have a bad temper."

"You're not kidding," he interrupted, planting a swift kiss between her eyebrows as they knit into a frown.

Laughing, she gave him a push. "I'm revealing something here! The whole Amber Maly case rocked my world. Janna helped me see I was reliving my own adoption trauma by fighting for Kaleb to stay with his mom. I can't keep running away from the past." She took a deep breath. "I've found my birth mother through the orphanage records. She emailed me last week, and she wants to meet me. I'm planning a trip to South Korea next year."

Bricker ran a hand over his forehead, his eyes wide. "Wow." His fingers rumpled through curls from the crown of his head to his neck. "You're taking a big step. Have you told your family?"

She nodded. "Brett had a fit. She said I would have my heart broken, and I'd break our mom's heart, too, when she found out." Lee licked her dry lips. She'd quailed at her sister's criticism, but she'd made up her mind. "I told her a part of me was missing, and I had to find it in the country where I was born. In the end, Brett actually volunteered to accompany me to Korea. See, I told you she means well." She tilted her face to Bricker's with a smug smile.

Chuckling softly, he repositioned her beside him and lifted her feet onto his lap, peeling back the long sweatpants to take the soles of her foot into his hand. "Sounds like you're ready to start living life on your own terms." His warm fingers kneaded the balls of her feet.

She stretched her arms overhead, yawning. "Can we write foot massages into our contract?" she asked, giggling as the tips of his fingers tickled her instep.

"Anything to hear you laugh," he whispered, gathering her back in his arms and lying against the pillows until the steady roll of the waves rocked them both to sleep.

Epilogue

Bricker tucked a light blanket over his mother's lap. "Do you think you'll be warm enough?" With the sun behind the clouds, the breeze nipping across the stern was chilly.

Corinne smiled from the port fold-out bench, the color high in her cheeks. "I'll be fine. I have a jacket if I need it."

Casting a glance toward the ocean skies, Bricker frowned. "The cloud cover should burn off soon."

She put her hand on his arm and squeezed. "Don't worry. Hector will take care of anything I need."

"Where do you want this?" Hoisting a cooler, Hector stepped into the cockpit.

Taking the container from the older man, Bricker lowered it to the floor and unloaded cold cuts and fruits into the mini fridge.

"Nice day for a boat ride." Relocating Corinne's walker to the side of the bench, Hector settled next to her.

From the corner of his eye, Bricker noticed Hector re-tucking Corinne's blanket. He smiled to himself. Lee had been right about his mother's aide. His attention to Corinne was above and beyond a caregiver's watchfulness. Would Corinne one day see Hector as more than a companion?

Swinging up into the helm, Bricker slid behind the

wheel and flipped the ignition to check the gauges. Corinne's resilience amazed him. As he'd feared, she'd been furious when she learned she'd been lied to for ten years. But instead of collapsing from shame at her husband's behavior, she'd rallied. She'd told Hector to put the wheelchair in the closet and return with her walker. "I've lived in Grant Kilbourn's shadow for long enough. My life begins today." Now that she was no longer bound to the wheelchair, she'd agreed to take a day trip on his boat with her family. Bricker glanced in his rear-view mirror.

Corinne was tucked into Hector's shoulder, shading her eyes and looking for whatever he was pointing at onshore. She called to her son from the cockpit. "Tatum's here."

He could hear the clicking of her high heels before she appeared. Grabbing the air horn, he leaned out his window and blasted her as she rounded the corner.

Her shoulder bag clattered to the planks. "Dammit, Bricker!" Sliding her sunglasses to the top of her head, she glared at him before swiping the handle of her bag from off the dock.

"Hi, Sis." He used his calm voice to annoy her, just like old times. Stepping back into the cockpit to help her across, he gave her an extra yank so she fell into his arms. Wrapping her in a bear hug, he held her until she squirmed. "Kind of dressed up for a boat ride, aren't you?"

Tatum made a face, holding up her bag and shaking it. "I left straight from the office. Some of us work for a living, you know." She poked her tongue at her older brother. "I'm going down to change. Is Lee here yet?"

"She's on her way." He glanced at his phone. No more updates, which was a good thing. She'd already texted twice to say she'd been held up. This morning, Amber and Dan Maly regained custody of Kaleb, and they'd asked Lee to be present when Children's Services drove their son home. The case worker was running late—unsurprising, considering Gloria Marshall's objections. The foster mother was no doubt dragging her heels over the whole process. Lee had told him of the rift between Gloria and her "practically adoptive son" Daniel as he and his wife completed couples counseling. Lee suspected Gloria coveted the extra money earned by caring for a special needs child. But Bricker, after seeing the dynamics firsthand in the Marshall household, believed Laurie showed a narcissist's need for praise and attention. Either way, Daniel Maly's family had been an easy target.

"Did I tell you how much money Lee's painting raised at auction?" Corinne asked Bricker as he opened a bottle of water. "Five hundred dollars!"

Swallowing, Bricker pointed the bottle toward his mother. "I forgot to tell you. She submitted her portfolio to the art program at the circus museum. They loved her eye for color. She's got an interview next week."

Fine lines blossomed around Corinne's eyes as she beamed at her son. "Oh, Bricker, how wonderful! I'm so glad she's finally believing in herself and taking her talent seriously." She raised a mischievous eyebrow and smiled. "Amazing what love can do for a person's self-esteem, isn't it?"

Tatum banged open the hatch door from the cabin. "Are you referring to Bricker studying for the bar exam? Yes, Mom told me your little secret." Tatum linked her elbow through his arm. "High time you got back to the law. I'm proud of you."

Shaking his finger at his shamefaced mother, he tousled Tatum's hair until she dodged away, sinking onto the starboard bench across from Hector and Corinne. Of all the changes he'd experienced since opening the window on the past, having his sister back in his life was one of the best. He tossed her a water bottle from the cooler.

"So when do we get this show on the road?" Tatum reclined her neck against the gunwale, stretching her bare arms to the sides. "When's the sun coming out? I planned to refresh my tan today."

"The cooler the weather, the better the chance of seeing the manatees moving around. I wanted to get down to Fort Myers by eleven o'clock, though. I hear they're friskier in the mornings." He glanced at his watch again. He hoped nothing had gone wrong with Kaleb's discharge.

Hector pointed toward the shore. "She's here."

A small figure in an orange dress clambered onto the dock, struggling to secure an oversized tote bag over her shoulder.

"Her bag's as big as she is." Corinne chuckled as she waved.

Pausing, Lee waved her arm in a wide arc over her head. Slipping out of her shoes, she carried them on two fingers as she trudged ahead.

Bricker hopped off the side of the boat, rocking the wooden platform as he landed. He jogged the length of the walkway to Lee, his heart racing from more than exertion. He hadn't seen her all week.

She lifted her head at his approach, a wide smile breaking through her frown of concentration. "Sorry I'm late! Trish Nichols caught me in the driveway and wanted assurances I'd stick with Amber during the transition." She swung the tote off her shoulder and handed it over.

Dropping it to the dock, he grabbed her by the waist and lifted her above his head, spinning her in a circle.

"Stop it! Your family's watching," she scolded, kicking him with her bare feet and trying to scowl.

"Let them watch." Inch by inch, he lowered her feet to the ground. Lifting the bag to his shoulder, he grimaced. "What are you carrying? Bricks?"

She shook her head. "A change of clothes, a towel, sunscreen, my camera, extra shoes, a book..." She tallied each item on her fingers. "Makeup, two bottles of water, some cut-up fruit..."

Cupping her face in his hands, he brushed his mouth over hers, savoring her lower lip for an extra instant before he let go. "Ready for anything. That's my girl."

She giggled, the delicious trill he still couldn't get enough of after all these months. Laying her palms flat against his chest, she sighed, her face sobering. "Are you sure you can take the day off today? You don't have much time left to prepare for the exam."

She'd called herself a mediocre college student, but she couldn't be more supportive of his need to study, even when it interfered with their plans. He wrapped his hands around hers. "I've passed the bar exam before, and I'll pass it again. Besides, I promised you a trip to see the manatees. I've been looking forward to this all week." He delivered another kiss to her full lips, drawing back with a sigh. Anything more would have to wait. Today was a family day. He held out his right hand.

Just then, the sun broke from behind the clouds, dazzling their eyes. Lee slid her hand into Bricker's, her other palm shading her forehead. "The heavens are smiling down on us."

He lifted her palm to his mouth and kissed it. "Not just today, but from now on."

Fingers entwined, they ambled up the sun-warmed dock to join the others.

A word about the author…

Nell writes contemporary romances about complex women and the men who can't resist them. Her sweet but sexy stories feature everyday people overcoming modern obstacles to love.

A mother of three, happily married for more than twenty years, Nell believes every person deserves to be the protagonist of a great love story. She spends quiet mornings walking her dogs and working out details of her novels, and afternoons in private practice as a reading instructor for children with dyslexia.

Visit her at:

https://nellcastle.com

~*~

Also by the Nell Castle
and available from The Wild Rose Press, Inc.
A Leap Of Faith